DUDI SINGS

M.E. Oren

River Lake Press

Also by M.E. Oren:

The Dallas Mercenary

DUDLHAM SINGS

M.E. Oren

River Lake Press

First published in Great Britain in 2012 by River Lake Press (UK)

This paperback edition published in 2012

A CIP catalogue record for this book is available from the British Library.

ISBN 978-0-9568870-1-6

This is for my mother

PROLOGUE

The changing room was an open space under the dwindling shade of a dying umdoni tree west of the pitch, ten yards behind the goalpost. Fourteen players sat silently on the dry ground that, despite the shade, was still scalding their backsides with oppressive heat. Some odd patches of wilting grass hung weakly over the soil as if mocking their despair. The young footballers sat with hands resting on their knees and stared solemnly at the ground; maybe beseeching the withering plants to hold on just a bit longer, maybe willing the earth to open up and save them from this misery.

The coach paced quietly in front of them. He was glancing at his wristwatch with increasing frequency now, and the players could sense the panic behind his gallant façade. It was their second game of the season, six minutes before kick-off, and not a word had been said. Sebastian, the left back, was still not here. He was the problem. They waited and waited and waited for Seb till tears started welling in some eyes.

Exactly two minutes before kick-off, the coach cleared his throat and spoke his first words.

'Right.' He slapped his palms together. This jolted everyone and some heads shot up. But the blank gazes quickly fell back to the ground or the few remaining leaves of the umdoni. 'Looks like we'll be missing a defender today.'

None of them raised a question. Had Seb suffered an injury, or an illness maybe? Had he encountered a family situation? Or was it just laziness? Coach Bill Tierney took his time studying each of their debilitated faces. He knew they had lost this game before a ball had been kicked.

'Jojo,' the coach finally called out at the skinny boy on the far side of the tree who was twiddling a stray blade of drying grass. 'You are going in at left back.'

That was it, the extent of his pre-match team talk.

As they had all feared, Seb never turned up for that game, or the next game, or the one after. And they lost every single one of those games.

The scene was replicated three weeks later when they sat down under the same umdoni for the start of game five. This time there were only thirteen players under the tree. They were waiting for JP, their main striker. The Butterfly Wanderers sat in silence with heads drooping lifelessly over hunched shoulders, but this time there were no tears. Other events had occurred to prepare them for today in the three hot, dry weeks after Seb. The players already knew they would never again see JP. But the coach didn't give up till three minutes before kick-off.

‘Right, we are another player short. Tema, you are going upfront.’

He said this too quickly, leaving himself a good part of three minutes with nothing else to give his desperate team. Fifteen seconds before the whistle, with all players in their positions, he shouted from the touchline: ‘Boys...! Let’s do this for Seb. Let’s do this for JP.’

They did not win.

Games six and seven came and went, without a win, or Seb, or JP.

Mwami and Beni were best friends. They worked as a pair, played as a pair, and sometimes called themselves brothers. The coach did not wait for them at the start of the eighth game. He already knew. The whole team knew. The whole village knew.

Two days before, Mwami and Beni had been taken, together, by three masked men with machetes; in broad daylight, with their friends watching.

It had come to that. Even daylight could not offer them safety now. These were hard times. The rains had not come. Drought was upon Gitaramuka. And with the times growing more desperate, so did the hunt for The Butterfly Wanderers.

Coach Tierney sat quietly with his players and pondered his tactics without Mwami and Beni. He was left with exactly eleven players and no substitutes. So there was no issue with team selection, just tactics. He decided that motivation was the key. He had to fire these boys up and keep them running on adrenalin for ninety minutes. But when he stepped in front of his players he realised that his own inner strength had deserted him. He opened his mouth and his lips quivered. His attempt to cheer and rally his team fell hopelessly into a melancholic drone.

'They were our friends...' he started waveringly, and paused to steady his voice. 'They were our brothers... We are going do this for our brothers.'

And they did it for their brothers. In games eight, nine, ten and eleven, the eleven players played ninety minutes with no substitutions. They played for their lost friends. But they did not win.

Game twelve came three months into the season. The coach looked hopelessly at the ten grave faces under the giant umdoni. They were waiting for Ngeze, the goalkeeper. They sang a few hymns to pass the time while waiting for their goalkeeper. Then the coach led them in prayer. He prayed for rain and peace and forgiveness and more rain. One minute before the whistle, the coach declared that he himself would be going in goal. But even the coach's best performance in goal did not save them from another humiliating defeat.

It was the last time they would see Coach Bill Tierney.

The next team talk was delivered by Sylvie, the midfielder and team captain who was, at fourteen, the oldest in the group. The coach had provided them with plenty of inspired phrases for this pre-match ritual, but Sylvie didn't think they would sound right on his tongue. Instead, he gathered the players and led them in a prayer his mother said with him every morning before school.

The star is my way
The wind is my chariot
The Lord is my shepherd
Heaven is my home
I am not afraid.

When they finished, he wiped away his tears and added, 'He was our friend. Today we are doing it for the coach.'

And on that Saturday morning, a mighty gust of wind with a swirling brown cloud of dust came from nowhere and swept away the remaining leaves of the umdoni. It blew haphazardly, sweeping the leaves one way, then another. In the first half, with The Wanderers attacking west, the wind was blowing west. When the teams changed sides, so did the wind.

They were the weakest team in the league. They were one player short. But on that windy Saturday, they knew a higher power was with them.

They knew that day, that the rain would come. And peace would come. And The Butterfly Wanderers would win.

BOOK ONE

The Crook

CHAPTER 1

A crime had been committed on the Dudlham Farm Estate; that remained the sole undisputed fact. There was as yet no victim or criminal or even a clue as to what exactly this crime was. Nine days had gone since the discovery of five severed human ears in an abandoned transit van, and no one was coming up to claim them. The crumbling walkways and dark corridors of The Farm echoed the same questions and flipped about some wild theories. Were there five dead bodies out there, each missing one ear? Or was it three bodies, one missing an ear and two missing both? Or were these earless people alive and walking amongst us?

The news had been rolling through all the major media outlets around London and beyond for more than a week, and still no credible ideas or explanations had surfaced. Tests on the body parts had returned nothing from the United Kingdom's DNA database. No one had been reported missing and no one had reported losing an ear.

In any other circumstances a crime, in such a place, would never have attracted this level of media attention, especially one with no victims turning up. The authorities would have pondered the mystery for a while, then quietly let it slide. This was Dudlham Farm. Things happened in Dudlham Farm.

However, in this case the mysterious body parts were white, and clearly belonged to fair-skinned Caucasian individuals, all five of them. The population of Dudlham Farm Estate was ninety-five per cent black. It didn't take long for a theory to start taking shape in the surrounding suburbs.

After three days, Tom Clarke, the leader of the extreme right British People's Party (BPP) called a press conference, which was of course ignored by all the major media channels. Only a couple of the pirate digital stations founded by his own supporters turned up. But very soon after, almost all the major stations were conducting phone-ins on the controversial political party and their Nazi leader. Some BPP supporters who had attended the conference phoned in to air their views. Most of them repeated exactly what Tom Clarke had said in that supposedly ostracised press conference:

...What if this were the other way round: black body parts found in white suburbs? It is time for white folks to make noise too...

Tom Clarke got his message across alright, press boycott notwithstanding.

And the demonstrations started almost immediately.

It was this group of placard-waving middle-aged roughnecks that Orelius Simm was trying to avoid by taking the long way round Lordship Lane to get to Northolt House on a particularly bright Saturday morning in mid-April. He had left

Dudlham to a relatively tranquil dawn at around seven a.m. for an intense two-hour workout at a gym in Bounds Green. His aim was to avoid the impending chaos, at least for now. The protestors had organised a march from the Met Police headquarters all the way to Dudlham Farm, to proclaim what most people already knew but were too British to say. To call this crime what it really was. To give voice to the muted white opinion in a ninety per cent white country. The irony was not lost on Orelius, and he allowed himself a small smile as he listened to an update from his car radio on the disruptions the protest was causing. He figured they were still at least twenty minutes away. He could be in and out again before they got near the estate.

He pulled up outside the Northolt House tower block at ten minutes before ten and parked on the ground floor between a beat-up Land Rover and a lime green Ford Fiesta. Since the entire estate had been built on swampland in the early sixties, the ground floors were used only for parking, with stilts holding the buildings above the floodplain. The dark shadow of a disintegrating deck-level walkway loomed from above.

'Hi, Oz,' a tired female voice called from behind, as he locked his car. He turned round to be greeted by the petite figure of Miquitta Simmons, in a short blue dress and three-inch black boots. She was swaying drunkenly from the Griffin Road entrance. Wood Green High Street, with a host of hardcore nightclubs, was only about two miles away. Orelius suspected Miquitta had spent most of her Friday night there, and part of her morning in some poor gentleman's bed.

'Hey, Miquitta,' he said dropping his keys into his hip pockets. 'Big night, huh?'

'Yeah, man...' she was slurring. 'First night out of the tags, man, had to go celebra–' her hands suddenly went towards her mouth as she bent forward and unleashed a jet of projectile vomit which landed a yard off Orelius's feet.

'Oooops... Sorry, Oz,' she said, collapsing to her knees to contain the stream. The strong stench of stale alcohol and rotten eggs wafted to his lungs. It was not yet ten o'clock in the morning.

'You OK, girl?' he asked as the little woman struggled to retch off the remainder of the phlegm stuck somewhere in the back of her throat.

'Yeah, I'm great... just wonderful.'

'Good. I've gotta go now. You take care, Miquitta.'

Miquitta Simmons had just finished probation and been relieved of the electronic ankle-tag after doing time for child abuse. The child in question was her own two-year-old son Jade, who was now in the care of social services. While most pushy parents train their toddlers to do fancy stuff like ballet or the Greek alphabet to mesmerise their guests, Miquitta Simmons had decided to teach her twenty-two-month-old baby how to smoke a cigarette. Two months short of his second birthday, Jade was capable of holding a cigarette between his two fingers, raising it to his lips to take a decent drag, and puffing out the smoke amidst the cheers of Miquitta's many unemployed alcoholic friends. One of the fascinated junkies even filmed one such show on his mobile phone and posted it on You Tube, where the authorities picked up on it and took it from there.

Orelius took one more look over his shoulders at the young mother who was now struggling back to her feet before he turned and headed into the block. He was ten minutes early but that was fine, Timmy would have been ready and waiting for maybe the last hour.

The Northolt lift squeaked to a stop in front of him as he walked past, heading for the stairs. Its rusting silver doors slowly opened with more squeaking, to reveal the frail figure of a rugged white woman in a greasy denim jacket and what appeared to be pyjama bottoms. Her mouth was wide open, with a string of mucous spittle hanging from one corner down to the breasts of her jacket. Her tongue looked like it was beginning to stick out but the tip disappeared somewhere between her teeth and lower lip. She made no move to step out. Orelius ignored the lift and strode nonchalantly towards the graffiti-stained stairway.

He knew the woman in the lift would not be getting off on the ground floor or the first floor, or any floor at all. She would probably still be there when he brought Timmy back later in the evening. Her name was Kelly-Jo; she lived at the Haringey Hostel for the mentally impaired, about a mile away, and that is what she did: she woke up, came to Dudlham Farm, rode the Northolt block lift, and then she went back home.

Orelius half-jogged up the nine flights of stairs to the fifth floor, then paused, leaning on the banister for about a minute to regain his breath. He turned right at the landing and walked past the green door belonging to the old cleft-lipped man all the kids around here referred to as The Hog. About five yards further, he stopped and knocked at number 91.

The door flew open with the first gentle tap. As usual, Timmy had been sitting on the other side with his ears pressed to the door, listening out for his footsteps.

'Hey,' the little boy yelped, hugging his bent shoulders. Then he half-turned and shouted in the direction of the kitchen: 'Mum, Orelius is here.'

Apart from the slightly oversized light blue Nike tracksuit jacket, he was wearing all tennis whites. They had nicknamed the blue coat *The Nile Jacket* because a few months back, when the slanted leg of the *k* in *Nike* started peeling off from the label on the lower back, Timmy decided to get rid of the curves altogether and only leave the straight vertical line of the *k*, thus

Nile; turning a giant sportswear manufacturer into an African river at a stroke of a fingernail.

There was a black tennis bag lying next to the door with the word *WIMBLEDON* inscribed across it in big slanting letters. A tennis racquet head was sticking out from one end, but this was only for show because the bag was big enough to fit it all in. Timothy Lewis wanted the good folks of Dudlham Farm to know that it was a Saturday and he was off to play tennis. One day, when he was world number one and kicking arse at Wimbledon, they would remember these Saturdays.

'Hello, big man.'

'You are two minutes early.' The boy raised two little fingers across his face for further clarity. 'Well done.'

'Yeah, I try. Do you wanna tell your mum we are going now?'

He hesitated as the old man from next door, Mr Hog himself, emerged from down the stairwell and trotted briskly up the hallway, his slight limp barely noticeable.

'Hi,' Timmy whispered weakly in the man's general direction, and the old man acknowledged this with a slight nod as he fumbled with his keys and hurried into his house, clearly uncomfortable with staring eyes. The kids called him The Hog, as in warthog, because of his cleft palate, and the old man was no doubt aware of this. He was a small man with thick facial hair that was probably kept in a desperate effort to hide his disfigured lip. Orelius couldn't help feeling sorry for him. Timmy had once been sternly chastised with a long lecture for referring to him as The Hog, and he hoped the boy had learnt his lesson. It was hard to imagine going through life with such an impediment, but Orelius suspected that this man, a refugee from some African country, had experienced worse. This was the kind of man who, rather than bemoan his deformity, would go down on his knees every day and thank God for the roof over his head and the food on the table.

'Come on then,' Orelius said once The Hog was safely inside his house. 'You need to say goodbye to Mum.'

'Muuum...' he prolonged the word as only kids under a certain age can, till it almost sounded like a song, 'we are off.'

'OK, Tim. Have fun,' she called from the kitchen. She did not come out to shake hands with Orelius, didn't even shout a greeting out to him. It had been that way for six years. In fact Orelius could not remember ever speaking more than two or three whole sentences with Timmy's mother since their explosive encounter six years before.

They walked back to Orelius's car, and just as he was driving out of Dudlham he saw the group of protesters through his rear-view mirror, turning into the street behind them. They were relatively quiet, not chanting or singing, just marching up to Dudlham en masse, holding various placards aloft. Most bore witty messages relating to justice and freedom but Orelius spotted an unusual one proclaiming THIS IS HOW WE DEMONSTRATE; PEACEFULLY! HOW ABOUT YOU? A sarcastic reference to the previous year's infamous riots that started right here in Dudlham as a protest but soon turned nasty, spreading throughout London and beyond, and resulting in at least five deaths and more that 200 million pounds-worth of damage. It had been mostly blacks causing the trouble that time, and some of these people were clearly still bitter about that.

'Who are those people, Oz?' Timmy had also spotted them in his side mirror as they turned onto Lordship Lane.

'They are protestors, Tim. Do you know what that is?'

The boy shook his head.

'They are a group of people who come out onto the streets in large numbers when they are unhappy about something. They want everyone to know that they are not happy.'

'Why, what are they unhappy about?'

He thought for a few seconds. He didn't feel it was a good time to be talking about mutilated body parts, but he also didn't want to lie. 'They think there is someone in Dudlham who is going around killing white kids. But what they are mostly unhappy about is that the police have refused to come out and say that there is a racist serial killer out here. So they are here to say it in their own way.' He looked over at Timmy and thought he saw him stiffen. 'This is just what they think, Timmy. It doesn't mean that it is true.'

'This person is only killing white kids?'

'That's what they are saying.'

'Orreeelius...?' he was doing his prolonged words again, and Orelius found it infectious.

'Yeeeessss...'

'Some people think I'm white.'

Orelius instantly knew this had been a mistake: he could see fear in Timmy's eyes.

'Well, that is not the worst thing one can think about someone else, is it?' he said jokingly, trying to steer the subject away from serial killers. 'Do you know my friend Cory?'

Timmy nodded.

'Do you know what most people think he is?'

'Tamika's mum said he's a twat.'

'I'd warn you about repeating such language, Timmy, but this time you've actually raised a good point. Even though he's got darker skin, Cory is half-black and half-white just like you. But because he's nearly thirty and has had enough chances in life to define himself in other ways, Tamika's mum probably has a good reason for thinking of him only as a twat.'

'I didn't know Cory was half-caste. He looks darker than you.'

'Exactly my point; in the end the colour of your skin doesn't really matter, you will always get a chance to decide for yourself who you want to be.'

'But it matters if there's someone killing only white people.'

There was no way Orelius was going to win this, and he didn't know how to end it.

'Timmy, there is no serial killer in Dudlham. I just told you what those people think, but they have no reason to. None of them actually knows of anyone who has been killed.' He paused to asses the effect of his words. Timmy didn't look convinced, so he tried again. 'It's just a rumour someone started to cause trouble, so please stop thinking about it now, will you? Let's talk about how many games we are going to win today.'

The boy clearly wasn't sold but he decided to let it go. The protestors had disappeared from their vision. But the old sprawling tower-blocks of The Farm refused to go away, their fading images swishing across the rear-view mirror as they sped along Lordship Lane.

*

On their way to the restaurant after tennis, the radio informed them that the supposedly peaceful protests they had left behind in Dudlham had grown ugly. Altercations between the white protestors and black residents had resulted in a forceful and violent dispersal of the groups by riot police.

Orelius switched channels, to spare himself a further grilling from Timmy. He knew that by the time he got him back home this evening, the protestors would be long gone.

Apparently, there was a bigger march outside the estate being planned for the following day, which was a Sunday. This worried him slightly because Timmy and his mother went to church every Sunday without fail. Nikisha Lewis was a woman who spent her life trying to avoid human contact. He could not imagine her wading through a band of rowdy protestors outside The Farm to get to their church, which was based at the Dudlham Farm Community Centre, on the other side of the recreation grounds. So it looked like there would be no church for Timmy tomorrow.

CHAPTER 2

The Jolly Farmer, otherwise known as The Jolly, or just TJ, was a pub and grillhouse in Time Garden on the Adams–Gloucester Road junction. Although the redbrick edifice was as worn and depleted as the surrounding towers, TJ had actually been constructed twenty years after the rest of Dudlham Farm. There were other small cafés and chip shops but The Jolly Farmer was the only establishment of its kind inside The Farm.

TJ was right at the edge of Dudlham Farm. Directly opposite, on the other side of Adams Road, were three schools: Dudlham Farm primary, William C. Harvey, and Moselle. Some people had of course questioned the wisdom of having a liquor-serving facility in such close proximity to schools. And the management at The Jolly were always consistent with their response: *We are in fact a restaurant.*

It was inside this restaurant that Orelius conducted his regular Sunday afternoon surgeries. He had an allocated spot – a small round table with a cosy sofa-chair in a secluded corner at the farthest end from the bar area. The number of seats on the opposite side of his sofa varied depending on his clients. Currently there was only one wooden bar stool across from him, occupied by a young, light-skinned Ugandan woman in her early twenties called Naima.

Naima had gone from being a young single student to a mother of two in the space of one afternoon. The two children had previously belonged to her friend and compatriot Farida, a single mother who had never married. She was currently being held at the Yarls Wood Immigration Removal Centre in Bedford.

The British Foreign Office has Uganda on their records as a safe country. The UK border agency clearly states that any illegal immigrant from a safe country, along with his or her dependants, shall be deported with immediate effect. Naima had been babysitting the three-year-old twins when their mother's allocated one phone call came to her. The mother had tearfully explained to her babysitter the implications of her impending deportation, declaring that she herself was willing to accept her fate. Her only worry was for her children, who she had not yet mentioned to the authorities.

Naima immediately realised there was only one thing she could do. So she said to the twins' mother, 'Farida, I'm so sorry, I don't know how I can help you. But I know I can look after your babies. I will say a prayer for you, and the twins will be mine until you come back. Whatever happens, these children are not going back to Uganda.'

Naima had said this because she knew something that the UK Foreign Office, the Ugandan government and even most Ugandan people don't know: that there is a small village in the

North Eastern corner of Uganda where having a child out of wedlock was believed to bring a curse of perpetual drought unless the mother and the children were killed. Naima knew this because she came from there. If she told her clan back in the village about Farida they would ask her to find a way to kill her and the children in London, to lift the curse. Giving the children up would have meant sending them to certain death. Now her problem was that she couldn't afford to look after her new family on her minimum-wage job. She couldn't apply for benefits, a) because she was illegal herself, and b) she had committed a crime by taking custody of Farida's children.

Orelius removed a thick brown A4 envelope from his briefcase and placed it on the table.

'This is the guy you are marrying,' he said, patting the envelope. 'His name is Jensen and he is Danish. I've filed some basic information in there, but you are meeting him on Tuesday and Friday to learn everything you need to know about each other.'

Naima nodded and slowly picked up the envelope. TJ was relatively quiet for a Sunday afternoon. The small speakers above them were piping slow music at just the right volume for conducting business.

'The ceremony will be at the Barnet registrar's office on Sunday. Everything is in place, including witnesses. But it will be down to you two to make this look authentic. You have the whole of Tuesday and Friday with Jensen. Ask him everything, whether he snores, or talks in his sleep, or pisses sitting down.'

She nodded again with her head down, studying the plain brown envelope.

'Good. Expect a call from him this evening and let me know if you have any questions,' he said waving her away. 'See you on Saturday.'

She started getting up hesitantly, then sat back down. 'Orelius, I know how much I'm paying him for this, and I will use my savings for that,' she started. 'I was just wondering about your fees... if you could maybe let me pay in monthly instalments.'

'Don't worry about it. Let's call this one pro-bono.'

'You mean...?' Her small brown eyes darted left and right in confusion.

'You have saved two young lives, Naima. Maybe someday you will get the appreciation you deserve, but for now this is all I can do.'

She started mumbling a shaky thank you but Orelius waved her away.

'Off you go now, your children are waiting for you.' Then, as she started to rise, he added, 'Oh, could you send Mary over for me? She's sitting up the balcony.'

Mary had called him that morning and asked for a meeting. He still didn't know her problem.

'It's about my husband,' Mary started as soon as she hit the chair opposite Orelius. She seemed jittery and was speaking too fast. 'He went away three weeks ago and now they are saying... he called me and said they wouldn't let him through at the airport. I don't know what to do...' She stopped and looked at Orelius, expecting him to figure out the rest.

'OK, Mary, I need you to calm down,' he said, and allowed her a few seconds to settle. 'I'm assuming your husband is having immigration problems?'

She nodded. 'He went to visit in Zimbabwe and now they are saying there's a problem with his passport. They won't let him back in.'

'So he is not in England?'

'He's in Zimbabwe.'

'Mary, there is not a lot I can do when someone is out of the country,' he said after a brief thought. 'I don't bring people into the country. I help those who are already here. Have you spoken to a lawyer?' A long time ago when he was still a teenager, Orelius had tried the ugly business of human trafficking and decided never again.

Mary gave him a confused look, fidgeting and twiddling her thumbs. She was a big woman of indeterminable age due to the mess created on her face by skin-lightening chemicals. Her all-in-one blue dress with floral patterns and matching headscarf suggested she had dressed for an occasion bigger than this meeting, probably church. The Sunday morning church service was a big thing in Dudlham Farm.

'I wouldn't worry too much about your husband, Mary,' he said after a while, because he could not think of any other way of giving this poor woman some hope. 'He will find his way back in, just like he did last time.'

Mary's husband was a certain young man currently known as Gerald Kayange, but as with most Africans around The Farm, the name was arbitrary. When he was caught working illegally in a fast food restaurant two years before, his name had been Moses Sebanga. While most captured illegal immigrants chained themselves to council doorframes or threatened suicide, Moses surprisingly acted quite to the contrary. He did everything he could to hasten his removal. In a surprisingly eloquent tirade, he called the immigration officers all the despicable names he could think of. He cursed the Queen, the racist British swine and their terrible weather. He thanked them for doing him a favour and saving him from this awful nightmare, and begged them to hurry up and send him home.

In reality, the only nightmares Moses was being saved from were the three credit card companies and a vehicle financer who had been chasing him for money he had spent and was never going to make back. These creditors never saw Moses again. But the man who took their money was indeed back in the country seven months later, with a new name, a darker tan and a fresh set of IDs. He was also eight years younger, according to his new passport.

Mary remained silent across from Orelius, her eyes imploring like those of a small child denied his favourite toy. He thought she was going to break down.

'How many kids have you got again, Mary?'

'We have three children: eleven, six and two.'

'Do you claim benefits?'

'No, we both work. He has... had... two jobs.'

'Has your husband ever been convicted of any crimes in this country?'

'No.'

He took out a sheet of paper from his briefcase and wrote something on it. 'Call this man first thing tomorrow. He is a lawyer. Tell him I sent you.'

She stared curiously at the piece of paper. Orelius stood up.

'Eer... how much do I owe you?' she asked.

'You don't, Mary. I haven't done anything.'

The phone call came as he was hefting his briefcase off the table. He didn't recognise the number but he answered it, using his right shoulder to trap the phone to his ear as he waved goodbye to Mary with his free hand.

'Hello, Orelius?' The voice sounded weak and it took him a few seconds to place it.

‘Hi, Nikisha? Is that you?’

He had given Nikisha Lewis his number when he had first started taking Timmy out. That was nearly seven years ago, and she had never used it.

‘Yes it’s me, sorry to bother you. I was just wondering...’ Her voice was beginning to tail off; as if she wasn’t sure she was permitted to talk.

‘Are you alright?’

‘Yeah I’m fine. I was just wondering if you have Timmy by any chance.’

‘Timmy? No, I had him yesterday, remember? It is Sunday today.’ Orelius couldn’t claim to know this woman at all, but sometimes he found himself worrying about Nikisha’s mental health, given her past.

‘That’s OK then. Sorry to bother you.’

‘Nikki?’

‘Yes...’ There was a trace of fear in her reply.

‘Do you know where Timmy is, Nikisha?’

‘Mmmh yeah... yeah. I think he might have...’ Her voice started dying out again. Then Orelius heard the voice suddenly break down into a shrieking sob. ‘I can’t find him, Orelius. I can’t find him anywhere.’

The last part of the sentence reverberated in his head like a ghastly drum roll. He could not breathe. ‘Are you at home now?’

‘Yes.’

‘I’ll be right there.’

CHAPTER 3

The protests had descended into outright riots outside the Gloucester Road entrance when Orelius got there. Some young black Farmers fed up with the white carnival in their backyard had decided to up the excitement by introducing weapons to the dance, with teenagers throwing bottles and flashing switchblades at the white protestors. For Orelius, the only surprise was that it had taken so long for it to get to that. And it was surely heading for worse. The police were out in full gear, forcing the residents back into Dudlham and trying to disperse the white protesters back into the streets.

He took the Adams Road entrance and darted through the narrow alley between Manston and Lympne, and got to Northolt in less than three minutes. The lift opened in front of him as he rushed for the stairs, and he caught a glimpse of Kelly-Jo in an unusual posture. She appeared to be squatting or kneeling, it was hard to tell. Once upon a time Kelly-Jo's behaviour used to freak out the residents, especially the younger children. Then, when they grew up into teenagers, the fear would go away. Some of them turned into bullies, taking great pleasure in abusing the lift-retard, sometimes spitting or even pissing on her. But in time they had all grown to learn that Kelly-Jo Pretty was just another human being whose problems just happened to be different from theirs. The Farm, and Northolt House in particular, had come to accept her for what she was.

Orelius knocked on number 91 and for the first time Nikisha herself let him into the house. He could not see her eyes behind the thick glasses but some tears had escaped onto her cheeks.

'You OK?' It was a stupid question but he couldn't think of anything else to say.

She snorted something, then broke down again. Orelius walked into the living room and sat down in the middle of the big brown-fabric settee. She took the chair opposite and continued to cry. When she was finished she started recounting events without being prompted.

Contrary to Orelius's assumptions, they had in fact gone to church in the morning despite the riots. On returning they found the protestors in full swing outside the main entrance, so they took the side alley, the one Orelius had used to get here. Timmy had been strangely drawn to the protests, fascinated. He had hesitated too long to look as they walked past, and asked endless questions. When they got in he asked if he could stand outside the door and watch from over the deck. Nikisha said yes but asked him to leave the door open so she could keep an eye on him. She lost track of time in her usual household chores, and the door must have swung shut in the wind, or was never even left open as requested in the first place. But that still shouldn't have been any cause for alarm. Even in The Farm one could justifiably consider the hallway immediately outside their own front door safe enough for a ten-year-old to hang around at midday. However, when Nikisha went out to look for him, he wasn't there. She asked her immediate neighbours first, starting with The Hog next door, and got nothing. So she headed down and walked around the block, and then towards the epicentre of the commotion at main entrance, questioning people along the way. There was no sign of Timmy anywhere.

'This was how long ago?' Orelius asked.

'The service finished just after eleven. We were back here by midday.'

He looked at the clock on the wall above the TV. Five minutes before five p.m.

Orelius stepped out onto the deck and scanned Dudlham Farm from above. The setting sun was hanging somewhere behind the imposing structure of Kenley. Old cars lined the narrow streets like foot-soldiers. There were groups of rowdy kids wandering about haphazardly, grateful for the mayhem that had come to their doorstep on a Sunday afternoon. Some protestors were still out there. A couple of them were being bundled into a police van along with several Dudlham residents. The rest of them assembled in the middle of the road with their placards, blocking the police vehicles and chanting over the sirens.

Someone caught his eye in the crowd, a small figure in the midst of a group of much bigger boys who were creeping in towards the action from about two car lengths behind the police van. He stood out due to his size and bright-coloured jacket as he darted randomly within the labyrinth, like a stray atom vibrating inside a molecule seeking stability.

'What was he wearing?' Orelius asked through the open door without taking his eyes off the stray atom. 'Was it the Nile Jacket?'

'What?' She first sounded confused as she came out to the door to join him. 'Oh... yeah, he had the light blue Nike jacket you bought him,' she answered. 'With a grey shirt underneath and...'

Orelius did not get the rest because he was already on his way. He kept his eye on the flickering blue figure in the crowd as he stamped towards the stairwell with rapid but precise steps. His pace quickened down the stairs and he broke into a jog halfway there. He didn't even realise that Nikisha had been following not far behind till they were at the scene on Gloucester Road.

The section of the crowd he was seeking was a safe enough distance away from the real trouble. He waded in with ease.

He spotted the blue jacket. And read the label on the back:

Nile.

*

The kid's name was Byron and he looked about twelve or thirteen. He was defiant at first. Without batting an eyelid he claimed the jacket was his: that his mother had bought it for him, he'd owned it for months and had never heard of Timmy Lewis.

'Where do you live, Byron?' Orelius asked without letting go of his hand.

'Debden.'

'OK, let's head to Debden and have a word with your mother about that jacket, shall we?'

'My mum is not at home.'

'Where is she?'

'At work.'

'So who's at home?'

'No one.'

'Then we are going to have to go and see this *No One*, Byron,' he said, and began dragging him towards Debden. 'That jacket belongs to a boy about your age who is missing. If you don't tell us the truth about where you got it, something bad might happen to him, and you will be to blame.'

Nikisha wasn't as patient. She yanked the back of the jacket forcefully, as if trying to rip it off his back.

'Tell us where he is,' she yelled, shoving him back and forth. 'Just tell us where he is forgodsake!' Then she let go as the tears once again got the better of her.

And that was all it took to break the little tough guy. He started shaking, his eyes fluttering submissively before welling up.

'I just found it,' he mumbled, then collapsed into sobs. 'I didn't do anything, I swear. I just found it.'

He was still crying when he showed them where he'd found it: by the roadside about fifteen yards from where his troop had been parading. That, he said, had been about an hour ago.

Orelius stripped him of the jacket and held it up for closer inspection. The patches of dirt and footprints were consistent with the boy's story. There was a partial pimply footprint on the lower back and at the top of the sleeves near the shoulders, with a clear space in between. It was as if someone had trodden on the jacket while it was folded diagonally almost in half – which would have been hard to achieve with a person inside it. There was no blood or any other alarming marks.

He flung the jacket over his shoulder and held onto it with a forefinger hooked into its hood as he surveyed the rioters one more time. The crowd was thinning, the farmers slowly retreating into the estate and the protestors back down Gloucester Road. Stern-faced police officers were marching along in packs, sweeping up any obstinate offenders and dumping them in marked vehicles.

'Hey, excuse me,' Orelius called after one of the uniformed officers who was helping bundle a captive into the van.

'You are going to have to step back, sir,' said the young policeman. He was brown-haired with a smooth boyish face, a new recruit. 'We are trying to deal with a very serious situation here.'

'My boy is missing. I believe he's been caught somewhere in this.'

'What?'

'I said my boy has somehow been caught in this. He is missing.' Then, noticing the officer's puzzled expression, he added. 'He is ten years old.'

'With all due respect, sir, I've had six-year-olds chucking bottles at me, so I can't pretend to be shocked,' he said, swinging the back doors of the van shut and turning to face him. 'But I don't think we've arrested anyone that young today. Have you looked for him in other places? Like his friends maybe... it is a Sunday, you know.'

'We have, officer. I wouldn't be coming to you if I didn't think it was serious.'

'You are going to have to report this to the local police. We are here to deal with this situation.' He swept both his arms to indicate the rioters.

Orelius started to protest but the officer was already moving away towards two placard wavers who were getting too close to the van.

Another police vehicle arrived, screeching to a halt right in front of the group and blocking their path. A piercing sound tore through the air as loudspeakers from the new vehicle came to life: 'These protests have been declared illegal. You have five minutes to disperse or you will be arrested and charged.'

The dwindling group was suddenly reinvigorated. They held their ground and started chanting even louder. The officers stayed in the vehicles and watched, counting down after every minute.

'Four minutes. You now have four minutes...

'...Three minutes. You now have three minutes...'

They counted down to one, before the group reluctantly started drifting away through Hornchurch into Freedom Road.

Orelius watched them, knowing that the group could be walking away with the answer to where Timmy was. He realised he was not thinking rationally. Perhaps they should have asked around, talked to some neighbours and scoured The Farm with reasonable thoroughness first, before thinking about the next move. But Dudlham Farm and the neighbours were not going anywhere; these people were. And one or more of them probably knew something that could help locate Timmy. Or even worse, God forbid, one of them could have done something to him.

He quickly committed a few of the departing faces to memory. Then he asked Byron for his house number in case he needed to ask him more questions, before dismissing the boy and beckoning for Nikisha to follow him back to the house. He needed to think. His gut instinct told him he needed to speak to the rioters. But they also needed to keep calm. He looked up the local police station and asked Nikisha to call and report a missing child. While they were waiting for the police to arrive, he started questioning her again.

'Are there any friends in the neighbourhood? People he's been hanging around with lately?'

'Timmy hasn't got any friends. He goes to school in the week, spends Saturdays with you, and we go to church on Sundays. He's had trouble making friends, even at school. His visits with classmates are rare, and when they do happen they are always prearranged.' She started crying again. 'My baby never gets out of my sight, we do everything together. He wouldn't just walk away like that.'

'OK, Nikki.' He allowed her some time to cry. Telling her to calm down would have appeared patronising in the circumstances. 'We'll wait for the police and see what they make of this and how they want to proceed. But I personally feel we need to speak with one or two from that group that was out there today. Tim was very intrigued by the protestors; I think he was drawn out there.'

It took more than half an hour for the police to arrive. They were two local officers, both in their late twenties or early thirties, a black male and a white female. They introduced themselves quickly, with names and titles Orelius could not grasp, then went through the motions of asking the obvious questions: about friends, relatives, neighbours, and Has he ever done this before?... They only changed tack when the jacket was brought up.

'Uh... huh, so, shall we assume he was out there amongst the riots?' the male officer asked Orelius.

'Why would you want to assume? You are police officers.'

The man grunted awkwardly and nodded his head. His face suggested he was not charmed by Orelius's attitude.

'Yes, I do think it might have something to do with the riots – not that he was involved,' Orelius said. 'He was out on the balcony watching them; we believe he went down there and that's when something happened. But there is no way on earth he could have been involved in the actual riots. Not Timmy.'

'We are not here to judge, sir,' the woman said, raising her eyebrows sardonically. 'No problem, we'll check with the officers who attended the scene. I understand a few people were arrested but I'd be surprised if any of them were ten years old. If he somehow got injured out there and ended up in hospital, you would probably have been informed by now. But we will check that too.'

'Please do that,' he said. Then, choosing his words carefully, he added, 'I've also got some other, slightly bigger fears. That mob out there – we assume most of them were here to make a political statement. But a mob is made up of people, and there are all kinds of people in this world. Who is to say that someone amongst them wasn't just a sick individual out to fulfil their perverted needs?'

That took the officers by surprise. They stared at each other before the man spoke.

'Well, that is one theory, and we'll certainly keep it in mind. But we have to start via the obvious channels. We will need to keep this jacket. Then knock on a few of your neighbours doors and ask some questions before we decide how to proceed. Assuming Timmy does not turn up in that time, obviously.'

Orelius had expected this; Timmy was ten years old and this was Dudlham Farm. If they were lucky, the police would start taking this seriously after twenty-four hours; only someone with some understanding of Timmy Lewis and his close relationship with his mother would know that only a few minutes of unexplained absence was enough. He asked to be excused and started heading for the stairs as the two officers began their inquiry by knocking on The Hog's door.

He had asked Nikisha to call him if the door-to-door routine yielded something. He couldn't simply hang around.

*

Within the next hour Orelius had found five Farmers he remembered seeing at the Gloucester Road gate and asked if they had seen Timmy in the fracas. None could remember. But after further grilling, two of them dug deep and said they might have seen him. But that was all, there was nothing else to tell.

This only supported Orelius's logic. There had been two groups of people out there, the Farmers and the outsiders, and right now he only needed to worry about the latter. He had lived here all his adult life and had witnessed burglaries, muggings and drug dealing. These were the kinds of crimes associated with The Farm. He had never heard of a child going missing. Besides, he could always come back and talk to the Farmers later; the outsiders on the other hand were a group of random individuals brought together by a racist campaign. He didn't know them, and aside from their common cause, he doubted that they themselves knew each other.

He retreated to his Croydon House flat to draw up a plan. His friend Cory, whom he had left a message while still at Nikisha's, had still not got back to him, so he picked up his phone again and tried the next person he had in mind.

The man everyone called Mega answered straightaway. They traded pleasantries over loud rap music that was blaring from somewhere in the background before Orelius hit him with the news.

'Listen, Mega, I've got a bit of a situation,' he said as calmly as he could and heard the music in the background stop dead; *situations* was Mega's life. 'Timmy has gone missing.'

'Holy pig.'

'We think he went over to see the riots and he hasn't come back. He definitely wasn't arrested, the police have been notified and they're asking around with some neighbours.'

'Holy pig.'

'He's been gone since around the time of the protests, so we are slightly worried. But we'll try not to panic just yet.'

'Holy pig.'

'I've got one more place to check and if I don't get any luck, I might require a search party. I'd like you to give Cory and some of the boys a heads up and I'll let you know if I need you.'

'Let me know ASAP. I'm getting a team on standby right now,' Mega said with the authority of a seasoned colonel.

Mega, or Megaman, was a six-foot-five seventeen-stone bare-knuckle cage fighter. Real name: Adrian Gibbs. He boasted a string of criminal convictions, most containing the phrase *Bodily Harm*. Orelius hoped it wouldn't come to that, but if things got out of hand Mega would be useful; because when Megaman spoke, people generally listened.

'We'll all stop whatever we are doing,' Mega assured him, 'find Timmy, then maybe everyone can go to sleep in peace.'

'Thanks, Mega.'

'No worries, bro. I gotch' you.'

CHAPTER 4

It was a few minutes after eight p.m. before Orelius started making his way to a pub in Palmers Green known as The Fighting Cocks. He had made some inquiries and found out, among other things, that this was the pub where those white rioters had gathered to plot their activities and where they would have reconvened afterwards to relive their adventures over drinks. It was well known that The Fighting Cocks was a Whites Only pub and that only the law prevented them from putting up a big banner across the gates advertising the fact. But today, Orelius Simm was going to The Fighting Cocks.

He heard the news of a breakthrough in the Ear-Slasher case on his car radio as he drove down the high street. A press conference was being held at New Scotland Yard and the emerging news was that one of the owners of the mysterious severed ears had turned up. The victim was not present at the press conference and his identity could not be revealed because he was a minor.

The first part of the puzzle, the actual crime, had been cracked. After all the talk about race, this turned out after all to be a drug-related crime, with no hint of racism whatsoever. Some drug baron, confirmed as a white male, had sent his henchman to deliver a special warning to some kids who had messed up one of his drug deals. The henchman got overzealous and chopped their ears off. This henchman, they said, was black. He was believed to be the person who abandoned the van with his human-ear souvenirs at the Lympne House car park. Neither the black henchman nor his white master had been apprehended, but this was nevertheless a significant break. They now had a victim and a motive. The police were so grateful to this kid for coming up that they agreed, as a gesture of goodwill, not to pursue the drug charges against him. He was a victim, they said. A small-time drug runner caught in the middle of a sour deal. The unnamed victim would instead be put on counselling and full rehabilitation programme, whatever that meant.

The police spokesman more than once commended the victim's bravery for coming forward to shed some light on this case.

Orelius heard this and wondered whether the thugs he was going to confront at The Fighting Cocks were also listening. How would they be feeling about their stupid protests now? Probably nothing, maybe even gratitude for the fun they had had while it lasted. These were racist thugs who needed no excuse to terrorise blacks.

He walked through the front door of The Fighting Cocks a few minutes before nine p.m. There were two sections, one on either side of the bar. Everyone seemed to be on the right-hand side, giving the fleeting impression that the place was packed. But the slightly lowered section to his left facing the giant flat screen was empty and the TV was off. There was a skinny young man standing at the bar with a microphone and a stack of papers in front of him reading out the Sunday night pub quiz. This was the reason for the lopsided population distribution: only this side of the bar had working speakers.

They noticed him one table at a time, and the whispers quickly spread. The silence cascaded spectacularly from front to back like a well-orchestrated musical arrangement, starting from the skinny quiz master, who spotted him mid-question.

'Question twenty-five: which were the last five states...' He hesitated here after seeing Orelius standing next to the front door, then proceeded in a slightly subdued tone: '...which were the last five states to join the USA?'

By now everyone was aware of his presence and he could feel the malicious stares.

A big man with beefy tattooed arms walked up. He stopped about five yards away from Orelius and stared hard at him without saying anything. Then he walked on to the bar and whispered something to the quiz master, who nodded earnestly before getting back on the microphone.

'Right everybody, Pistol Pete has made a special request. He wishes to be allowed to read the next question,' he announced. 'So I'm passing you over to him.'

There were giggles from the table Pistol Pete had come from. Orelius looked over to that group and saw a pretty young blonde he recognised as Rachael Sutherland. He knew Rachael through his friend Jermaine back at The Farm. And he knew a few things about her that made her presence here surprising.

At the bar the young barmaid and the quiz master exchanged conspirators' smiles as Pistol Pete took the microphone.

'OK, number twenty-six is a multiple choice question,' Pistol Pete started without looking at the sheet in front of him. 'What was the role of Africans in the great British empire? Were they... (A) Shooting-range targets...?'

This time the giggles came from all round the bar and Pistol Pete smiled, keeping his eyes on Orelius as he read on.

'...(B) slaves...? Or... (C) Pets.'

There was a thunderous roar of laughter. People clapped as Pistol Pete squeezed his way back to his table.

Orelius had come here hoping for empathy, expecting hostility, and prepared for a fight. He could tell now that he was going to get the latter. And someone was going to get hurt.

He watched on as Pistol Pete's team welcomed him back with high fives all round. When his tattooed arms got to Rachael, he held on to her hand, pulled her up close and gave her a hard, lingering kiss on the lips.

'Excuse me...' a sharp voice drew his attention away from Pistol Pete. 'Can I help you with anything?'

Orelius had not seen the short man approach. He was dressed in a white shirt and plain grey tie. His posture remained firm as he stared up unflinchingly at Orelius, juggling a big bunch of keys in his right hand. It wasn't hard to work out that he was the manager of the house.

'Don't worry, I'm not here looking for trouble,' Orelius said. 'I just need to talk to some of your punters.'

'Well, I'm afraid I can't let you do that. I can't let you go around bothering my guests.'

'Like I said, I come in peace... Why don't you let them decide for themselves if they want to talk to me?'

The man shook his head slowly with a derisive smile. 'You just don't get it, do you?'

'Oh yes, I get it alright. I know I'm not welcome here, believe me. I'm only here because I have to be, so please excuse me.'

'OK, let me make this simple for you, let's just say you are barred from this pub. So no, you are not excused! Now will you kindly step–'

'Barred?' Orelius smiled. 'Since when?'

'Since the moment you stepped in, OK? I don't have to give you a reason. Just do us all a favour and step outside.'

Orelius was already walking away but not in the direction the small man expected. He was ducking between the closely packed tables, heading towards Pistol Pete's group.

'Hey!' the manager shouted but Orelius ignored him as he pushed past the middle-aged couple who were standing with their drinks next to the group. The table was cluttered with paper and drinks and there were no available seats. He leant forward with his elbows on the edge of the table and flashed his best smile at its dumbstruck occupants.

'Sorry for the interruption, people. But I've got a problem, and I know this is not going to be easy but I can't think of any other–'

'Listen, buddy–' This came from a stocky bald man seated on the other side of the table, directly opposite him. '–I don't know where you come from, but in this country we don't just walk into parties uninvited.'

'Don't be nice to him, Lee. Just tell him to fuck off,' said Pistol Pete, who had now settled back in his seat with his beefy arms around Rachael. He turned to Orelius, and to show Lee how it was supposed to be done, he spat out: 'Fuck off!'

Behind him, the manager was also yelling. 'I told you to leave, mate. Don't blame me if this gets ugly.'

Orelius turned round to face him. 'I am not leaving till I'm done, OK?' Then he spotted a sudden movement off the corner of his right eye and swung back instinctively with his guard up, blocking the left hook from Pistol Pete's fist and simultaneously planting his right knee into the big man's groin.

Pistol Pete went down like a puppet whose strings had been snapped.

Orelius spun back towards the manager and, keeping a straight face, he said, 'Looks like it's already got ugly, mate.'

He sensed another movement from the same table, and this time he didn't turn round. He simply stretched his right arm behind him without looking.

'Sit down, Lee,' he said calmly. But there was a black Glock 17 semi-automatic pistol in his hand, pointing the bald man back to his chair, in case Lee didn't understand his words.

A collective gasp of horror rose from the table, followed by absolute silence, which quickly spread and once again engulfed the house.

The barman tried to dart for the door from behind his counter and Orelius turned the gun towards him. 'Get back behind that bar, soldier. I need everyone in here.' Then, back to the manager, 'Have you got the door keys on there?' he asked, pointing at his bunch.

The manager was trying to remain stoic but his quivering lips let him down. He mustered a nod, holding out the keys.

'Good, now, I'll walk you to the doors and you are going to lock them for me, OK? You are free to try any clever tricks at your peril.' He quickly scanned the crowd and, waving the

Glock in the air, he shouted, 'That goes for every single one of you.'

They got to the door and back to Pistol Pete's table without incident. The seating arrangement favoured him: with everyone huddled on one side of the bar, he had them all within his field of vision.

'Right, I didn't want to do this, but it has come to this,' he started, when he was happy he had the situation contained. He was juggling the manager's bunch of keys passively in one hand while the other held the Glock face down. When he looked into the eyes of the girl he recognised, he saw her face drop.

'Is this your boyfriend, Rachael?' Orelius asked her, pointing at Pistol Pete with the Glock.

Rachael nodded but her whole body was shaking.

'So, what does that make Jermaine then? Your slave... or your pet?' Orelius looked down at Pistol Pete, who was still on the ground. 'I bet the emperor here didn't even know you are sleeping with slaves... Did you, Pete?'

Pistol Pete winced again.

'I bet that hurts, doesn't it, Pete? My grandmother once told me that hate is a golden retriever with a wicked sense of humour: picks out all your cast-offs and drags them back up to your feet.' He smiled down at the big man. 'You hate gays... your brother turns out to be one of them. You hate niggers, your girlfriend starts fucking them.'

Then he thought of something and headed for the bar. There were three people there: the two staff behind the counter and the quiz master. Orelius waved them with the Glock to join the other captives and all three complied with a swift cowering retreat. Then he walked over to the now completely incapacitated Pete and, with relative ease, dragged him to the front of the room. He sat him on the floor against the counter a yard or so from his feet and took the microphone.

'Good evening, ladies and gentlemen,' he said on the mike. 'I believe you were having a wonderful evening before I came in, and I hope you can continue having a wonderful time once I've left. But it looks like the bit in between is not going to be pleasant. I came in here looking for some information regarding a missing boy. The reason I chose this place was because this boy went missing from Dudlham Farm Estate around midday today and we all know that most of you here were in Dudlham at that time. His name is Timmy and he is ten years old. He went down to the entrance to watch the riots and hasn't been seen since.

'I'm going to walk around and show each of you a picture of Timmy. If someone knows something useful and they can help me, I will thank them, then apologise to the rest of you, and let everyone get on with their evening. If I think someone knows something and they are lying to me, I will try not to hurt them – because there's no way I can be sure it is a lie, and I am a fair man like that. I will, however, hurt Pistol Pete here instead,' he said tapping Pete's back lightly with the pointed tip of his boot. 'I will hurt him a little bit more every time I think I hear a lie, and keep it going till I get the truth. If I don't come out with a lot of true stories from this pub tonight, the big man here will be left wishing he was dead. I want the liar to always remember, every time they go to see Pistol Pete in hospital, that they could have saved him. And for this I will not apologise. Because this man has hurt my feelings. I get emotional when people remind me of those slavery days.'

He put the microphone on the counter and reached into his back pocket for the picture of Timmy he had borrowed from Nikisha. To keep a clear view of everyone and the front door, he stayed where he was and started calling them up one by one and showing them Timmy's picture.

First up was a stumpy young man with greasy curly hair who slowly shook his head at the picture. Orelius stared hard into his eyes and knew this was a person who'd never been in an arm-wrestling contest in his life, let alone a fight. The sight of the Glock would scar him forever. Orelius waved him back into the crowd and called the next.

He was with the fifth potential witness and had kicked Pistol Pete hard on the shin only once when he realised his mistake. Despite being armed, he was still gravely disadvantaged: a single man trying to control a crowd of thirty drunks. There was no way of making absolutely certain that no one reached for their mobile phone. He was relying solely on fear. However, by locking the doors, he had calculated that he could buy himself enough time to get *something* from these people; some hope, some glimmer of information to give him a start.

This was a mistake. Other than keeping his hostages contained, locking the doors had achieved very little with regard to a potential ambush from outside. He had underestimated the speed of CO19 – the Metropolitan Police's Armed Response Unit – and their special skills in gaining entry to buildings undetected.

They appeared like ghosts, from the lowered left section of the bar that had been deserted, maybe through a concealed fire-exit he had not spotted. Thick black armoured police vests over white shirts, approaching stealthily with submachine guns. Orelius turned and caught a glimpse of the muzzle of a Heckler and Koch MP5 carbine.

And that was it.

The pain was only a momentary flash, all the muscles of his body tensing simultaneously and collapsing into a searing spasm.

Then nothing.

BOOK TWO

The Cop

CHAPTER 5

He had been up for about fifteen minutes and was still trying to figure out his location when he heard a movement on the other side of the metallic door, a series of quick shuffling footsteps, followed by a light tap and a click of the door. A face appeared in the peephole, and Orelius could make out a small section of the pale skin around the sharp blue eye that was peering unblinkingly at him. He stared back, trying to work out whether it was a man or a woman, but the face shifted as the figure began to speak.

'Hellooo there. You up?' The voice was male, slightly shrill with a slight Midlands twang.

Orelius walked to the door and rapped loudly on it in reply.

Whoever he was – most likely a police officer – he seemed happy enough. He said, 'OK, I'm going to get my colleague to open this door and we'll lead you to the front desk where we are going to formally place charges. Then we will bring you back here pending bail hearing. Do you understand that?'

Orelius was still thinking of what to say but he heard the man's footsteps heading away from the door without waiting for an answer. He trudged back to the shelf-like outcrop at the far corner of the cell that served as the bed, and sat on it, covering his face with both hands. The inch-thick mattress with a blue plastic cover did nothing to alleviate the pain in his lower back. The cell was about ten foot by ten, with cold concrete flooring. Other than the bed, there was a small rusty sink-toilet combination in the corner right of the door, and nothing else.

He had no recollection of anything after the arrival of the submachine gun-wielding uniforms at The Fighting Cocks. But since he was still alive, with no visible flesh wounds, he could guess that the Firearms Response Unit had not used the MP5s on him. Instead, they had pumped 50,000 volts of electricity through his body with a Taser gun. Someone had indeed done something clever and dialled 999 as soon as the trouble started. He never stood a chance.

The door clanked open five minutes later and he found himself face to face with two Met operatives. They were both blonde and of average height, but one of them was considerably wider than the other, especially around his waist. The slender one looked neat, with an intricately trimmed schoolboy haircut. He started by reading Orelius his rights, formally placing him under arrest. Then he stepped aside and motioned him to walk ahead of him, with Big Hips already on his way, thus sandwiching him between the Uniforms.

At the front desk, a grey-haired custody sergeant had just started asking him routine questions for the paperwork when the man was informed that there was an urgent call for his attention. In a clearly sarcastic display of courtesy, the sergeant asked Orelius to excuse him, before he disappeared into an office.

When he came back five minutes later he appeared brusque. He rattled out some drivel in police-speak, then ordered his officers to take the suspect back to his cell. From what little Orelius could glean, something more important had come up which meant they would have to finish booking him some other time. Ten minutes later he was back in the cell, lying prostrate on the thin plastic mattress and plotting his next move when a thick chain rattled loudly once again. The sound of the door opening brought a muffled sigh of relief. The short stint in solitary was already driving him close to the edge.

'We are going for a walk, mate.' The announcement came from a dark Asian officer with a moustache. He held the door open and nodded towards it. 'Come on, this way.'

Orelius began to feel a strange itching around the back of his neck as the officer led him out past the front desk, through a series of corridors, to a dull-coloured room about the size of an average lounge, at the back of the station. Other than an old beechwood table and two chairs, the room was bare. The officer pointed him to one of the chairs and left the room.

A blonde-haired man walked in as he left. This one was carrying a green plastic folder, which he dropped on the table before taking the chair opposite Orelius. He wore a short-sleeved black shirt and a grey tie with blue stripes, and looked tanned, like he had been on a holiday. The man loosened his tie, then started flipping though his folder without looking at Orelius. He was snapping through the pages way to quickly to be actually reading the contents.

'Orelius Kendrick Simm,' he said when he finally looked up. His voice was deep and assertive. Then he went back to the file, nodding silently, as if giving Orelius time to respond.

It was not a question, so Orelius looked straight back at him and continued to scratch the back of his neck, saying nothing.

'Hmm...' The officer nodded again, like he understood the lack of response. 'Do you know why you are here, Mr Simm?'

'Yes, I know why I'm here.'

The man calmly nodded.

'You are not here to represent me, are you?' Oreluis scratched the top of his left arm. The itching was getting worse and he was convinced it was some mystery plague from within that dingy cell, or perhaps the Taser gun. 'I haven't asked for a lawyer yet.'

'No, I'm here to ask you some questions, although you don't have to answer them. That is your right. You could also choose to talk to me at a later time, once you've spoken to your lawyer, if that's what you want.'

Orelius stared at him and he stared back, before going back to the file.

'OK, Mr Simm, there is CCTV footage and at least twenty witnesses saying that at around nine p.m. last night you held an entire public bar hostage, armed with an illegal weapon. You shot at an individual from close range in an obvious attempt to murder, and you assaulted at least one man, causing grievous bodily harm.' He looked up from the file. 'These are only some of the charges they will be putting on the booking sheet.'

He spoke articulately, with a cockney accent but without the rough East London edge, like a man who gave a lot of presentations. Again he didn't give Orelius time to respond before resuming his pitch.

'Orelius–' they were now apparently on first name terms '– it sounds to me like you are in a lot of trouble, my friend.'

Orelius chuckled, flashing a quick sarcastic smile even though the irritating itch was still travelling along his arms. He could feel it now on the inside of his palms.

'You OK? Looks like you are coming out in a rash around your neck.'

'No I'm not OK. I'm sure this is from whatever you lot shot me with, and I will be taking action.' Scratching the inside of his palms was proving tricky. 'I want my lawyer, now.'

'That's fine, it is your right. Who is your lawyer? You got a contact number?'

'Andre Boateng, I'm sure you'd know how to find him.'

'Of course... of course. Dr Dre himself,' he said in a childish singsong tone through a dry chuckle. 'I'm sure Dr Boateng would love to represent all black people who find themselves in trouble in this country. But he is therefore a very busy man. You might want to pick someone we can access right now. Besides, I doubt Lord Boateng would want to be associated with someone like you, I really do.'

Dr Andre Boateng was a famous human rights lawyer, a young black man who had made a great impression nationwide, tackling famous cases for the downtrodden. The good doctor first made his name about five years back when fresh from law school; he won a landmark case for the residents of Aylesbury estate, forcing the City of London to foot the bill for the relocation of liquor stores from the area. He had sued the council claiming that the number of licensed stores within and around the estate selling cheap alcohol was disproportionate to the residents' needs, and their concentration there did not compare evenly with other areas. These stores, he argued, were taking advantage of vulnerable young people and their presence could directly be attributed to antisocial behaviour. The council had first tried to settle things out of court, proposing to relocate a small proportion of the shops. All the stores in question had been established there legally, sold many everyday essentials other than alcohol, and had officially never fallen foul of the law. The shop owners decided the easiest way to stop this madness was by demanding ridiculously large sums of compensation if they were to be moved through no fault of their own. They plucked a sum from the air that they knew the council could never afford, and threw it at them – after all, it was the council that set the terms of the licence, and they had fulfilled their part of the deal. If the council wanted to break the agreement because of some overexcited kid, fine, but there was a price. It was widely expected that the council would come to its senses and realise that Dr Boateng had no case; that some judge would simply tell this grumpy black kid to get a life. So to the courts it went, and after three weeks of highly publicised arguments it was the council that was sent home with its tail between its legs to clear up the mess.

Dr Boateng was now a regular on the news and current affairs programmes, and had just been awarded a peerage. So he was in fact Lord Boateng, although he remained known to the masses simply as Dr Dre.

Orelius ignored the officer's insult and continued to scratch his arms.

'You are a very interesting character, aren't you Orelius?' The man leant back on his chair to study him from a different angle, and Orelius couldn't help thinking this man was performing to some unseen audience. His appearance and demeanour wouldn't have been out of place in Hollywood:

sharp chiselled facial structure covered in a wave of golden blonde locks; articulate speech and generally confident aura.

When Orelius gave no response, the man edged forward again, plumped his left elbow on the table and, with his right hand, started tapping at the open page of his file with a silver pen. 'You have a wide range of business interests ranging from trafficking illegal migrants into the country, selling fake identity documents, brokering the recruitment of illegal workers... in fact they tell me in Dudlham that Orelius can solve any problem. "Orelius will fix it" seems to be quite a slogan down there.' He chuckled mirthlessly before going back to a random page. 'You have a Masters degree in Business Management from Manchester but it hasn't been utilised in quite the way your professors intended.

'Excluding your flat in Dudlham, which you bought under the Tenant Purchase Scheme, you own two other properties: a three-bedroom semi in Hampstead and a luxury flat in St Albans, both let out to rich professionals and providing you with a rental income of approximately seven grand a month. Great job if you can get it, Orelius.' He whistled, shaking his head dramatically. Then he picked up his narrative again. 'And yet, astute businessman that you are, you still choose to live in your Dudlham Farm flat, closer to your clients. What is the ultimate goal, Orelius? When does it stop? When is it going to be enough so you can cash in, pack up and join your father on the beaches of Barbados?'

The man paused and loosened his tie some more. 'Do you want to say anything at this point, Orelius?' He was smiling at Orelius as he said this, clearly expecting him to be impressed.

'I take it that is a serious question.'

'It is. Have you got anything you want to say?'

Orelius couldn't help smiling back. 'No, *sir*. I do not wish to say anything.'

'Great.' He slapped his palms and rubbed them together in a *let's-get-down-to-it* gesture. Then he swept his hands along his arms as though rolling up his nonexistent sleeves before proceeding. 'There is of course a point to all this. I understand your little boy is missing... I also know that he is not your biological son, but no matter...' He shrugged. 'Anyway, this is how I see it: you were very keen to find your boy yourself because you didn't believe in the police. And that's why you did what you did at the pub last night. Some people would consider that gallant and admirable, and I have to admit that I am one of those people.

'However, things haven't turned out quite as you planned, have they? Because now you are facing the prospect of not only being unable to do anything about finding your boy but also of not seeing the outside of these walls, or the walls of the prison they will send you to, for a very long time.'

He stopped and waited, but he had still not asked a question, so Orelius stayed silent, closing his fists tightly to control the urge to scratch.

'Wise move, Orelius. Silence is a great weapon around here, but most people don't understand this. I can see why you are successful in your endeavours.' He covered his mouth behind clenched fists and cleared his throat, again just for effect – there was nothing wrong with his throat. 'Orelius, did you really believe that those people took Timmy?'

'I only went up there to ask them a few questions. But yes, I do believe that any one of them is capable of taking Timmy. Human beings do inhuman things. Surely, as a policeman, you know that.'

'You think right in the midst of a mob of dozens of citizens and police officers someone had the time to grab a boy, strip him naked and take off with him without being noticed?'

'What do you mean strip him naked? We only found his jacket...' He looked up at the man's expression and knew straight away that he had missed a lot whilst in that cell. 'Oh no... what are you talking about... what happened?'

'I'm sorry, I thought you knew. I guess this happened about the time you were on your way to The Fighting Cocks.' He shook his head apologetically. 'They found the rest of his clothing... including his underwear... everything except his shoes.'

The items had been found early last night, when the investigating team went back to the scene of the riots where the jacket had been found. They had been scattered within about a fifty-yard radius but in plain sight, as though no effort had been made to hide them. Forensic techs were still working on them but initial inspections revealed no obvious signs of trauma.

Orelius listened with his head down, muttering '*Oh my God*' repeatedly.

'The most important thing of course is Timmy. Everything is being done out there.'

'What exactly *is* being done?' Orelius snapped. 'Why are you telling me all this... who are you... where the hell is my lawyer?'

'Like I said, you don't have to talk to me, Orelius.'

The man's calmness had some effect: Orelius's tone became imploring. 'I need to get out of here, please. I know I did wrong but I was just looking for Timmy.'

'You committed a serious criminal offence.'

'I was desperate. These were people who were going to be lost back in the wilderness by the time the police took the case seriously.' The inflammation had now reached every inch of his body and he was scratching away frantically without shame. 'I was just trying to get something I could hold on to.'

'But why them, Orelius... why them?'

'If something happened to Timmy out there,' he placed a hand gently over his heart, 'if this happened at the riots, then I believe one of the outsiders was responsible. Dudlham Farm is my home and I know everything that goes on up there.'

'So it's us against them, huh?... None of your fellow Farmers would ever harm your little boy, eh...? If you know everything that goes on in Dudlham, would you care to tell me which one of you friends recently chopped off some kids' ears and left them in an abandoned vehicle?'

Orelius said nothing.

'Exactly, I didn't think you would,' the man quipped. 'The group you targeted are a few ignorant drunks with nothing better to do. But taking a little boy? Orelius, if you really want to save Timmy, you need to calm down and think logically. The truth is the majority of us are appalled by the likes of Tom Clarke and his thugs, but this is about Timmy... Don't you think your emotions are just getting the better of you here?'

'You are thinking of them as a mob. I'm thinking of them as individuals.'

The man's blue eyes shot up, almost in admiration.

'This world is full of sick, twisted people, sir,' Orelius continued. 'Dozens of them were marching at the exact location where Timmy disappeared yesterday. How can you be sure none of them is involved?'

'I'm not sure about anything but I know that was an organised group who made a list of everyone who participated in the rally. Investigating them will be the easier task, and someone is doing that now. They are disgraceful low-lifes, but my initial feeling, after talking to a few of them, is that you are looking in the wrong place. But don't worry, they are being dealt with by very capable officers, and we shall see.

'I personally would be more worried about another, more complicated situation, if I were you. Less than a week ago five human ears were found in the car park on the block right opposite where Timmy lives. And then yesterday the boy goes missing. Two highly unusual and disturbing occurrences in the same place in the space of one week. I wonder why that never struck you as odd – unless of course you knew all along the story behind those ears.'

'That was a drugs thing, and I only know that because it was on the radio. It's not my scene and it's definitely not Timmy's.'

The man froze, as if Orelius's response had thrown him off track.

'OK, I will admit you got me there,' he finally said. 'I assumed that news broke while you were locked up in here and that you hadn't heard it yet. But never mind, I do have a good explanation for that, and I will give it to you, just bear with me. First I need to talk to you about why I'm here.'

He closed the folder and shifted it to one side. 'In the last week, while trying to investigate this Ear-Slasher thing, we have found it very difficult to get any real cooperation from the residents of The Farm. There are fleets of abandoned vehicles stolen from scrapyards, sitting on those car parks, some of them with no wheels or roofs. Nobody owns them; someone just drags them there after they've been removed from the DVLA records, in case one of his good neighbours might find a use for them. Sort of like communal ownership: if you can make use of the windscreen or a tyre, chop away; if you can get it started, drive away. The van with the ears had no number plates; but even if it did, tracking the owners would be a dead end.

'We know some of these vehicles come alive late at night, with false stick-on licence plates to commit crime. And they're back again by early morning, lying dormant between the Dudlham stilts as ownerless junks. We know that Transit is drivable, was in fact driven recently, and that its latest trip probably resulted in those ears. Yet somehow all the people we've managed to question know nothing. They don't know how the cars get there, never seen anyone touch them, never seen them move... they are just junk. These... *Farmers*, as you call them... they don't like the police much. They simply want us to go away.'

This was clearly a reference to last year's violent riots, which had severely worsened the already sour relationship between the police and the black community.

The man proceeded. 'But I found out that they do like you very much, Orelius. That is why I'm here, to make you a simple proposition: if you can help us in Dudlham Farm, we can help you with this.' He patted the green folder.

'What do you mean, help you?'

'We need to find the person who drove that Transit into Dudlham.'

'You mean the drug dealer's henchman?'

'Forget why they were there. We just need the person who last drove the van.'

'You want me to be a snitch?'

'We are looking for a police informant, yes.'

Orelius chuckled, 'You are joking, right? When you walked in here you made it sound like you knew everything about me. So you must also know that I should be the last person to ask to be a snitch. And to pick a time when I'm sitting here helpless and worried sick about my missing boy... some sense of humour you have.'

'On the contrary, I think I picked a great time. Right now you could walk around Dudlham Farm with me, fingering suspects, and it wouldn't affect your reputation because everyone would assume you were working with the police trying to find Timmy.'

'If you want to release me on a tag or something so I can finger your drug dealers, I will not say no. I need to be out of here. But I'm sure you are not that stupid, you know I won't care one bit about your ear-slashing drug dealers. I will spend all that time doing what I can to find Timmy.'

'Not if you can kill two birds with one stone.'

'What's that supposed to mean?'

'You know when you keep referring to the Ear-Slasher as a drug dealer... it's because that is what you heard on the news, right?' He held up a finger signalling him to wait even though Orelius had made no effort to respond. Then he opened his green folder and removed a passport-size colour photo which he placed face up on the table, slowly sliding it towards Orelius. 'Is this Timmy?' he said, tapping the picture.

Orelius nodded.

The man dug into his back pocket and came out with a brown leather wallet. He removed another photo of about the same size and placed it next to Timmy's. It was of a smiling blonde boy with a missing tooth.

'That's my little boy, Connor. He is nine, one year younger than Timmy,' he said. 'Now let's play a quick game of "spot the difference" with these pictures – or, more importantly, the similarities... Do you get where I'm going with this?'

Orelius did, but said nothing.

'Come on, work with me here, Orelius.'

'I know what you are saying,' he said, his eyes still on the photos. 'I'm just waiting for you to start making sense.'

'Good. Now try and take your mind back to just after you realised Timmy was missing but before you heard the news about the drugs connection to the Ear-Slasher. Let's make it a hypothetical situation: Timmy has gone missing... you've looked everywhere, you're panicking, you can't figure anything out... then I come up with these,' he pointed at the two photos, 'A reminder of how easy it would be for someone to mistake Timmy for a white kid. Tell me then, hand on heart, that you would still not be interested in the Ear-Slasher.'

A sound escaped Orelius's lips as he shook his head with an incredulous smile. It was like Timmy's words had come back to haunt him: *Some people think I'm white...*

He had personally dealt with a few cases when Timmy had suffered abuse from other black kids because of his skin colour. He had been called *white trash*, and a *no-race*, among other things.

'And even if this suspect knew that Timmy was of mixed heritage, a real racist sociopath would hate the mixing of their race with the enemy's,' the man carried on. 'Timmy could have still been punished for that very reason by our man.'

It sounded like a joke, a silly trick to get Orelius on his side. But the man had a way about him that suggested he could pull much better tricks if that was his aim. This man was onto something.

'What is this?' Orelius finally asked. 'What are you telling me?'

'I'm trying to tell you that we need someone on the inside to help us figure out what the hell is going on with those ears. And now that you understand that this thing might not be a strictly white problem, it would be very helpful for both of us if that person was you.'

'This is not a good time for mind games, sir. What is going on here? Why do you keep asking me to imagine I hadn't heard the news?'

'We've got a public order situation out there. You saw the scenes yourself; the last thing we need is a repeat of last year's riots. Thus, until I know for sure that you are on my side, everything I tell you will remain hypothetical.'

'So let me get this straight. You are asking me to be a snitch, and my reward, thanks to this ridiculous link you have forged, would be that I will be helping find Timmy. At the same time you have also admitted that you only tried this because you thought I hadn't heard the news about the ears. How then were you expecting to get away with it when I got out there and found out the link was bogus?'

‘I promised you a good explanation for that, and that’s exactly what I’m trying to do. But you could make my task a lot simpler if you just work with me on the hypothetical situation I’ve given you,’ the man said with an impatient sigh. ‘Simple question, simple answer... Say you never heard anything on the news and the situation was as it was before yesterday. If I then sent you out there to find me the driver of that van, what do you think your chances would be?’

‘Thanks for trying to make it simple, but I’m afraid I still don’t understand.’

‘You understand my question, Orelius. That’s all that matters right now. Whether or not you understand anything beyond that will depend on your answer to that question. This time if you choose to remain silent I will take it as a no and walk out of that door, and leave you in the hands of Her Majesty’s authorities.’

‘I need to know what I’m saying yes or no to.’

‘All I will tell you is that this is a classified matter, and that I know some things that you don’t. I will not divulge any more without seeing some form of commitment from you.’

‘I thought we were talking hypothetically.’

‘We are, Orelius. We are.’

There was another long silence as the men eyed each other.

Orelius broke it first. 'Sorry, who did you say you are again?'

'Aha, we must have skipped that part.' The blonde man chuckled as he reached into his back pocket and fished out the same brown leather wallet. He flipped the transparent ID flap and slapped it face up on the table. Orelius was still staring at the photo on the badge as the man stuck out his right hand and said: 'Detective Inspector Greg Downing, New Scotland Yard.' He said it like they do in the movies, and seemed impressed by his own delivery because he flashed a confident smile.

Orelius looked at the badge one more time, then at the man's flashing teeth, before reluctantly reaching out to shake his hand. Downing gave a firm handshake, with a vicelike grip that held on longer than necessary. Orelius saw a network of veins rippling through his forearms and realised that, like himself, Downing was a man of immense strength. Orelius was six-foot tall and Downing about an inch or so shorter. Their physiques were identical, and the handshake felt like that of a couple of boxers sizing each other up before a bout.

'So is it a yes or a no, Orelius?' he asked after finally releasing his hand. 'Can you help us find that driver?'

'Well, I want to find Timmy. If this thing you are proposing gets me out of here...' he shrugged, 'I will do anything that has to be done.'

'We are asking you, a well-known... excuse me, I can't think of a better way to put this...' he raised his hands apologetically, '...I'm asking a well-known thug to help with a sensitive police operation. We are taking a very big risk here and I need to know if it's a risk worth taking, if you can get us some results.'

Orelius took a moment to think. 'I could tell you that if someone in Dudlham Farm knew something, and I wanted to find out what this thing was, then it is very likely that I would find out what I wanted to know.'

'A bit vague, but that is good enough for me.' He smiled. 'It's always advisable to be cautious with statements, especially when you are sitting inside a police station.'

Orelius folded his arms across his chest, managing to control the urge to scratch again.

'Now, like I said, what I'm about to tell you is highly sensitive top-secret information known only to very few people.' The detective paused and stared hard at the table in front of him, as if weighing up what was about to come from his mouth and wondering whether it would be too heavy for a civilian to handle. 'About twenty-four hours ago a decision was made at a very high level to release a statement to the media about the Ear-Slasher case, with the sole purpose of restoring public order. The statement was carefully worded but may still be deemed by some to be misleading, and could lead to a disastrous fallout should things not go to plan. Thus we find ourselves under even more pressure to solve this mystery.

'Policing that area of London is difficult at the best of times. But inside the Farm right now we are dealing with an almost impenetrable wall. No one trusts the police, period, notwithstanding our best intentions. So we need someone on the inside, someone well placed and trusted. And I can't think of a better candidate.'

'OK, you have used some big words there but this is how I understand what you've said so far: you needed to change public perception from this being a racist crime to a mere drug-related crime, so you fed a lie to the press. Is that right?'

'At some point we are going to make this agreement formal, and you will have to sign some papers which will bind you to confidentiality. After that I will answer all your questions, but for now I will only give you enough to get you there. You can interpret it however you want.'

'So what exactly am I signing up to? I help you find the person responsible for those ears and I can walk away from this?'

'Someone in that estate cut off at least five people's ears. That's what we know; but we believe there is a whole world of evil behind this. We need you to use your status and contacts in Dudlham to get us that person and everyone else involved, including witnesses who know and can testify to what they know. In return we will review the list of charges against you for this–' he nodded towards the file, '–and try making it shorter. We can't just let you walk away.'

'That doesn't sound like a great bargain to me. My lawyer could cut most of those charges for nothing.'

'Then maybe this would be a good time to call your lawyer,' Downing said, gathering his file from the table and pushing his chair backwards. 'You are welcome to try and find me once you've checked what your lawyer is capable of, but I can't promise you the deal will still be on the table. I'm sure I can find someone else.'

'Hey...' Orelius held up a hand. He knew this was another tactic to push him into a corner but he couldn't bear the thought of spending another minute in that cell. 'I'd like to help. I want to help. For Timmy, I will accept any conditions, as long as you can let me back out there. But if I leave here with even a hint of suspicion that I'm being tricked, this will turn into a game between me and you. And that wouldn't be good for either of us.'

Downing was now back on his seat, leaning forward calmly, with steepled fingers. 'To be honest with you, sir, right now I don't trust you. And if I can't trust you, you shouldn't trust me either.'

Downing hiked his shoulders in a *Well-what-can-I-do?* shrug but said nothing.

‘If you can get my lawyer down here to look at what you are proposing before I sign anything,’ Orelius continued, ‘that would be a good start, something I can work with.’

Downing stared at him for another few seconds, tapping an index finger on the table absently, before finally saying, ‘OK, who is your lawyer?’

‘I told you already. Andre Boateng.’

Downing jerked backwards harshly against his seat in frustration. ‘Orelius, you do realise the urgency of the situation, don’t you? We would love to get you Andre Boateng, but we haven’t got time.’

‘I am serious, Andre Boateng really is my lawyer. Why don’t you just ask him? I’m sure Scotland Yard won’t have any trouble finding him.’

*

The second coming of Andre Boateng

Fifteen years ago, when Orelius was still a teenager starting out in the immigration scam, they brought in a young African, maybe only a couple of years older than him. They had found him as a vagrant drifting in Calais after a couple of failed attempts to get on the ferry to the UK. The man was in such a sorry state they felt compelled to bring him in on purely compassionate grounds. He did not have a penny to pay for their services.

Ninety minutes later the poor African emerged from the back of the food container lorry in Dover, dehydrated, bedraggled and close to suffocating. Orelius and his gang fed him, watered him and sent him on his way to a begin life as an alien with only a fifty-pound note and a passport. The passport proclaimed him to be a Belgian citizen named Tobias Ndebele – Belgian by marriage. It got Tobias a National Insurance number, a bank account, and eventually a job at a warehouse packaging imported fish.

Tobias spent eighteen months in the country working fifteen hours a day, six days a week, and sharing a single-bed flat in Dudlham Farm with three other immigrants. He worked, he slept; and generally kept to himself.

After a few months with a steady income flowing through his account, the bank started tempting Tobias with irresistible credit card offers. He took all of them, along with three other high street store cards. Yet after eighteen months all these credit cards remained unused, and his bank balance was still growing. With a flourishing bank balance and perfect credit rating, most British banks can lend up to thirty grand without security, maybe more at a push. Tobias managed to borrow thirty-five, with minimal fuss.

Then, at the end of his eighteenth month, Tobias maxed all his credit cards and overdrafts, cleared his accounts, and left the country as quietly as he had arrived; with a grand total of just under sixty-thousand pounds.

Three months later a Boeing 747 British Airways jumbo jet landed at Heathrow with a young student named Andre Boateng. He had a five-year student visa issued by the British High Commission in Ghana to study law at University College, London. The immigration officer at the airport welcomed him with a warm smile and wished him the best in his studies. He was self-funding his course, and nobody bothered to question how this could be managed by an orphaned African who had barely scraped through high school in Ghana by selling all of his late father's land and livestock.

Nobody even noticed that his initial application to UCL had been sent from within the United Kingdom.

CHAPTER 6

Two extra chairs were brought into the room where Orelius had remained sipping bad coffee. Downing walked back in first and took his original chair, then two men in suits followed him in almost immediately, flanked by a uniformed officer. The officer showed them to the empty seats either side of Orelius and Downing, and left, closing the door behind him. One of the suits was black and notably shinier than the other, which was beige. The owner of the shiny black suit was taller and leaner, with a presence that seemed to make everyone else in the room uncomfortable. He was a black man they had all seen on TV, heard on the radio and read about in the papers: Dr Andre Boateng QC, popularly known as Dr Dre. The beige suit belonged to a representative from the Crown Prosecution Service, a short pot-bellied lump called Rolly Wilkes.

Refreshments appeared: tea, coffee, fresh juices and spring water. And within half-an-hour of his arrival, Dr. Boateng had in his possession a copy of a deal signed by the representative from the CPS stating that in three weeks' time, Orelius would have to appear in court to answer to one charge of possession of an illegal weapon. The CPS would not be pursuing any further charges relating to the incident at The Fighting Cocks.

Rolly Wilkes had tried to impose some conditions on the deal, but Dr Boateng fended him off, turning to Orelius. 'That rash on your neck looks pretty nasty. You got that from here, right?'

Orelius nodded.

'Do you want us to file something for it?'

The other two men looked at each other incredulously before Downing intervened. 'Gentlemen, let's not lose our heads here, OK? A boy is missing and none of this lawsuit bullshit is going to help with that. Orelius, you are probably just suffering an allergic reaction, we will give you some medication and a written apology if you want.' Then he turned to the CPS guy. 'Let him loose, Rolly, we need him.'

'I understand, sir. But you know this has nothing to do with me. There were victims in that incident at The Fighting Cocks, and they will want action.'

'Victims? They're a bunch of thugs, Rolly. Did you know they had a list of everyone who came to the protests? Yes, we found it at the pub; that's how organised they were. I looked at it, and every single one of them has got something on them that we should prosecute. So I guess we could go ahead and prosecute everyone, or we could talk to them and come to an agreement for the greater good.'

Rolly still wasn't convinced, so the detective got up and asked him outside for a private conference, which lasted about five minutes. When they came back, the CPS guy scribbled his signature on everything in front of him and began hurriedly gathering his papers. He left the room cowering, with his head down, looking even smaller than his five-foot-five microstructure.

Lord Dr Boateng stood up and gave Orelius a streetwise chest-bumping handshake. He also whispered that he would try and get him a non-custodial sentence on that single charge, and declared that he was otherwise available if needed, at any time.

*

'I can tell you now, Orelius, that no victims with slashed ears have come up to explain this mystery,' Downing said, finally clarifying what he knew. 'There is no mysterious white drug baron and his black henchman. They do not exist. There is no one in custody. In fact nobody knows anything at all about those ears today, just like no one did yesterday or a week ago.'

'So the news was all made up.'

'A spin, yes. To restore order,' he said with conviction. 'Did you ever wonder why this news came in the form of a press release with no questions answered, rather than a full press conference? Wasn't it convenient that the person with missing ears who finally came up just happened to be a minor and thus could not be named?'

Orelius tried to piece it all together in his head. It made sense, and he had signed the deal on that basis, yet he still couldn't allow himself to believe it.

Inspector Downing seemed to be reading his thoughts. 'Things were getting out of control, and this is the last thing we need right now after last year's riots. Something had to be done. There was no time to worry about the truth, but word had to be put out that might stop another senseless bout of violence. So we had to engineer an angle that would allow us to do that without compromising the operation.'

'Is that legal?' Orelius's voice was low, almost a slur. The lethargy and severe light-headedness had begun soon after taking the medication from the custody physician for his allergies. 'How can you get away with that?'

'We probably can't, entirely. But if, in the ensuing calm, we manage to solve this case, we can at least try to justify our course of action. Those demonstrators were out there to voice the racial aspect of this crime, but most of the real anger is due to the lack of progress in bringing someone to justice. The idea, as you guessed, was to switch the angle from race, throw a theory out there to counter the BPP's own theories – which are also just that: theories. No one really knows anything about the bloody ears. However, in the circumstances, looking for a white drug baron and his black henchman sounds much better than looking for a black racist serial killer. And I have to say this has achieved its purpose. The white activists have put their placards down and gone back to their day jobs, most feeling rather embarrassed by their actions of the past few days.

'The original problem hasn't gone away, however. The police still hold five ears belonging to some white human beings somewhere. We have a crime but we know neither what the actual crime is, nor who the victims are. The idea was to try and solve this quietly, hoping that as long as all the responsible criminals end up behind bars, few questions will be asked. The press statement only said that someone came up to claim that their ears had been cut off recently in a drug-related dispute. It didn't state that this person's ears had actually been confirmed as one of the five that were found in Dudlham. This sounds a bit far-fetched but at least it gives us some room to manoeuvre. If things go wrong, we can always maintain that our supposed victim turned out to be some publicity-seeking nut who chopped their own ears off. This way, we've got the choice of going back to our original strategy of appealing to the general public for information.'

'The connection to Timmy... was that forced for my benefit?'

'That is a valid theory that we are taking very seriously. We are keeping the cases separate for now. I'm on the Ear-Slasher, and there is someone else on Timmy's case. But we're sharing intelligence, and we believe the two cases might well converge at some point.'

Everything was beginning to blur before Orelius's eyes. The doctor had advised him to sleep off his medication but he'd elected not to mention this to the detective. Sleep could wait.

'What happens if we do find this guy and it turns out he has nothing to do with Timmy?'

'It wouldn't affect your deal if your help is deemed to have been significant in making that discovery.'

'I'm not worried about my deal.' He was struggling to keep his voice steady. 'What I'm asking is, where does that leave Timmy's case? It sounds to me like the ears thing has become the priority because of the lie that was fed to the public. So say we find this guy, sort out your side of the problem, but it turns out it has nothing to do with Timmy, what then?'

'Like I said, there is a dedicated missing persons' team on Timmy's case as we speak. They will continue that work regardless of anything else that might be going on in Dudlham Farm. And it would continue in the same spirit whether or not you were in jail.

'However, the deal you've been offered here falls on my side of the case, and requires that in your three weeks of freedom before you appear in court you help us figure out who put those ears in that van. The possible connection with Timmy is a bonus but I personally believe in that bonus and I need you to believe it too. We are officially hunting the Ear-Slasher, but I need you to believe that this person also took your boy.'

Orelius tried to open his mouth but it proved too much effort.

'You alright, Orelius?' It wasn't the first time the detective had asked him that question since taking the medication. They were back in the same room, and the detective now had a sketchy map of Dudlham Farm, about twice the size of his green folder, spread out on the table. 'You look kind of dizzy. I think they gave you something very strong.'

'I'm fine,' he mumbled. The small yellow tablet and two tablespoons of thick sweet syrup seemed to have helped with the itchiness alright, but not his need to stay awake. 'Go on, I'm listening.'

'You sure you don't want to go and lie down for a few minutes, and maybe do this later?'

'I'm fine, Gregg.' The detective had insisted he would be Gregg to him for the duration of their mission.

'Like I said,' the inspector went on, 'this case was only handed over to me two days ago. I studied everything that had been done and was struggling to see anything else I could do differently, before we heard about Timmy and your subsequent attempts to take the law into your own hands. And I figured... well, there was nothing to lose.' He smoothed the edges of the map with his palms and used a black marker to draw circles on it. 'Anyway, the previous team worked The Farm progressively from the point of incident, which was here.' He drew a circle round Lympne House. 'This is where the van was found, so, after collecting all evidence and doing the usual tests, they knocked on doors within this block and asked a few questions. When nothing useful came up they progressed to the surrounding blocks, here and here.' He drew two more concentric circles. 'By the time they finished with them, they realised that this approach was never going to work, so they stopped.'

Orelius had drifted close to semi-consciousness by the time the detective finished speaking. He noticed Downing eyeing him suspiciously, and snapped back to full alertness.

'Did they come up with a suspect? A name... anything?'

'No, nothing at all. Like I said, those people didn't seem to like us being there asking questions.'

'So they just stopped? Was that it... case closed?'

'Well, that is when they handed the case over to me.'

Orelius had immediately spotted two major flaws in their strategy.

First was their mode of questioning. At The Jolly, he had already heard three or four names bandied about as the suspected Ear-Slasher. This was from only a single visit to the pub since the incident. Yet these people had knocked on close to four hundred doors and not one name had emerged. It is one thing for Farmers to speak their minds inside TJ, but if a uniform knocks on your door and starts asking questions, you keep your answers short and pray they don't ask to see your passport or have a look around the house.

The second flaw was the area they had covered. When the detective drew those circles on the map, something stood out. They had probably placed a similar map on the table, and a red dot on Lympne, then more circles around the blocks, based on geographical proximity to Lympne. Stapleford House stood at the bottom corner of the detective's map, furthest from Lympne, which was on Gloucester Road behind TJ. So Stapleford was not within Downing's boundaries. Stapleford was tucked towards the south-east corner of Dudlham, slightly removed, as though it had been constructed as an afterthought. Its design was also different to the rest of the buildings. They didn't have the deck-level walkways, and more importantly in this case, they didn't have the ground-floor car park. Furthermore, the structures were so closely packed in the immediate area that the small space left between Stapleford and the Willan Road houses was not enough to park cars. Most of the residents used the adjacent streets, which were thus always busy with cars parked bumper-to-bumper, and many residents often had to venture further afield.

Only an expert in the unusual tapestry of Dudlham would have known that through a series of alleys and informal paths etched over time with the gradual disintegration of some of the original structures, you could get to the Lympne car park quicker than any other from Stapleford. If someone wanted to avoid hassling for space and find a guaranteed parking spot, they could park at Lympne as they entered The Farm and walk through the alleys. Not only would it guarantee a spot, it would also save the extra five-minute journey around Willan to hassle for a spot in the jammed outer streets. It was a trick some of the Stapleford residents had found useful over the years. In short, if someone parked in the Lympne car park, his destination was almost as likely to be Lympne House as Stapleford. The police had covered Lympne, then Hawkinge, Hornchurch, Kenley, Manston and Northolt. They had left Stapleford untouched.

'It was never going to work at The Farm, that door-to-door thing,' Orelius said. His voice had fallen to a weak monotone as he battled to stay awake. 'I know it, you know it, and I'm pretty sure *they* knew it. They were doing it because it looks good on the records: number of doors knocked on... number of police officers used... number of hours... These people were not really looking for a result, they were just checking the boxes so they could file everything neatly and put it away.'

The detective stopped studying the map and looked up at him. 'There is no need for that, Oreluis. They followed a tried and tested procedure. Only this time it didn't get a result, so we are here to try a different approach. Making wild allegations is not going to help us one bit. And you've also got to consider that if we were to leave Timmy out for now, there officially aren't any victims...' He took another look at Orelius's face with growing concern, and pushed the map to one side. 'You sure you are OK, mate? You look pretty off colour.'

'Did anyone talk to Kelly-Jo?' Orelius murmured, his upper body tilting over the table in slow-motion. His head jerked just before hitting the table, and he straightened up with a start, breathing heavily.

'OK, Orelius, I think that's enough for today. I'll take you home and we can finish this tomorrow.'

'I need to talk to Kelly-Jo... about Timmy... if he used the lift...'

'Who is Kelly-Jo?'

'She... she is always...'

This time his head hit the table and it didn't come back up.

CHAPTER 7

Orelius woke up to the dim orange glow of a lightbulb directly above his eyes, and it took him a few seconds to work out that he was in the same cell in which he'd spent the previous night. He could hear a continuous banging from across the hallway, as if someone was hitting the bars of the cage doors hard with their palms. He walked up to his door and peered through the peep-hole down the hall. The bright lighting and relative lack of activity suggested it was night time. He turned round and saw a small white sheet of paper lying near the head of the bed. He picked it up and read the note, messily scribbled in capital letters with a black marker: it was addressed to him, instructing him to go to the front desk as soon as he was up so someone could give him a ride home. The last line stressed that he was not under arrest, with underlined words and three exclamation marks at the end.

He tried the door again. It was not locked.

*

'Sorry about last night, mate,' Downing said, after waking him up with an eight a.m. phone call. 'You passed out and the doctor said you might be out for a few hours, so I left with instructions that you be sent home as soon as you got up. How are you feeling now?'

'Yeah I'm fine.'

'Good, because we've got work to do. You said something about Kelly-Jo...?'

'She's a mentally retarded woman who spends all her time in the Northolt lift. If Timmy used the lifts to get down to the riots, she would have most probably been in there.'

'And you think she might have something to do with this?'

'No, but she might know something. She could confirm that Timmy did get out of the building at that time.'

'We'd have to also consider that he might not have used the lift. He's ten years old and may be scared of this peculiar woman.'

'Actually, I think if Timmy was going out, he would particularly use the lift if she was there. He likes Kelly-Jo, chats to her, and sometimes even brings her snacks.'

'OK, this sounds like useful information. But listen, don't talk to someone you think is a suspect without my presence, it could seriously mess things up for us legally. If you have a good reason to suspect someone is involved, call me and I will be down there right away. Remember, my case is officially the Ear-Slasher only, but while I'm with you our front will be that we are looking for Timmy just like the other team. Detective Garret's team will go the old-fashioned way and search every crease and corner of Dudlham. Our approach will be to investigate individuals based on intelligence provided, hopefully, by your contacts.'

'OK.'

'So off you go, start fishing. I'll call you after noon to arrange a meeting and chat about anything you've got for me by then. But first I want you to take down a few numbers. You got a pen?'

Orelius reached out and fumbled over his bedside table.

'Yes,' he said lifting a black pen and an unopened envelope, 'go on.'

He wrote down several numbers. The first was the direct mobile line to Downing, then a special line to his office at Scotland Yard. The others were for his local constabularies in Wood Green and Tottenham, where Orelius had spent the previous night and a half. The detective said there was an ongoing situation at Scotland Yard which meant he could be pulled off this case at anytime without notice. These last numbers were in case Orelius was to come by some useful intelligence when Downing was no longer in charge.

'And of course you've always got 999 in case of emergency,' he added. 'These numbers are your back-up. Anything happens, you call me first. I will be here,' the detective said before putting the phone down.

Orelius got out of bed and pushed a few chin-ups on the bar across his bedroom door, barely breaking sweat before jumping into a cold shower. He preferred cold showers in the morning. In winter he would make the exercise longer and the shower shorter, but it had to be cold.

He picked up his cordless landline as he sat down with a strong cup of coffee and two bars of dry wholegrain wheat cereal. He called Nikisha Lewis first, and almost immediately regretted it. Her voice was weak and empty, the last ounce of soul gone with Timmy on Sunday, and Orelius had nothing to give her other than patronising consolations and meaningless promises.

His next call was to Cory Dillinger, a friend and a useful pair of eyes around The Farm.

'Cory D. Talk to me,' Cory answered with his standard phone salute.

'Hello, mate.'

'Oz...?' His voice brightened, as though he had not checked his caller ID. 'Good to hear from you, cuz. I heard about the shit that went down at The Fighting Cocks. Mega gave us the word and we've been canvassing the perimeter last two nights. Still no sign of Tim, cuz. This is unreal.'

Dillinger was a twenty-eight-year-old Farmer who had never expressed any desire to leave. His contacts in Dudlham made him quite a respectable living. The latest of his ventures was rap music. Cory had converted his living room into a state of the art studio that he promised would be the future voice of

UK urban music. He hired it out to young Farmers dreaming of becoming the next Tinie Tempah or Dizzie Rascal.

However, this new scheme was still a Work In Progress, not quite bringing in enough to make a living. So for now Dillinger was still holding on to his two main money-makers: his position as broker between drug users and their suppliers, and his role as a negotiator in minor disputes between good, hard-working citizens and authority. When it came to the latter, he specialised in driving offences. If you got caught speeding, you were at your points limit, and your job depended on driving, Dillinger was the man to go to. He could find someone else, for a small fee, to take the points for you. The DVLA would write to the registered owner of the vehicle caught on camera, asking them to state the driver at the time of the offence. The owner would write back with a name and address provided by Dillinger and located in Jamaica. Sometimes the DVLA were persistent enough to follow up, and they would find that the names and addresses did indeed exist. But if they still wanted to issue the points they would get a reply saying that the named respondent had unfortunately passed away – in a road accident. If they further persisted and demanded proof, it could be arranged. But it hardly ever came to that.

'I need a favour, Cory,' Orelius said after the pleasantries.

'That's what I do, cuz. Favours.' Cory laughed dryly at his own joke.

'You know that Gutierrez kid? The one with–'

'Gutierrez...? Course I know him, the lanky little pest, who doesn't?'

'Can you find him for me?'

'Now?'

'As soon as you can, bruv. Now would be great.'

Cory paused for a moment, making a distant humming sound as if consulting a diary that Orelius knew did not exist. 'That's cool, cuz. I will get on his case right away. What do you want me to do with him when I find him?'

'Call me as soon as you do, and I will meet you both at TJ. Tell him I just need to ask him a few questions.'

'Already done, cuz. Already done.' Then he changed his tone. 'Sorry about this whole thing with Tim, man. First the freaky ears, then this. That kind of shit doesn't happen around here, cuz. People here commit crime to put food on the table... this is fucked up.'

'Now that you've brought it up, what's the street saying about those ears anyway? Who was last seen using the van?'

'There are all kinds of rumours flying around. You know how it is with those bangers, they've been sitting in the car parks since way back when and no one remembers how they got there. Kids mess around in them–'

'What is the biggest rumour flying around though? About the ears?'

‘The Bogeyman. Some people say he’s been seen inside that whip late at night.’

Orelius was aware of the old man from Stapleford whom everyone referred to as The Bogeyman. He was invariably credited with most of the inexplicable happenings in Dudlham.

‘Did anyone seriously say they saw him in the van? Is there any credibility to this?’

‘Hard to tell, cuz, because sometimes they also say he flies around on a broomstick in the middle of the night.’ He let out another awkward chuckle before picking up again in a more serious tone. ‘Why, you think the ears have something to do with what happened to Tim?’

‘I don’t know, bruv. Never mind, just find Gutierrez for me.’

*

Gutierrez was a notoriously loquacious fifteen-year-old black African boy. Real name: Obafemi Obi Obierika. Everyone called him Gutierrez because his father, despite being Nigerian, was named Juan Carlos Gutierrez. Old Gutierrez was a recluse who made no great efforts to explain this misnomer. It was left to his charming son to spin elaborate yarns about how his father acquired the name. Gutierrez Jr claimed he had a Puerto Rican great-grandfather who had met and married a Nigerian woman in the US and they ended up moving back to Nigeria, where his father, Juan Carlos, was born.

Like most of Gutierrez's stories, it was bullshit. And everybody knew it.

A long time ago, during his brief stint with trafficking, Orelius had been responsible for matching black Africans and West Indians with names from all parts of the globe, Spanish, German or even Burmese Ghurkha names. Most of them were names that were on the Home Office's database of legal residents but which their owners would, for one reason or another, never use in Britain. Some of them were dead. They had put in place a good network dedicated to finding these names. One of the basic immigration packages that such gangs offered was to transport clients through the channel tunnel, often in the back of a lorry. This deal would simply get you to this side of the pond alive; then you were on your own. Another and slightly more expensive package, the one Gutierrez's dad had no doubt taken, would get you in and give you some ID and immigration documents. You became whoever the papers said you were. Some people got John Smith, some people got Gutierrez. Nobody complained.

Until about three months ago, little Gutierrez had been well known as a loveable door-to-door salesman pushing all kinds of merchandise, from international calling cards to ethnic cosmetic products. There was no question this boy was gifted with a very useful gob, which served him wonderfully in that line of business. Most salesmen in Dudlham Farm got the doors slammed in their faces with a barrage of profanities. Gutierrez was welcomed with open arms and warm coffee. He would sit and talk to elder residents about his father who was incapacitated and unable to work, and how he was working hard selling this merchandise after school to subsidise their meagre social services handouts. He had intelligent conversations with folks, mostly housewives several decades older than him, about life in this country as a second generation immigrant and what they could do as a people to improve their prospects.

On a good day Gutierrez could make about fifteen pounds per household from the sales, and about ten times as much from the visit itself. Because, as little Gutierrez cheerfully greeted his hosts at the door, his eyes would secretly be working out the mechanics of the lock. As he sat sipping his coffee and chatting about the drug problems facing the youth, his eyes would be wandering around, noting anything worth stealing. While he helpfully offered to wash up the coffee cups, he would also be quietly rendering a subtle sabotage to the kitchen widow, to allow entry for the thugs that he would go on to sell this information to.

About three months before, one of Gutierrez's clients, desperate to cut a deal with the CPS after a burglary went wrong, snitched the boy as their inside man. But while the other burglars went down, the case against Gutierrez fell apart when

CHAPTER 8

'I'm in trouble?' Guttierrrez asked with an uneasy smile as he dropped his lanky frame onto the seat directly opposite Orelius. At fifteen, he was already pushing six foot tall, but he was slight, and his facial features were soft, almost feminine: full red lips, high cheekbones and a pair of wide brown eyes that were hard not to trust. Cory Dillinger, in contrast, was five-foot-six-ish but as wide as a tank, with broad shoulders and muscled, tattooed arms. He took the other remaining seat on his right and slouched back, his arms folded across his chest, keeping the tattoos on full display. They were at Orelius's usual corner spot in The Jolly.

'No you are not in trouble, son.' Orelius said with reassuring calmness. 'You want a drink?'

Gutierrez thought for a beat. 'Yeah, I'll have a straight brandy on the rocks, please.'

'Don't be silly.' He reached into his pockets and peeled off a twenty from his wallet. 'Cory, get me and little Gutierrez here two Cokes and whatever you want for yourself.'

'Nice one. Cheers, Oz.' Cory grabbed the money and made his way to the bar.

'You know I'm not doing any more scams, Oz, I swear. That's all in the past. I've turned a new chapter.' Gutierrez started protesting his innocence as soon as Cory was out of the way. 'I'm not even going into people's houses anymore. I'm getting a website, that's where all my business is going to come from now. All legit... just chasing the Ps, bro, you know how it is. I've got to help my old man pay the rent.'

'Take it easy, Gutierrez, no one's accusing you of anything. You are here because I need your help.' Given the way Cory had grabbed him and frogmarched him to The Jolly, aggravated further by his recent near-jail experience, it was easy to understand the kid's concerns.

'Oh, OK. That's fine then. I just thought...' He shrugged, and let the thought go.

'I need to tap into your good brains, young sir.'

'Huh?'

'I need your inside knowledge of The Farm – but don't worry, I'm not going to rob anyone. I'm just trying to find Timmy.'

Gutierrez's thick eyebrows furrowed.

'I take it you've been inside most flats around here and that you know most of the Farmers well.' He smiled, and the boy relaxed.

'I've been everywhere, Oz. I'm a people person, that's how I make a living.' He said this proudly, now that he knew it was not thought a bad thing. 'The households I haven't been inside I can probably count on my fingers.'

'Good. Then I think you can help me,' Orelius said with a nod and another smile. This time boy smiled back contentedly. He was privileged to be in a position to help Orelius Simm. 'First of all I want you to tell me if there's anything you've heard about that van with the ears. Not just the baseless rumours but something that sounds legit.'

He thought for a couple of seconds then started hesitantly, 'OK, I know this is going to sound exactly like the usual Bogeyman rumour, but Sofia, the Turkish woman from Lympne, is a respectable person and a good friend of mine. And she told me she thinks she saw an old, bearded black man sometime last week, inside that van late in the night. I don't see any reason why she would make this up, she doesn't even hang around with folks from here enough to know about the Bogeyman myths.'

So it's back to the Bogeyman, Orelius thought, with slight disappointment. He had always had him in mind but somehow The Bogeyman sounded too convenient, to easy a target.

'Right, thanks for that,' he said. 'Now we are going to try something different. Let's call it an exercise on your knowledge of this estate. I will start by taking you over to Stapleford House. Not literally, but in your head. I will go through the flats and ask you some questions about each one. You just think and tell me everything you can about them, OK?'

He nodded.

Orelius removed a pen and a notepad from his shoulder-bag. Cory arrived back with a tray of drinks and dumped it on the table. He had got himself a brownish coloured drink in a long glass with an assortment of sliced fruits floating over it and red and blue straws sticking out.

'What's that?' Orelius asked placing the notebook on the table next to the tray.

'Pimms and lemonade.' Cory answered taking a sip. 'Beautiful drink, you should try it.'

'Looks like a girl's drink,' Guttierrez sniggered, safe in the knowledge that Orelius Simm was on his side.

'You will be screaming like a girl in a minute if you don't shut the fuck up,' Cory snapped pointing the rim of his glass at him. 'You little vermin.'

Orelius looked at them both with a bemused expression which soon turned grim. They fell silent.

'Right, Gutierrez.' Orelius clicked his pen ready. 'All set?'

'Ready, Oz. Fire away.'

They travelled up and down various flats of Dulham Farm for more than an hour, concentrating mainly on Stapleford and Lympne blocks. Orelius would single out individuals from Gutierrez's general assessment and ask specific questions about them, then maybe make a phone call or two, and come back with some follow-up questions. By the end of it all he had a list of nine names. Nine possible suspects, but it was hard to look past the fourth name down the list.

The Bogeyman.

However simplistic it seemed, this man had now come up from so many different angles he could not be ignored. Gutierrez's revelations about the Turkish woman's possible eyewitness account, especially, gave The Bogeyman new credence. It was a name that had been lingering on his mind ever since he had sat in the small room at Tottenham Police Station and watched Downing drawing circles round The Farm. It was also a name that was being bandied around this pub. But more importantly, the man lived in Stapleford, a block that had not been covered by the police.

Markus Isaacs, The Bogeyman, lived at number 59 Stapleford House.

*

Markus Isaacs:

When I was nine years old my mother and I left Jamaica for a better life in the United Kingdom. I never saw the United Kingdom, I saw Dudlham Farm. I am now fifty-nine years old and I have stopped dreaming of the United Kingdom. What began in Dudlham will end in Dudlham.

I landed at Heathrow airport in 1963 and disappeared inside a one-bedroom flat in Croydon House, never to be seen again. Every once in a while I would step onto the balcony to marvel at the structures of Kenley and Northolt, towering high above the rest in the endless field of bone-white blocks. On the other side of my window was the manicured green of Lordship Recreation Grounds. My mother told me stories of the Battle of Britain and the Second World War RAF fighter-bases which these blocks were named after. I couldn't wait for my next visit back to Jamaica to retell these great tales to my old friends; to flaunt the pride of our new home and sing at the top of my voice about Dudlham Farm.

Little did I know that I would never leave Dudlham. That my old friends and the land of my birth would become but distant memories.

I would never have guessed that one day those haunting words would come from my mother's mouth:

'Today, son, you are going to fight back . . .'

*

Orelius knew as much about Markus Isaacs as every other Farmer, a mishmash of half-truths and myths created by the underworked creative minds of Dudlham. Markus Isaacs was The Farm's own bogeyman, a mysterious thickly-bearded face most people only saw in the shadows late at night or in the early hours of the morning. He was an old man who had come back to live the rest of his days in Dudlham after almost forty-years of a life sentence at Grendon maximum security prison. Apparently, in another lifetime long before Orelius was born, a thirteen-year-old Markus had lost his mind and hacked his family and two of his friends to death with a kitchen knife. Neighbours had heard the screams and rushed out to find young Markus outside his door, wrestling with a knife through his mother's chest, with two other thirteen-year-old bodies, both blood-soaked, lying next to her. He had been living with his mother and stepfather at Croydon House. The stepfather was later discovered in the bedroom. He had also been butchered by that knife.

Since his return to Dudlham, Isaacs had remained an aloof eccentric who preferred to keep to himself. He was a sixty-year-old man who had watched life pass him by from the bars of his prison cell. His slight weirdness was understandable, but Orelius knew that the rumours about Isaacs being the Ear-Slasher only gained credence because no one really knew him. He was a man with no family or relatives, a troubled soul who had been branded one of Britain's worst psychopaths. The racist angle also favoured him, considering that two of his victims had been white boys in 1960s England. And he had been put in prison for forty years by white people.

One could only imagine what such a prisoner would be subjected to inside Grendon for forty years. And who knows what that experience could turn him to? A monster... serial killer... child molester? It was possible. Orelius would have to find out.

He picked up his pen and wrote the number 2 next to Isaacs's name: he was the second person he would be talking to, his second suspect.

His first suspect was not on this list, and lived in a flat that had not been discussed in this meeting. In fact he had deliberately missed off this address as he explored Gutierrez's incredible knowledge of The Farm. This one, he had decided, he would deal with personally. Not even detective Downing was going to be involved. The fact that he had even thought of this name was making him uncomfortable, and he hoped that he would quickly clear its owner of any suspicion so he could proceed without any further reservation.

He looked at the list once again, and before knocking on any doors or asking any questions or twisting any Dudlham arms, he realised the answer lay somewhere on this single sheet of paper. These nine names would tell him something about what the hell had gone wrong in Dudlham Farm. Because, like Dillinger had said, people here committed crimes to put food on their table. But this – this was fucked up.

He left the bar before midday and headed straight to his first suspect.

most of the Dudlham Farm housewives he had helped rob refused to testify against him. They instead started a petition to save their good boy from getting a criminal record. In their opinion, he was just an innocent kid who had experienced a misguided moment. They argued that if Gutierrez was to be sent away to Feltham, he would surely come out a real criminal. And thus they saved their young master.

CHAPTER 9

'Hi, Nikisha,' he said as the small woman opened her door. 'Sorry, I tried to call but I keep getting your voicemail.'

'That's OK. My phone's battery must have been dead.'

'Can I come in?'

'Sure.' She stepped aside and motioned him into the sparsely furnished living room with an old worn-out fabric double sofa set on one side, a stand with a TV at one corner, and an array of toys in the middle, including a red BMX bike.

'You heard anything...?' he asked, settling down on one corner of the sofa. Nikisha had taken the single seat chaise.

'I spoke to the detective yesterday and today. He said they were doing everything they could.'

'You mean detective Downing?'

'I think he said his name was Garret. Keith Garret.'

This sounded like the name Downing had mentioned as the man heading the other search team.

'How about you though, you OK being here on your own?' he asked. 'Is there anything that could help take your mind off things? Friends... relatives, maybe?'

It was not the best thing to say to a mother with a missing child, but what was, other than that you had found their baby?

'My son is missing,' she said with a grim snicker. 'I don't need anything to take my mind off things.'

This sounded like a pretty strong and assertive statement, especially coming from Nikisha Lewis. Before today, he knew her only as a woman who would recoil in horror at the mere prospect of talking to another human being. This newfound toughness was surprising, suspicious. For a long time Orelius had inwardly questioned Nikisha's mental stability, considering what he knew about her past. He had never thought her dangerous, but her account of the events leading up to Timmy's disappearance worried him. Was she troubled enough to harm her own child?

He would never forget the time he decided to find out more about her, after their explosive first encounter, almost seven years ago.

Despite everything else that occurred that day, it is the *beeping* that still dominates Orelius's memory of that afternoon. He recalls other fragments: his trip to Manchester that morning... his heart being shattered into tiny pieces... taking the news without shedding a tear and somehow ending up at the Northolt House parking lot without any recollection of his journey back. But this is where that beeping sound found him, and it has never left since. He hears it in his head every time he is faced with a temptation to slip back to his old lifestyle. It has become the stimulus that snaps him back from a hypnotic trance.

On that day seven years ago, however, that sound had been real. It was coming from a car behind, because his BMW was blocking everyone's path. There was a queue of about five vehicles behind him waiting to get into the car park, and this suggested he must have been stopped right there in the middle of the road for a long time. But at the time nothing made sense.

He turned the key in the ignition and the engine squeaked for a few seconds, then died. Two further attempts to fire the engine brought the same result. That at least explained why he had stopped in this spot and was holding up traffic. His car had broken down.

Orelius stared blankly at his steering wheel, trying his best to ignore the hooting from behind. He glanced in his rear-view mirror and saw that the driver most offended was the one directly behind him in an old blue Ford Fiesta. Not a sound from any of the other cars in the queue, and he guessed that they were the smart ones: they had recognised his BMW and decided to take the safe option. This was the height of Orelius Simm's reign of terror, when the mere mention of his name had grown men quaking. He saw one of the cars pull out of the queue and turn round. The person in the Fiesta, obviously a visitor at The Farm, continued beeping relentlessly. The probability of that hooting sound turning to tears was growing every second. But in the light of what had just happened in Manchester, Orelius did his best to block it out and give the impatient driver a chance to walk away.

He tried his engine one more time, and this time it started turning weakly, then jerked, and collapsed yet again. The beeping grew louder and louder in his head till he could hear nothing else but the grating honk. He stepped out of his car, leapt the few strides to the Fiesta, pulled the door open and yanked the driver out by the collar. He met no resistance whatsoever as he started shaking the driver like a leaf. It was hard to believe this was the same person who had been hooting aggressively seconds before.

'What the fuck is your problem!' Orelius screamed.

He did not notice that the driver was five-foot-three and only weighed about a hundred pounds. Or that she was woman.

'I'm sorry... I'm so sorry,' she cried, shaking with fright. Tears were flowing down her face through her thick round glasses. 'Please don't hurt me.'

Other motorists had joined the queue either side of the entrance but none of them made a sound. Some kids appeared from different directions and gathered around the scene with curious stares. No one intervened. They were here for the show.

Orelius never hit the woman but he gave her a damn good shake till she collapsed to her knees, squealing and panting like a dying animal. Then he picked her up and shoved her back into the Fiesta. He slammed her door and kicked out with his right boot, denting the outside. The woman let out another sharp squeal.

He looked round at the spectators and other waiting drivers and shouted, 'What the fuck are you all looking at!'

The watching kids dispersed. The other drivers recoiled into their cars and tried their best to make themselves invisible.

This violence would turn out to be the therapy he needed for what had just occurred in Manchester. For after this, he jumped back into his BMW and got it started at first attempt. And by the time he had parked it properly in the ground floor parking lot, tears were flowing down his cheeks.

He wept quietly in the darkness of the Northolt Block car park for thirty minutes. It was the only time he shed tears for his lover and his unborn child.

Orelius would later learn, among other things, that the bespectacled woman he had assaulted that day was a nineteen-year-old single mother from 91 Northolt House. Nikisha Lewis. A kindred spirit. A broken woman, just like himself, whom life had already dealt the most wretched hand imaginable even before the cruelty Orelius had inflicted on her that afternoon.

Two days later, Orelius was waiting outside 91 Northolt House when Nikisha and her four-year-old son emerged from the flat, heading for school. He was sitting on a wooden stool that had been left on the deck, with a black briefcase on the floor to his right, a yard or so off the neighbour's door. When she spotted Orelius, the mother let out a gasp of horror, and instinctively reached out to put a protective arm round her son.

'Please don't hurt my son.' Her low husky voice trailed off. She stayed still, and for a moment she appeared in control. But then Orelius saw tears creeping under her glasses.

The little boy's arms went round his mother's hips. 'Please don't hurt my mother. She is not well... she is feeling a bit ill.'

Orelius lowered his gaze to the owner of the small voice. He stared straight back at Orelius, his almost colourless eyes pleading. Orelius dropped his gaze first. Then he turned away and raised his eyes over the balcony, to face the sea of disintegrating tower blocks that was the Dudlham Farm Estate. Mother and son remained locked in their embrace.

He did not tell the little boy that he already knew about his mother's illness. He did not tell him that he now understood that, for Nikisha Lewis, sickness was normal life; that frequent visits to the doctor had been routine for her since she was eight years old. He looked at the boy's innocent face and wondered if he was aware that his mother had been abused at school and at home, and again at the second home where she had run for refuge.

Even though Orelius was at this time well known as a ruthless gangster, the incident at the car park had been random. Nikisha had been in the wrong place at the wrong time. But as soon as he began checking on her, he realised that someone up there with almighty powers was still laughing at him.

Of all the people whom his wrath could have befallen, he had picked on a young woman who had been repeatedly raped by her aunt's boyfriend before she turned fourteen, and had run away to live with a distant cousin in Dudlham Farm. Then, after a relatively unremarkable twelve months at The Farm, coming home late from a babysitting job one evening, she gets accosted by a gang of drugged-up youths. Orelius could only imagine what must have gone through her mind: was there a big sign on her forehead saying '*RAPE ME*'? Because that is exactly what these boys went ahead and did, all four of them taking turns on her already battered fifteen-year-old body. This, he learned, was the encounter that resulted in this sweet boy who was talking to him now. A young child seemingly destined to follow his mother's doomed life path, surviving on the grinding poverty of the dole system, and already being bullied in school. Orelius Simm had picked on a woman who had known nothing but pain and cruelty in her life.

Almost two minutes passed in silence, as Orelius searched for the right words. Then he lowered his eyes back to the boy's level, widened his lips into a tight smile, and spoke for the first time.

'Actually, Timmy, I'm here to see you.'

The only response was a further tightening of the mother–son embrace. Nikisha Lewis's lower lip was trembling.

Orelius hunkered down and lifted the briefcase to his lap, clicked it open, and removed a square white box about ten inches square by four deep. 'Brand new Nintendo Wii,' he said, patting the package gently. 'A little birdie told me that this was your Christmas wish that never came true.' He tried the smile again but it did nothing to light up either mother or son. 'It's yours, Timmy. I want you to have it.'

The boy looked up at his mum. The mother looked down at her son, her left hand reaching up to her face to suppress a snivel as the tears continued rolling down her cheeks. Neither of them moved.

'OK, Timmy, I will just leave it down here. Take it inside whenever you want, it's yours.'

He got up from the stool, holding the case in his right hand and pausing momentarily to brush a speck of dust off his shirt with his left. Then he started walking away, heading towards the stairs.

He was waiting again at the same spot that Sunday when they got back from church. This time he had brought a new pair of Nike trainers, which were received with the same wall of silence. But as he started walking back down the hall, the boy turned round in his mother's tight grip and mumbled a quiet '*Thank you.*'

It was at this point that Orelius decided that, as long as he lived, no one was ever going to hurt this boy. His mother had suffered enough.

In the following weeks he bought more toys, and sweets and school essentials. He personally paid a visit to the families of the kids who had started on Timmy with racist taunts. Most of them, remarkably, were black. They didn't see Timmy as one of them. Some, he understood, even called him gay because he didn't share their level of interest in football. Orelius had a few quiet words with the parents. This was six years ago, a time when no one wished for a visit from Orelius Simm. He even managed to draw the occasional thank you from Nikisha.

As expected, there was plenty of speculation about the nature of his relationship with Nikisha Lewis. But for the fact that Timmy was clearly a mixed-race child, while both he and Nikisha were black, obvious conclusions would have been reached. Little did they know that while Timmy soon grew up regarding Orelius as a father, his mother remained a stranger to him.

His regular visits soon turned into a duty. About three months later he forced an uncomfortable conference with Nikisha in which they agreed that he could always have Timmy for the whole day every Saturday. After establishing his indifference to football, Orelius tried to introduce him to other hobbies. Tennis became love at first attempt. He enrolled him in an academy in Finchley where during the early years he spent the first three hours of his Saturday mornings. This turned into half-days in latter years, with the other half spent in parks, restaurants, movies, or whatever else they could agree on for their boys' days out.

While Timmy loved his mother, he lived for Saturdays. He would wake up early, get himself ready and be waiting with his ears pinned against the door for Orelius's footsteps. There had been tantrums of untold proportions on the two or three occasions Orelius had been forced to cancel. Orelius became acquainted with other parents from the tennis academy, and his gangster image began to soften.

He would later consider it another ironic act from that almighty Master above, that, through Timmy, he ended up achieving what he had set out to achieve on the day he travelled to Manchester.

He had allowed someone into his life unconditionally, and learned to give back love where he received love.

*

Now, after more than six years, Orelius was closer to Timmy than anyone besides his mother. This somehow worked despite the fact that the mother had always remained an enigma to him. Every time he showed up, it would be Timmy getting the door; his mum would only offer a weak barely audible 'Have fun' from somewhere in the house, safely out of sight.

'So you are holding up OK then?' Orelius asked.

'Yes, I'm stronger now,' she answered.

'Now...?'

'Yes, I have to be strong for my son. When he comes back he will have a strong mother who can protect him, a mother he can be proud of. I won't ever let him down again.'

Orelius felt a momentary discomfort. Maybe he had misread her, but this woman seemed more confident and upbeat now than at any time since he'd known her. She was not the terrified Nikisha who would stumble when someone looked at her. Could it possibly be because she was now rid of something she had considered a burden...? Surely he would have known through Timmy if his mother was heading towards a complete breakdown. Timmy would have mentioned something. Unless... he couldn't bear to let his mind dwell on that thought.

'Nikki, the man you spoke to is officially handling Timmy's case. I've also been asked to help look at this from a different angle with another detective. They think as an insider I might be able to spot something they might have missed, and I need your help. I know you've probably done this already with detective Garret, but I need you to walk me through your activities on Sunday again, from the time you woke up till the time you realised Timmy was missing,' he said, getting a small notebook and a pen from his pockets, which he had no intention of using. He was doing it for show, to keep this looking impersonal. 'Take your time, give me as much details as possible. You never know what might be important.'

'I told you: we went to church, came back, saw the protestors at the main entrance, so we used the alley. We got in, Timmy asked to watch the protests from the balcony, and I let him. That's it, haven't seen him since.' Her voice was steady, with no sign of emotion.

The fact that Nikisha had braved the riots and gone to church bothered him.

'OK. What route did you take to church?'

'Same route as usual, through Gloucester then Adams Road.'

'Who conducted the service?'

'The church service...?'

'Yes.'

'It was done by Pastor Sara, the wife of–'

'It's OK, I know who she is.' Orelius waved that one off and shifted in his chair to have a better look at her. He was indeed familiar with the all-singing, all-dancing Victory Gospel Church and their infamous pastor. 'And in church, did you or Timmy meet any friends or acquaintances? Anyone pop over to say hi or have a chat? Or maybe Timmy had a quick run-around with some friends?'

She hesitated, still with no trace of emotion on her face.

'Obviously we've been going there a while so we recognise many of the faces, but I wouldn't call them friends.'

'Anyone you can name?'

'What?' she looked confused.

'I mean anyone from the church service you can name off the top of your head right now. Someone who recognised you too.'

'Yes, I saw Tracy Billing from Martlesham.'

Orelius had no idea who Tracy Billing was. 'Did Tracy say hi or acknowledge you in any way.'

'Yeah, she waved, I think.'

'And you waved back?

'Yes, I did.'

'So if I went to Tracy now she'd confirm that she saw you and Timmy in church on Sunday morning.'

Nikisha started to say something then stopped. The implication of this route of interrogation was beginning to sink in.

'Yes,' she said quietly. There was the slightest hint of pain in her voice but her face gave away nothing. 'I believe she would.'

'And when you got back here, I assume people saw you walking through the estate or up the stairs maybe?'

'The old man next door was coming out just as we walked past his door.' She was referring to The Hog. 'He saw us. I believe he can confirm that.'

'And he would confirm that Timmy was OK.'

She swallowed and closed her eyes to absorb the pain of the question.

'Yes,' she nodded.

'OK, that's good,' he said, then remained silent for a while, as if unable to think further.

'What is this, Orelius? What are you trying to say?'

'I spoke to a few people who were at the riots and pretty much none of them remembers seeing Timmy. But they saw you there.'

'Because I was there looking for Tim.'

'And somehow you didn't see a boy running around in Timmy's jacket? It took me seconds to spot that jacket from up here.'

There was no reply from Nikisha.

'The police believe that Timmy wasn't really anywhere near the riots and that the clothing was left there by somebody as a deliberate misdirection,' he explained without looking directly at her. 'Now, try and look at it from my point of view, Nikisha: you pointed me towards that gate where I just happened to find the jacket, after you'd already been there on your own.'

She swallowed again and said nothing.

'Nikisha, you allowed me to share your son, and he shaped my life. I'll be forever grateful to you for that. I'm sorry I never got to know you enough in the process. But I come to you now as just a man who also loves Timmy and wants to help protect him. I hope this is enough for you to trust me and be able to talk to me at this difficult time. If there was an accident or something that you think no one will understand...' He paused to let that sink in but still couldn't look at her. 'You do realise the police will soon come to this line of thinking too, by which time it will be too late for explanations. The world will then become a very lonely place for you.'

He did not see the missile till it was an inch away from his face but he moved his head in time for it to miss his left eye by a whisker. It smacked the wall behind him and landed back on the settee next to him. It was a black two-inch heeled size six female boot. When he turned to look back in shock at the source of the missile, she was already coming at him. She flung herself over the coffee table and bore down on him with her claws out, punching, slapping and scratching at his face.

'He is my boy! He is my life!' She was crying. 'He is my *life*,' she said repeatedly as she attacked him.

Orelius was initially too shocked to react, and took the beating before he summoned enough strength to hold her off. He wrapped his big arms around her flailing arms and stood her up so they were facing each other. He kept hold of her even after her wild rage had waned and she had crumbled to helpless sobs. Then he gently lowered her to a sitting position on the sofa and sat down next to her. He leaned forwards with his elbows on his knees and rested his head in his laced hands, listening to her sobs.

'He is my life,' she said again, her voice now hoarse.

'I'm sorry,' he said.

'Please help me find him, Orelius. Help me find my baby.'

'I will,' he said, and slowly got up to let himself out of the house.

CHAPTER 10

Orelius called Downing as he walked back down the Northolt stairs. He told him about the suspect list, and Markus Isaacs, but did not mention his encounter with Nikisha Lewis.

'Well done,' the detective said, after he explained the process he had used to generate the list. 'It's not exactly a breakthrough but it's an inside angle; we would have struggled to gain that without you. So now at least we have some names. I'm heading down there and we'll see this Isaacs guy first. Don't attempt to question him or anyone else till I'm there.'

'OK. But a quick word of advice: if you are coming down to The Farm you might need to tone everything down a bit. I mean what you wear, the car you drive, and even how you talk. Don't make it too obvious you are the police, or things could get tougher.'

'I know that, Orelius, which is why we needed you in the first place. Don't worry, I never wear uniform. That's why I've got the D in front of my rank.' He chuckled but Orelius didn't get the joke. 'I'm coming alone and we are going to play this as just two regular guys asking some questions. You could do most of the talking. I will be there to make sure things are done in the right way in case it goes to court.'

*

They met up twenty minutes later outside Kenley on the northern edge of the estate. Downing seemed to have got his point about toning down alright. He came in an old silver Corsa that Orelius was sure had been acquired specifically for the tough Farm terrain. His grey short-sleeved T-shirt, hanging loosely over a pair of faded blue jeans, looked almost ragged enough to blend in. Orelius was also in jeans and a white T-shirt, and the detective's almost matching choice of attire made him feel at ease. They left the Corsa at Kenley car park and took Gloucester then Willan Road on foot.

'Before we go further I'd like to lay down a few truths, Orelius,' the detective started as they marched along the path. 'I picked you because I believe you can get results in this case. But I also did it because, to be honest, I am not the best man for this kind of case. I mostly work white collar crimes.'

'White collar crimes?'

'Yeah, corporate stuff, hardly any violence involved.' He paused, and Orelius nodded to keep him talking, sure that this was heading somewhere. 'Anyway, at the time I was handed over the files this was still an ambiguous case involving a few severed human ears and with no sign of the victims. We didn't know what kind of crime had been committed and I was only meant to be looking after the case temporarily, while things were being figured out. But here we are now investigating a missing child and possibly multiple homicides.'

'Right,' Orelius nodded him on again, still waiting for the point.

'I just happened to be around, and even though I could have pretty much just sat on this case till they figured out who they really wanted to assign it to, I realised something had to be done. From your records I knew that once you'd come to your senses and left Tom Clarke's thugs alone you would end up back here, tearing the place apart with your associates, searching for Timmy. All I've done essentially is offer my authority, contacts and badge as a police officer to a search that you would have been doing anyway. But that also means that whatever we do, we cannot break the law, or this could all backfire catastrophically on me. So if you are uncomfortable with that, you should let me know now and I'll call the deal off, and you can see how far your friends get trying to find Timmy with you in jail.'

Orelius tucked his hands in his pockets and walked on. 'I have to say I appreciate your honesty,' he said. 'And you got one thing right: whoever Scotland Yard sent down here would have needed me, regardless of their experience. I have passed word around for everyone to cooperate with detective Garret and his team, but it would have been a whole lot easier if I'd actually been there with them.'

'If you are thinking you'd rather be in the other team, forget it. DI Garret is running an official police investigation, and teaming up with a civilian, let alone a known felon, is out of the question. I'm the one who made the connection with my Ear-Slasher case and engineered an unofficial way into Timmy's inquiry. Our relationship will remain very much off the record.'

'How did you manage to get me an official deal with the CPS then? Assuming there isn't any funny fine print in that.'

'No, your deal is legitimate. The bosses are keen to resolve the Ear-Slasher thing, especially since the resulting public disorder forced us into a very risky bluff. I told them you could give us the person who left those ears there.'

'So they don't care whether the connection with Timmy is true or not? I do.'

'So do I, Orelius, so do I. And I'm telling you once again that if you show me that person, I will show you what happened to Timmy. If you don't want to believe me, fine, but just stick with me anyway. This is the closest you will get to the police investigation.'

The need to clarify these things baffled Orelius slightly because he had already bought the detective's theory that the incidents were linked. He chose not to comment further and walked on, his mind contemplating the possible realities that could be awaiting them behind the enigmatic character they were about to meet. If half the things that were said about Markus Isaacs were true, then he was capable of abducting a child, and he was capable of collecting human ears.

*

Markus Isaacs:

In Dudlham Farm Estate, I knew I had walked into the heights of a dream. I knew Dudlham would make me. Those were the good days of The Farm. When the newly built blocks gleamed, and the corridors and walkways breathed hope. When fresh immigrant children played side by side with their adopted compatriots and dared to dream that they too would one day call themselves British. Oh yes, those were the days. But I enjoyed them only from a fourth-floor window in Croydon House, never once venturing beyond my front door. I spent my only two summers of freedom watching other kids out in the playgrounds, longing to be out there making friends. But they were never even aware of my existence. I started school the following year, but I still could not make any friends, only enemies.

These kids turned my dreams into nightmares.

Sometimes I blame them for what happened. Sometimes I blame my mother's husband, for he too made my life a misery. Sometimes, I blame myself.

But never my mother. Not once.

Not even when I hear her final words to me:

'Today, son, you are going to fight back.'

*

It took Orelius and the detective ten minutes to get to Stapleford. They were approaching the block, about twenty yards from the entrance, when Downing stopped abruptly and raised his right hand to Orelius's chest. His gaze was fixed on a point in space around one of the top-floor windows.

'What is going on up there?' he asked. His mouth had curled into an O, with both eyeballs dancing around his raised brows. 'Is that someone dangling a cat out of their window?'

Orelius followed his gaze. 'Yeah, kids. They are playing a game.'

'Aren't they supposed to be in school?'

'I think they've just started their Easter holidays. But most of them would rather play this game than go to school anyway.'

There was a cacophony of chants and giggles from a group of about seven or eight kids on the ground who were looking up with arms outstretched, ready to catch the ginger cat.

'He's not going to throw it, is he?' Even as Downing said this, he was already striding purposefully towards the group. 'Hey!' he started shouting.

Orelius scurried to catch up and hold him back. 'What are you doing?'

'What do you mean, what am I doing? I'm not going stand here and watch this happen.'

'OK, Gregg. Let *me* stop them if this really upsets you that much,' Orelius said tersely, stepping in front of the detective.

The boy in the top floor window had turned the cat upside down and was holding it by all four legs. The animal was snarling, twisting and turning wildly.

'Hey, you! Stop–' Orelius began. But the cat was already on its way down.

One of the kids on the ground dived and caught the cat spectacularly, like a pro goalkeeper, amidst jubilant cheers from his mates. The animal was lashing out, scratching, and snapping its fangs at the catcher. The kid eventually succumbed and let the cat go, and his friends started giving chase.

Downing remained rooted to a spot, gaping.

'Let it go, detective. The cat's fine,' Orelius said, beckoning him towards the entrance. 'For future reference, though, don't ever think of stepping in front of those kids and telling them what to do unless you've got a gun and maybe some backup. These children will wind you up so much you will want to arrest them all. And what would you achieve by that? Best you could do is get them a couple ASBOs after dozens of trips to the courthouse and endless paperwork. They'll keep you so busy you won't have time for serial killers and child abductors.'

The detective stared at him grimly and said nothing.

Orelius started towards stairway, and he followed. *Welcome to The Farm, Detective Downing,* he said to himself as they marched up to Markus Isaacs's flat.

*

Markus Isaacs:

Everybody wants to know why I did what I did. When I got out of prison some newspapers offered me money to tell my story, why I did it and how I survived forty years in one of the most hostile prisons in England. Some people want to know about my mother, a few are curious about my mother's husband. But most people want to know how I feel about my former classmates Anthony Hart and Ian McHugh.

I remember the events of that summer of '65 better than I remember what I had for breakfast today. But this story cannot be sold. My sins have been forgiven and these people have become my friends.

They are my only friends.

I see them everywhere. When I can't sleep at night they rise and walk with me. They rescued me in prison when I was first stabbed in the eye with a toothbrush in the exercise yard. Of course I was accosted in the showers too. And I never stood a chance against my attackers because there were always three or four of them, but Anthony Hart and Ian McHugh were there for me. They came and stood by my side. My mother's husband helped me look the other way. And when it was all over, my mother was always there to kiss my pains away. I survived because I spent those forty years with Anthony and Ian and my mother's husband. But not in the same way I spent them with my mother.

My mother's last words were, ultimately, what carried me through:

'Today, son, you are going to fight back.'

*

Markus Isaacs's flat was on the second floor of Stapleford House. Orelius knocked three times on the green door and nothing happened. He lifted the mail-flap and attempted to look inside. There was no sign of life. The next door down the hall cracked open, and a middle aged female head in a blue floral African headscarf popped out. The woman considered them suspiciously, then stepped into the hallway and leaned over the deck to stare out at nothing in particular, clearly offering her services if required.

'Excuse me,' Orelius called out, and pointed at Isaac's door. 'Have you seen him recently?'

'I heard him leave this morning. He goes walking, I presume...' she shrugged. Her teeth were milk white, accentuated by her dark lips. 'He leaves very early, while it's still dark, and is normally back before dawn. Not sure I heard him come back today, though.'

'So he's normally at home most of the day?'

'Indeed. He's an old man, hasn't got nothing else.'

'You two talk? I mean as neighbours, are you close?'

'He keeps to himself mostly, but I've managed to get him to talk to me a bit. Only because I pushed the issue, mind. I try to know my neighbours, it's in my culture,' she said, tapping her heart proudly to illustrate the origin of her compassion. 'He moved in next door and the whole block was worried because there were all these stories about his past. But I gave him a chance, didn't judge him. I thought I should find out for myself.'

'And what did you think?'

'I think he is a good man.'

The two men looked at each other. Neither had been expecting that.

'Could you just tell him we popped by,' Orelius said finally, deciding that this woman was an attention seeker looking for an opportunity to get involved. 'This is detective Gregg Downing from the Metropolitan Police.' He didn't need to introduce himself. 'We are following up my missing boy's case. So when he comes back, tell him we came by and we just need to talk to him.' He reached into his pocket for a pen, and tore off a bit of paper from his suspects list to jot down his mobile number. 'He can reach me on this number, but I might also try again later to see if he's in.'

'Sure, I'll pass that on.'

'Thank you very much. You take care now.'

They started walking back down the hallway towards the stairs.

*

Markus Isaacs:

The first time I came home from school with a swollen lip and a cut on my left eye, I was not crying. I never cried. But my mother did, sometimes. Not because of my injuries but because she too would be nursing a split lip or a black eye. Sometimes my troubles at school helped me forget the misery at home, but only for a while. Soon I found myself wishing to be somewhere away from school and even further away from Dudlham Farm. I longed for the land of my birth. But we had left Jamaica with dreams of a better life, and a black eye is a small price to pay for a dream. A cloud means nothing when the birds are singing.

After she was done crying, my mother would ask me three questions:

Did you start it?

I shook my head.

Did you fight back?

I shook my head.

Did you cry?

I shook my head.

Good, she'd say. You did good.

This was my mother: strong in adversity and gracious in despair. In a storm, her wisdom was my rock, and through darkness, her smile my shining star.

The person who uttered those fateful words in the summer of sixty-five was not my mother:

'Today, son, you are going to fight back.'

*

Ten minutes after Orelius and the detective had left, two young men arrived at Markus Isaacs's door. They were both five-ten, with light brown skin and similar dark curly hair. Their slightly bigger than average ears were the sole blemish on their otherwise handsome features. Also matching were the pairs of baggy blue jeans they had sagging loosely around their buttocks, showing off the labels of their designer underwear. In fact the only distinguishing mark between them presently was that one was wearing a large black bomber jacket while the other had a blue *New York Knicks* vest draped over a plain white shirt.

They did not knock on the old man's door. Bomber Jacket tried it to confirm that it was indeed locked, then removed a small grey toolbox from his jacket pocket, got down on his knees and went to work. Knicks leaned over him with his hands on the doorframe and watched.

A few yards down the hall a door cracked open and they saw a female face with the floral African headscarf peering out questioningly.

'What is this now?' the woman started. 'He puts up this big show with a policeman to hoodwink us, then sends you right behind him to do the dirty work. Just who does Orelius think he is fooling?'

Knicks, still with his left arm over the doorframe, glanced up at her.

'Get back in your house,' he said.

Then he lowered his head back towards his accomplice, who now had a thin silver wire stuck inside the brass door lock, and was twisting it left and right.

The woman stepped onto the deck and faced them, her arms folded boldly across her chest. 'I understand he is looking for a missing boy, but why get you into this? This is not the right way to solve problems. God, you are just kids.'

They both ignored her. Knicks didn't even look up this time.

'Do you know you two wanted to be pilots when you were little boys?' she asked. 'Every time I came to your house you would be sitting up on the kitchen worktops side by side, flying imaginary planes, pilot and co-pilot. All that purity and innocence is now gone, what a pity.'

'Shut up,' they both said, almost in unison.

The lock clicked, Bomber Jacket twisted the knob, and they were in.

'You will not find the boy in there,' the woman said, walking up to Isaacs's door. 'And he hasn't got anything worth stealing either, if you are thinking of that too.'

Bomber Jacket had moved swiftly from the kitchen through the living room and into the bedroom, banging doors and moving furniture haphazardly. Knicks was hanging around closer to the front door, staring menacingly at the woman, who appeared unfazed.

'Orelius Simm is the devil of Dudlham Farm, and you are his nasty little foot soldiers.'

Knicks reached into the right hip pocket of his baggy jeans and brought out a small black pistol.

'Get back in your house,' he said, pointing the gun at her.

'Oh, so you are going to shoot me now, eh?' she snapped. The gun seemed to have irritated rather than scared her. 'Come on then... do it. Shoot me right here.' she tapped at the middle of her chest then spread her arms wide 'Do it!'

Bomber Jacket came back from the bedroom and whispered, 'There's nothing here. Let's go.' Then he brushed past the woman as if she wasn't there and hurried down the hallway.

Knicks put the gun back in his pocket and followed him, his hands raised behind him in a poor imitation of a shield, trying to bat away the verbal assault from behind.

'...You dare point a gun at me, who do you think you are?'

A couple of strides in front of Knicks, already with one foot on the stairs, Bomber Jacket muttered, 'This woman is crazy.'

Behind him the woman's voice was gaining momentum.

'... I changed your diapers, Ray Kimani...'

Knicks and Bomber Jacket were indeed Ray and Mickey Kimani, a pair of twenty-one year old identical twin brothers. They claimed to be Samoan, a fact they were quick to point out to new acquaintances, right after their names. The Kimani twins were in fact London born and bred, with a Scottish mother and a Kenyan father. It was never clear how this made them Samoan. Or why they particularly wanted Samoan heritage. Their hobbies included touring the nearby suburbs with loaded pistols and collecting valuables from rich folks, often with their permission; the twins, despite their patience with the African woman, were generally very persuasive with their guns.

'... I changed your diapers, Mickey...'

CHAPTER 11

As Orelius and the detective stepped outside Markus Isaacs's block, they saw three boys of around ten carrying out what looked like a BMX stunt-show along Willan road. They were twisting, swerving, and flipping the front wheels of their three matching red bikes in a remarkable display. Their audience was thin: two girls of roughly similar age, and two equally scruffy boys. This didn't seem to deter them, however, as they rode along in tandem showing off.

The only problem was that they were in the middle of a busy road.

An old red Volkswagen screeched to a stop and avoided one of them by few inches. The driver threw his arms up in the air in anger, letting out a stream of expletives. The kids cycled round his car howling with laughter. The one in a Tottenham Hotspur shirt and black shorts stopped next to the driver's window and extended his right hand, with the middle finger sticking out.

'Hey!' Orelius shouted from behind.

The boys, none of whom had appeared intimidated in the slightest by the motorist, took one look at the speaker and stopped in their tracks. Then they turned their bikes round and started speeding away.

‘Hey, you, MJ… hold it, MJ. *Oi…*’ Orelius started running after them but changed his mind after a few half-hearted strides. He watched them disappear round the corner, then started walking back towards Downing who had not moved. The detective didn’t look like he was having a good time at The Farm.

‘What was that all about?’ he said when Orelius rejoined him.

‘What?’

‘Why were you running after them?’

‘I was trying to get MJ,’ Orelius said. ‘MJ is the one with the Tottenham shirt. His name’s Mic Bailey and I’ve got some business…’ He stopped himself mid-sentence as his focus returned to his partner. ‘Well, never mind MJ for now, you might hear his story again if you hang around here long enough. Have you got time to try some others on the list? Then maybe we can come back and see if the old man is back,’ he said pointing towards Isaacs flat.

‘Yeah, I’ve got time. I think we should find this Kelly-Jo woman first.’

To prove his point about the previous investigators’ errors, Orelius suggested they walk back to his car through the alley between Lympne and Manston, and drive it to Stapleford and back, before visiting Kelly-Jo at Northolt. By the time they parked the car at Northolt, the detective seemed to have bought his idea that it had been a mistake to overlook Stapleford.

Orelius had also told the detective a bit about Kelly-Jo and her lift. He had even got a slight cackle from Downing when he told him about the popular myth about the serious fault with the Northolt lift that somehow mysteriously fixed itself without any outside intervention.

'So this woman is obsessed with lifts?' Downing asked as they turned into the block and approached the lift.

'Yes, she is. And not just any lift, just this one.' He punched the call button, then released and punched it again harder to make sure. There was screeching and clanking as the lift came to a stop. The door slowly squeaked open.

It was empty.

Orelius took a step forward and stood still.

'Well, I don't see anyone here,' Downing said. 'Thought you said she is always here.'

'She is, most of the time.' He looked at his watch. It was nearly three. 'Maybe she is at The Jolly. She has lunch there and sometimes stays on a bit longer. Shall we go have a look?'

They drove Downing's Corsa about two hundred yards to TJ via Adams road. It would have been quicker to walk but the detective claimed he needed his car.

The Jolly was fairly deserted: a group of four young men in removals jackets dining on the top balcony; a middle-aged couple standing at the bar with no drinks, chatting to the barman; and a lone old man with a newspaper on the small table by the door.

There was no sign of Kelly-Jo Pretty. The barman had not seen her today. And yes, she usually came in for lunch around two, and always had soup and lasagne. On the odd occasion she skipped lunch, she was mostly likely to appear later in the evening for coffee. And as she had missed lunch today, there was a good chance she would come.

Orelius's phone beeped a text alert and he removed it from his pocket to read a message from Mickey Kimani:

Nothing @ da bogeyman's yard. But dere's a propa mouthy miss Africa nxt door hu's lucky she's a woman or I wud hav decked her

'Great,' he muttered to himself.

'Do you want to have a coffee and maybe try Isaacs again?' Downing said.

Orelius nodded, figuring that Markus Isaacs probably wouldn't be back yet, and that as long as the twins had been neat with the lock, there would be no way for the detective to figure out what was happening behind the scenes.

He quickly scanned the bar for a suitable seat. Retreating to his official table at the back didn't feel right, so he picked the one next to the door that had been vacated by the old man. The newspaper was still there and he wanted to scan through it.

They were sipping their coffee and discussing some of the other suspects on the list when the detective's mobile rang and he got into an animated conversation with whoever was on the other side. More than once he repeated the phrase: 'That's OK, Chief. I understand.' Then he said: 'I've got an interesting angle on this one, Chief. Maybe you should let me see it out. I'm working closely with the boy's father.'

Downing appeared uncomfortable with the conversation, and grew gradually more agitated, as if he wasn't quite getting his way. Finally he closed the phone. 'We should get going now, I think,' he said, looking at his watch. 'Let's knock on Isaacs's door one more time. You can try Kelly-Jo in the evening and let me know how that goes.'

They were back outside Isaacs' flat within ten minutes and still there was no one in. Miss Africa next door was once again on hand to inform them that the old man had indeed appeared a few minutes after them, and she had relayed their message. Then he had left again almost immediately. Yes, it was unusual for him not to be in at this time, she said. But no, she didn't think Isaacs had anything to run away from. He was a good man, she repeated.

Orelius noted that the door was locked. The twins must have picked the lock neatly without breaking. Or the old man had quickly fixed it and locked up again before taking off.

Miss Africa surprisingly failed to mention the Kimani twins' visit until they were turning round to leave.

'Oh, and by the way, I don't think he was very happy about the twins' visit either,' she said as she shut the door behind her.

Downing looked at Orelius questioningly but made no comment. Either he was too preoccupied with whatever Chief had told him on the phone, or he didn't want to know.

'I'm going to have to go now, Orelius,' the detective said hurriedly. 'But I'll be just a phone call away. Leave the suspect list for now and concentrate on Kelly-Jo. Find out if she saw Timmy on Sunday.'

*

Like most Farmers, Kelly-Jo Pretty had her own story to define her role in Dudlham Farm Estate. Once upon a time, when there were still a handful of white folks braving the influx of black immigrants in The Farm, a twenty-one-year-old single white woman occupied number 65 Northolt House. Her name was Marianne Pretty. She gave birth to a baby girl and named her Kelly-Jo. Marianne was a typical social welfare case: single mother, no job, no real family to speak of, just trying to make it one day at a time on state handouts. Gracing each day with neither complaint nor regret; dancing in the rain because yesterday was a storm. Unaware of anything better, for all she could see around were others like her, trapped in the same cycle of *pretend-normal existence.*

Except one day Marianne Pretty decided to stop existing.

Her two-year-old baby was found playing with a stuffed toy near the entrance to the Northolt block, about five yards away from the very lift that would later become her life's obsession.

Wherever it was that Kelly-Jo's mother went, she never came back.

Residents, most of them black immigrants fresh from Africa and the Caribbean, could not fathom a human being capable of abandoning their own flesh and blood. They blamed it on evil spirits. The whites from surrounding suburbs suspected foul play, some cynically pointing out that Marianne Pretty had it coming. What else did she expect, living amongst robbers and drug dealers?

CHAPTER 12

Orelius pulled up outside The Jolly and stayed in the car, watching the woman smoke outside. She was sitting on a ledge next to the back-patio doors, less than ten yards from where he was parked. With his windows down, he could clearly hear the desperate sucking sounds of a smoker who had never quite mastered the art. She battled with the cigarette, managing only a couple of half-decent puffs before giving up and lobbing it over the stairs. He watched her limp gingerly into the pub, and waited two minutes before following her in.

He found her standing at the far end of the bar, waving a shaky right hand in a bid to catch the barman's attention. The young barman had his back turned; he was facing the big square mirror on the back wall, sorting out strands of his long ridiculously-styled hair. There was also a light-skinned barmaid in attendance but she was busy wrestling with one of the beer pumps, pouring a pint of locally brewed ale for another customer. She spotted Kelly-Jo, and tilted her head to call out for her colleague.

'Jack, there's a customer waiting.'

Jack turned away from the mirror. He was a muscled black boy no older than twenty-two, with heavily gelled jet-black hair and a fake diamond stud in his left ear. He was wearing a tight-

Jack leaned closer over the counter with a childish grin on his face, and this only made it worse for Kelly-Jo. She froze, then her twitching intensified. The boy howled with laughter, as though he had expected this. Then he eased back and, having decided to give the terrified woman a chance, he relaxed and softened his tone. 'How have you been Kelly-Jo, my friend? I haven't seen you in a while.'

She too seemed to relax. She nodded her head and smiled.

'What can I get you this evening, then, my darling?'

The smile widened. The tongue finally released itself from behind those lips, and through a painful stutter Kelly-Jo found her voice. 'Can I have a bowl of soup please?'

Jack shot his female colleague a look and she giggled. Then he turned back to his customer. 'Sorry, Kelly-Jo, we are not doing any food today. Chef didn't turn up.'

Orelius looked around and counted at least four diners scattered around the pub.

'How about a latte? Can I have a latte?'

'The coffee machine is broken, sorry.' He shrugged.

In the alcove behind the bar, the barmaid had her right hand over her mouth in a poor effort to suppress a fit of laughter. She had smooth caramel skin, ample breasts and a stunning figure, probably the reason Jack worked here.

Kelly-Jo's shoulders slumped in dejection as she turned round and limped to the small table in the farthest corner. She sat there pitifully, her head resting in her hands, trying to lose herself back into a place where the Jacks of this world could never get at her.

Jack walked back to Orelius with a satisfied grin on his face. 'Sorry about the delay, mate. What did you want again?'

'Can I have a bowl of soup please? And a latte.'

The kid started to laugh, thinking this was another dig at Kelly-Jo, but he stopped when he saw the grim expression on Orelius's his face.

'Sure, Oz. No problem,' he said, then quickly punched some buttons on his till and turned round to start up the coffee machine. 'Just take a seat and I'll bring the latte and the soup for you in two minutes.'

'That's fine, I'll wait here.'

He watched him pour the coffee and serve it neatly into a mug sitting on a saucer, which was sat in the middle of a silver tray with milk and sugar on the side. Then he rushed across the restaurant into the kitchen and reappeared with a steaming bowl of soup and two slices of bread. He also brought cutlery and condiments and placed it all on the same tray.

'That will be two-fifty for the soup, mate,' he said placing the tray front of him. 'The coffee is on the house.' He winked, and smiled again.

Orelius pushed the tray to one side and leaned across the bar, beckoning the boy with a slight nod of the head. 'Can I have a word, Jack?'

'Course, Oz. Anything,' Jack said, leaning forward excitedly.

Orelius enticed him even closer with a hand gesture, like what he had to say was for his ears only. When he was close enough Orelius reached out with his right hand and grabbed him by his throat. Then he shoved his head back against the still-hot coffee machine. Trapped in a choking grip, with the back of his head against hot metal, the boy could only manage desperate gurgling sounds. The smell of burning hair gel floated in the air.

'Next time she wants soup, you will give her soup. If she wants coffee, you will give her coffee. You hear me, Jack?'

Jack's black face was beginning to go pale and his eyes seemed to be popping out, but he made his best attempt at a nod.

'Good.' Orelius let go, and the boy collapsed low on the floor holding his neck and wheezing, as if he was suffering an asthma attack.

All round the restaurant, the monotonous drone from the clinking cutlery and casual conversations died. Orelius didn't look round but he could feel the eyes on him.

'And that goes for you too, sweetheart,' he said, pointing at the barmaid, who had frozen in shock in her spot in the alcove. Her mouth opened wide, as though he had pointed a loaded gun at her. She looked like she was going to scream, but she only managed a nod.

Orelius placed a five pound note on the counter and carried the tray to Kelly-Jo's table.

'That's for you, Kelly-Jo,' he said, placing the tray in front of her. There was no other chair available so he grabbed one from the next table and sat opposite her.

'Thank you very much.' Even though her head was bobbing up and down like a basketball, she said this quickly without a stutter. She didn't seem surprised that he had joined her uninvited. Orelius had feared he might overwhelm her and send her into that mute, twitching state he had witnessed at the bar.

He looked on as she began to eat: he had to be careful. If he pressed the wrong button, her system would crash and everything could be lost. Kelly-Jo wasn't a person whose memory could be easily refreshed, not even with a little help from Megaman.

He waited patiently for her to finish, using the time to review his day's work. He had spoken the Turkish woman at Lympne and she had seen a man in that van alright. It had been very late on the night before the ears were discovered, but the interior lights had been on briefly and she had caught a decent glimpse. She was sure the man was black and had a bushy beard. Orelius had asked if she had seen the man actually drive the vehicle, and she answered no; but she had heard the engine running as he sat inside fiddling about with the interior light on before getting out. She had stopped peeping just as the man was shutting the door behind him, so she couldn't be sure which direction he went in. Sofia's account had sounded like a genuine lead towards Markus Isaacs – until he asked if she could tell how tall the man was. She had hesitated to think before deciding that the man she saw could not have been taller than the height of the van; she had not seen his head clear its roof. This was a problem because Markus Isaacs was about six-four. Even those who had never set eyes on The Bogeyman knew him as a gigantic red-eyed monster. The height of the Transit van was about a hundred and eighty centimetres, so anyone over five-eleven should have been visible over its roof. Orelius had no reason to doubt Sofia, but he was left with questions about this height discrepancy. Maybe a simple error had resulted from her use of the van's roof to gauge the man's height from her first-floor vantage point fifty yards away. Or there could have been another reason why she couldn't see Isaacs's head over the van. He was a very dark black man with a bushy beard, so if he had dark clothing on top, it would have been difficult to see him in the night. Or maybe she had not seen Isaacs at all, but another person altogether, a kid perhaps, cleverly disguised by a stick-on beard to commit crime. These were questions that could possibly be resolved by talking to the old man himself. If only he could find him.

The *dip, dunk, chew... chew...* sounds of Kelly-Jo eating stopped.

Orelius reassembled his thoughts.

'Kelly-Jo,' he started, trying to sound as pleasant as he could. 'I need your help with something.'

She lifted her head once, then dropped it back down.

'You know Timmy from Northolt, don't you? Little boy... about this tall...' he illustrated by positioning his hand about five feet off the floor, '... with very light skin, almost white. Do you know him?'

She nodded. 'Yes, he's a good boy.' She said this with relative ease.

'Can you remember the last time you saw him?'

She lowered her head and went quiet for a while. Almost a whole minute passed, so Orelius was forced to prompt.

'Kelly-Jo you remember Sunday... the day before yesterday? I saw you in your lift on Sunday afternoon. Did you happen to see Timmy that day?'

She thought for another couple of seconds. 'Yes... he gave me cookies.'

His heart rate shot up: Nikisha had not mentioned anything about Timmy handing out cookies on the day he went missing. 'Timmy gave you cookies on Sunday, are you sure?'

'Yes... he's a good boy.'

'He is, and that's why I need you to think very carefully if you really saw him on Sunday,' he said. Then, speaking very slowly, he added, 'Not yesterday... but the day before, did you really see him? Because Timmy has been missing since then, and if you remember correctly, you could help us find him.'

'Timmy missing....? Is he in trouble...?' The stutter was back, her lower lip shaking.

'Yes, he is missing. He's been gone since Sunday and if you saw him in the lift, it could help us figure out where he might have gone.'

'Timmy gone...?' She twitched, her head bouncing more frequently now. 'Maybe the lift took him when I wasn't watching. I was trying to watch out for them. I always watch out for them, but I... I...'

'What are you saying, Kelly-Jo? Did you see something happen? Did something happen in the lift?'

'I saw it... I remember... but I couldn't help.'

'You saw it?'

'Yes. The lift... the lift took... took...' The twitch had turned into a full body tremor.

'The lift took him?' he asked leaning closer, silently urging her lips to keep moving. 'Is that what you are trying to say?'

He waited; counting three... four... five beats, trying not to scare her back into that protective cocoon.

When nothing came he tried again as calmly as he could. 'Kelly-Jo, could you please tell me what happened after Timmy gave you cookies?'

'He just went off... I tried to tell him but he just went off.' Her eyes bulged out eerily under furrowed brows, as though a shocking truth was trying to push out from behind them. 'It wasn't my fault... the lift is bad, that's why I watch out for them... the lift took him... it's not my fault.' She started rocking back and forth in her chair amidst the twitching and head-bobbing. Her eyes were looking straight at him but were somewhere far away.

Orelius knew that he had lost her. There was nothing else he could do now but wait and watch her speak in tongues to her invisible audience till she was ready to come back to him. Her voice began to rise, and the bubbling turned almost spiritual.

He banged the centre of the small wooden table so hard it rattled both their chairs, '*Timmy*, Kelly-Jo!' he roared, and felt a chill, as deathly silence enveloped the entire restaurant. 'Where *is* he?'

The rocking stopped. Her eyes caught his, and she froze for a few seconds. Then she dropped her eyes, and tears started fitting short-sleeved shirt to display biceps that were probably a result of steroid abuse.

'Yes,' Jack said, his eyes scanning the bar. Kelly-Jo was standing right in front of him but she might as well have been invisible. Jack looked right through her, then turned and headed towards Orelius.

'Hi, Oz,' he said with an exuberant grin, as though they were best buddies. 'What can I get you, mate?'

'I think she was here before me.' He pointed to Kelly-Jo.

Jack turned and looked at her again with a scornful smile, then shook his head, 'Oh, her? She'll wait. She won't mind.'

'It's alright, I'll wait. You better look after her first.'

He hesitated, clearly shocked by Orelius' courtesy.

'OK,' he shrugged. 'I won't be a minute.' He dashed over to her in three quick strides.

'Yes, Kelly-Jo. What can I get you?'

Her permanently wide-open mouth began moving but her tongue seemed to be stuck. Her eyes darted around as if she was overwhelmed. Two more twitches followed in quick succession.

'I haven't got all day, Kelly-Jo,' Jack said, and Orelius could sense the boy stifling a laugh.

She tried again, and this time a sound emerged, an inaudible mumble.

flowing down her cheeks. Her sobs were muted. It was the tremors of her upper body that really opened Orelius's eyes to her pain.

'I'm sorry, Kelly-Jo. I'm so sorry.' He lowered his voice to a quiet, heartfelt plea. 'Just tell me if you know where Timmy is... please.'

She looked up at him again and the sobbing stopped, but he saw a slight twitch. She tried to form some words but they stuck in her throat.

'Take your time, Kelly-Jo. Just relax, we're just trying to help Timmy here, OK? I'm sorry for shouting; I'm not a bad man. I'm your friend, and so is Timmy... How was your soup, by the way? Was it good?'

She made another attempt to lift her heavy tongue but a twitch got in the way. Then another twitch... and another.

Orelius realised that he had heard the last words from Kelly-Jo Pretty tonight:

The lift took him... it was not my fault...

CHAPTER 13

Orelius had his phone out and was flipping through his list of contacts before he stepped out of The Jolly. The first part of his conversation with Downing was completely muddled, the detective having to continually stop him and ask him to slow down. He wasn't sure whether he was calling the detective for any particular kind of help, or if he just needed to talk to someone to keep him from doing something irrational with Kelly-Jo.

'She either did something to him or she saw something, Gregg. You should have seen her reaction.' He was hurrying along Adams Road towards Northolt. He needed to inspect the inside of that lift. 'Now she's gone into mute mode and I can't get anymore from her. Take her in and get an expert to question her. Check everything out, search her room at the hostel and her lift. I saw her there on Sunday just after getting the news and I'm sure she was doing something odd, only I couldn't figure it out then... this woman is way more messed up than I thought.'

It was only when he was inside the lift that he figured out that in the six years he'd been coming to this block for Timmy, he had only used the lift maybe four or five times, although it looked no different from any other lifts at The Farm. It creaked, squeaked and smelt foul, with stains and graffiti everywhere. He crouched, then got on his hands and knees to inspect the brownish stains. Most of them looked old, but maybe a couple of them looked fresh enough and red enough to be what he did not want them to be. He rode up and down with residents, pretending to be on his way somewhere. The strange image of Kelly-Jo in the lift on Sunday kept changing shapes in his head. Had she been crouching or sitting down, or maybe trying to *hold* something down?

It was nearly midnight before he finally accepted that the elevator was going to tell him nothing tonight.

He knew Kelly-Jo was now back at her quarters in the hostel and wondered whether there was something there that could help him understand this woman. Security at the facility was tight and it would be hard for him to gain entry and search Kelly-Jo's room without raising any alarms, but he knew a few people who could. He was just about to call one of them when he remembered something else she had said; about Timmy giving her cookies. If he wanted to offer snacks to the woman, Timmy would have asked his mother's permission first. And Nikisha would have probably accompanied him to the lift for this charitable mission. So if this had really happened on Sunday, why hadn't Nikisha mentioned it?

It was a bit late for a visit but he was already in Northolt and he hadn't checked on Timmy's mother in a while. Maybe this was the time. At the very least he could clarify this small detail before attempting any raids at the hostel.

He took the lift up to the fifth floor.

His first two knocks on her door were gentle taps, mindful of the sleeping neighbours. He waited a few seconds then knocked again three times, this turn loud enough to maybe bother mister Hog next door but no one else. Another minute went by with no sign of activity before he tried the door and found it locked as expected. Then as he was about to start walking back to the lift, he heard something from within. He pressed his ears against the door and listened.

The sound was low but unmistakable; a soft mourn, the quiet sobs of a person in distress.

Forgetting the time and the sleeping neighbours, he turned the handle and rattled the door violently against the frame. With his heart thumping wildly, he called out her name and only heard the painful mourn intensify. He backed up three steps, aimed his right boot towards the hinge side of the door and put all his momentum on it, again and again.

It took him three attempts to break in and not one neighbour stepped out of their door to inquire.

*

He found her lying prostrate on the old couch in the living room. Her left hand was hanging limply close to the ground with droplets of blood falling off her wrist to form a small puddle on the laminate floor. Orelius knew then that he should have seen this coming. He had, perhaps impertinently, accused her of harming her own son then forgot about her in the subsequent consuming efforts to find Timmy.

He could have blamed the authorities for not looking after her considering the trauma she was experiencing. Downing had advised that their work be kept apart from the official investigation, but did that mean staying away from Nikisha or had he just subconsciously decided that this was the right thing to do? He knew detective Garret and his team had kept in close contact with a couple of visits a day but that was not enough. As far as he knew no one had taken her in for counselling or even spotted that this woman had no friends to support her through this ordeal. But looking at it now, Orelius realised that this should have in fact been his own responsibility. He, of all people, knew that before Timmy, Nikisha Lewis used to be a weak near-suicidal manic-depressive. Timmy had given her strength and happiness and now someone had suddenly yanked it all away. He should have seen this coming.

Her moans were soft and muffled as if from a pain deeper that the cut across her left wrist. Her eyes were wide open staring into space, seemingly at peace with dying. Orelius figured her relative calmness was a good thing. Had she been scared of dying she would have panicked thus increased her heart rate and with it the speed of the bleeding.

‘Oh my God...’ he muttered, instinctively reaching for her loose lifeless hand and gently lifting it up to the couch’s armrest, above her head.

With his left hand still wrapped around her wound, he had a quick look through the room for something to contain the bleeding. Then he let go of her hand and almost tore off his own black jumper and tied it tightly around the wound. As he continued searching the house for better First Aid equipment, he dialled 999.

CHAPTER 14

'Sorry to hear about what happened with Nikisha last night,' Downing said sombrely as he got out of his Corsa. 'How is she?'

'She had regained consciousness by the time I left this morning,' Orelius answered. 'The doctors are confident of a full recovery, but she's still very weak. She lost a lot of blood.'

The detective nodded but said nothing. He was leaning against the driver's door with his arms folded across his chest. The collars of his blue shirt hung lopsided across his chest, with the top button undone. Beneath was the pair of jeans that the detective seemed to have decided was most appropriate for The Farm.

It was a few minutes after ten a.m. on Wednesday, the morning after Nikisha's attempted suicide. The sun was up, which seemed cruel for the young woman facing the prospect of eternal darkness unless someone could bring her baby back to her. Orelius had called Downing in the early hours as he drove back from Middlesex County Hospital, adamant their search had to continue as planned. If anything, he argued, the incident only highlighted the need for more urgency. The doctors could pump blood back into Nikisha and cover her wounds, but they couldn't really save her; only Timmy could do that.

'A family liaison officer spoke to her, and she gave me the impression she was fine. There was a woman there with her at the time, and we all assumed she was family, someone to support her through this. We didn't know she was alone,' Downing said almost apologetically.

Orelius simply shrugged.

'You think she'll be alright?'

'For now, yes,' Orelius said evenly. 'They are keeping a close eye on her at the hospital. They will be putting her on suicide watch and will offer some counselling when she leaves the ICU. After that...' he shrugged again, '...well, who knows?'

They were silent, watching patches of spring sunlight in the cracks between decaying tower blocks.

'Shall we start making a move?' Orelius finally said, tilting his head left to indicate the direction of Markus Isaacs's house. Downing had insisted that they continue to work the two suspects simultaneously.

Orelius himself was not so sure so about Isaacs now, not after the significant chats last night with Sofia the Turkish witness and then Kelly-Jo Pretty. The old man had made the suspect list because he was an odd character. It would be great to talk to him and find out who he really was, what made him tick, whether he was capable of chopping off his enemies' ears and collecting them as a trophies. But the twins had gone through his house and found no sign of Timmy. The man Sofia had seen had reduced Markus Isaacs to a *maybe*. The Bogeyman's status as a suspect was dwindling even before they'd had a chance to talk to him.

Kelly-Jo on the other hand had reacted in the most curious manner when questioned. Orelius had replayed the scene with her at The Jolly several times and tried to read between the lines, but there were no answers, only further questions. Maybe Isaacs had something to do with the ears, and Kelly-Jo knew something about Timmy, but the two seemed unrelated.

Downing checked that his doors were locked before stepping away from the vehicle. They started walking down Gloucester Road.

'What is happening with Kelly-Jo?' Orelius asked. He was striding briskly, one step quicker than the detective. 'Have they taken her in yet?'

'I issued the instructions. They should be on their way there now.'

'Are they also coming to check that lift?'

'She will be questioned first. If we feel there is probable cause, she will be placed under arrest and the crime scene techs will be down here to take that whole area apart.'

'How long is that going to take?'

'Well, a bit longer than usual. She is a special needs case, so we have to bring in a specialist to talk to her. A forensic interrogator,' he said. 'Listen, let's not put all our bets on this woman. Whatever she told you last night, you have to keep in mind that she is a mentally impaired person. Let's go try this elusive Mr Isaacs one more time; Kelly-Jo is being taken care of.'

They turned left and hit Willan Road but Orelius was not as enthusiastic as yesterday. Before dozing off on a hospital bench last night, he had added the name Kelly-Jo Pretty to his suspects, and spent most of the night evaluating the list. Sometime in the middle of the night, in some kind of delirium, he had started discussing the list with the unconscious Nikisha Lewis who lay on the other side of the wall. He had mumbled some of his thoughts loudly enough for a passing nurse to be alarmed, before eventually coming to the conclusion that Kelly-Jo was now his first suspect. Markus Isaacs still looked good for the Ear-Slasher, but any connection with Timmy now seemed tenuous. Other than these two, the other names on his list now seemed a waste of time.

Kelly-Jo Pretty had been up to something when he saw her in the elevator on Sunday. Of that he was sure. He had spent the night turning the fuzzy glimpse he had caught of her over and over in his head, and still couldn't work it out. But she was without doubt his number one suspect now.

*

Kelly-Jo's mental impediments became apparent at an early age, during the first efforts to foster her. Her speech and cognitive senses had taken way too long to develop. When she first began to utter semi-coherent sentences at the age of four, they seemed to come through a heavy tongue, with a thick lisp. Her first foster parents started her in a normal school but she remained a loner incapable of interacting socially, and liked to drift to unusual places for a child. She was particularly drawn to lifts. The psychiatric problems of this unusual child soon overwhelmed the first family and they decided to give her back to social care. Everyone who tried to foster her after that reported the same abnormalities. And they always included instances of Kelly-Jo disappearing, only to be found in a lift somewhere.

Psychiatrists and other specialists failed to pinpoint her condition, but they all agreed that she had one.

At the age of eleven she was sent to a mental asylum in Tottenham where, after a few years of attempting treatment, it was decided that she would never be cured. Kelly-Jo had an extremely low IQ. She also had an abnormally slow nerve synapse response system, which seriously impeded her cognitive abilities. But to the common untrained eye, her only insanity was her addiction to lifts. She was not a paranoid schizophrenic. There were no voices in her head telling her to cause harm, and thus she was never considered a danger. So her stay in the asylum was not a lockdown. Unlike other residents of the facility, she was allowed some freedom. She signed for her welfare benefit cheques herself. They also allowed her to wander around the city as she pleased, adventures which hardly ever went beyond a couple of miles and invariably ended at the Northolt block. And she always got back to her room before her curfew.

Kelly-Jo was in the asylum because she didn't fit in anywhere else.

*

They got to Isaacs's within five minutes and were met with the same locked green door.

'I think we need to concentrate on Kelly-Jo,' Orelius said as they descended the Stapleford stairs. 'At the very least she knows something.'

In reply Downing got on his mobile and called for an update on Kelly-Jo.

'They have her,' he reported back once the phone was back in his pocket. 'The specialist interrogator hasn't arrived yet, but he's on his way.' Then he saw Orelius's dejected expression, and added, 'This is for the best, Orelius. We want to get the correct information from her and we have to do it in the right way, or we are going to end up with nothing but figments of her imagination.'

'Sorry, I just don't feel like we are making progress.'

'Well, we've got a list of suspects. Which is more than we had before. I've also arranged to meet Isaacs's former parole officer to see if there is anything he can tell us about him that would give us probable cause to search his flat. I'm seeing him on his lunch break today. He now works for the National Offender Management Service, and he invited me to their Clive House HQ in Westminster. You are welcome to come along if you want.'

'That reminds me: shouldn't Isaacs have been on a tag or something? I mean... the man was a butcher, surely there must have been some strict conditions on his release.'

'They did have him on a tag for the prescribed period, and they kept regular checks afterwards to see how he was rehabilitating back into society. But you can't monitor them forever, he served his time. Let's see if the parole guys can give us something. This man has no other friends or relatives we can talk to. In the mean time, do you want us to check on those other names you've got?'

'We could, but I've got a feeling we'll be wasting our time.'

Despite his doubts, Orelius removed the list from his back pocket and scanned it, tracing down the rows with his index finger. He stopped at a point midway, then moved back up to the first name and stepped closer to the detective, tapping at the word. 'We could give her a visit. She's on the Northolt block and I'm sure she'll be in.'

'Anita Ahmed,' Downing read the name out loud.

'Yes. Let's walk this way. I'll tell you about her.'

CHAPTER 15

Anita Ahmed answered the door herself. She was wearing a red dupatta hijab with golden-yellow patterns. The headscarf fell to her shoulders but left her face clear.

'Hi, Orelius, come in.' Her voice was low, with a calmness that indicated little surprise at their turning up unannounced. Under the hijab was a pleasant oval face with full red lips complimented nicely by the red dupatta. She was a beautiful Asian woman in her late thirties or early forties.

'Sorry to bother you, Anita.' They had decided that Orelius would do most of the talking. Downing would look for an opportunity to inspect the house for anything unusual. 'I believe you've heard about Timmy.'

'Yeah, it's a big shock for everyone. I'm sorry.'

Orelius's eyes were already wandering. It was a relatively bare living room with an old wall-unit holding framed photos, and various Muslim artefacts against the wall opposite them. There was a television stand at the corner next to the window but the area in between was bare, without a table of any kind. Instead, a white rug, about three foot by three, occupied the space in the middle. A prayer mat, Orelius figured.

'That's OK,' he said, turning to face her. 'We are just going around the estate trying to figure some things out, and we thought we should come and have a word with you.'

She wrapped her hijab tighter around her shoulders and waited for him to proceed.

'Do you know Gutierrez, the kid who sells stuff door-to-door?'

'Yes, I do. Good kid. Shame he got involved with the bad boys and got himself in trouble. They must have put a lot of pressure on him, because he really is a good kid.'

'And do you make it a habit of sleeping with all good kids, Anita, or was Gutierrez an exception?'

She opened her mouth to answer, then stopped.

'Are you going to answer me, Anita?'

'Huh?'

'You heard me.' He started pacing round the room, inspecting the framed family portraits on the wall-unit. 'Do you know how old Gutierrez is?'

She shook her head but her mouth opened and she mumbled a yes. She was now leaning over, facing the floor with her head in her hands.

'He is fifteen years old. And he was a year younger when you started sleeping with him. What I want to know, Anita, is just how young can you go? Twelve, eleven... ten maybe? Do you know what you are doing?'

opportunities I never had: to be young and to be modern and to be a woman.

'I was seventeen when I got married, and I had all my three children before I was twenty. Then my husband stopped having sex with me. He brought in another woman from Pakistan, and then another. This was normal to me. I did not question anything. I simply carried on raising my children like I was supposed to.' She drew a deep breath, and what came out was the cry of an oppressed child. 'I was not aware that I was anything other than a carer for my children and a servant to my husband... but Gutierrez came here and... he made me feel like a woman, Orelius...' She broke into shoulder-shaking sobs. He stayed silent and let her cry. When she was finished, she wiped her face again and looked up at him. 'I'm a lonely woman, Orelius. I'm lonely and broken in many ways. But I would never harm a little boy.'

Gregg Downing was back in the living room. Orelius looked at him questioningly and he shook his head.

'Let's get out of here,' Orelius said as he got to his feet and started heading for the door.

Downing hesitated, trying to say something, but he stopped and followed him outside.

'What was that... did this Gutierrez boy tell you all that?' he asked, once he had shut Anita'a door behind him.

Orelius nodded.

'When?'

'Yesterday. I had a long chat with him and he was very helpful with our suspect list.'

'And did it occur to you to do something about the sexual abuse he was suffering?' the policeman asked. 'That woman was raping an underage boy.'

'What do you want to do, Gregg, Arrest her? If that's what we are going to do then maybe we should also arrest the drug dealer there,' he said, pointing at another door next to the stairwell. 'And the sixteen-year-old prostitute at the far end. If you've still got time, there is also a woman on the fourth floor who hires her twin babies out for anyone wishing to con the welfare system. Maybe we could pick them all up while we are here.' He stopped and looked at the detective apologetically. 'This place is full of criminals, Gregg. When this is all over, feel free to come back. And bring your colleagues. You'll have plenty of fun. But for now, please just help me find Timmy.'

'You know what, I might just do that,' the detective snapped. 'Arrest everyone, including you, Simm. And shut this whole goddamned place down if we have to.' He started towards the stairs, then stopped and turned, pointing a finger. 'I am sick and tired of you preaching all this spiel about Dudlham Farm. I'm not from another planet. Right now I need your help with this case and I don't know how long we'll be working together. We might be around each other long enough for you to think of me as a friend. But I'm a law-enforcement officer, Simm, don't forget that.'

*

Orelius caught up with him at the bottom of the stairs, next to Kelly-Jo's lift. The detective was leaning against the wall, with his hands folded across his chest, staring intently at the old, rusting vehicles on the ground floor car park, as if searching for any new signs of crime in this godforsaken estate. Orelius tucked his hands in his pockets and stood next to him, saying nothing.

Orelius was first to find his voice. 'Why did you pick me, Gregg?'

'What?'

'If all you wanted was a local connection to help you find your way around Dudlham, you must have considered others.'

'You wanted to find Timmy, I wanted to find the person responsible.'

'And that was good enough for you? You just assumed I could be trusted?'

'Well, I dug around a bit...' He appeared to be considering his next words carefully, and then decided not to say them at all.

'Dug around how?'

'I'm Scotland Yard, Orelius. I can find out pretty much anything I want about anyone.' He gave him a quick glance, then turned his eyes back to some mysterious point in space. 'Yes, I did consider a few others from around here, read a few files. All very interesting individuals, but if I had to pick something else that drew me to you, other that your relationship with Timmy, I'd say it was Gandhi.'

'Huh?'

'Mahatma Gandhi,' Downing said, and smiled at Orelius's incredulous stare. 'I looked at the transcripts from your interrogation last year during the London riots. And I was impressed, especially with the Mahatma Gandhi bit.'

*

The London Riots

The now infamous 2011 London Riots started with a small peaceful demonstration outside Tottenham Police Station after the cops shot dead Mark Duggan, a twenty-nine year old Tottenham resident, during a routine raid. The demonstration was supposed to involve nothing more than an honourable all-night vigil. But then someone threw a bottle (or a stone, or a coin, or nothing at all depending on who was reporting) through one of the Police Station windows and the demonstration quickly turned violent. The cops took the battle to the streets without considering that it was the summer of 2011 when schools were out, the economic recession had hit and jobs were scarce. Meaning the streets was overrun by hordes of idle, anxious and irritable youths. Before the end of the following day all units of the Met Police had been deployed to Tottenham to deal with the riots.

As they do with all disasters, the real savvy underground businessmen of Dudlham quickly saw an opportunity in the riots. Safe in the knowledge that this urgent call of duty had transferred London's entire law enforcement team to Tottenham, the businessmen packed vans and mini-busses with their men and headed the opposite way. Their first stop was at industrial area of Enfield where they knocked down CCTV cameras, disabled alarms and went about their business without interference. When they were done they used their mobile messenger technologies and social networking websites, where they commanded a great following, to alert yet more idle anxious and irritable youths of a fresh demonstration happening at the industrial estate in Enfield. The kids would arrive in Enfield to wide open gates, smashed-up windows and empty shop floors. But under the absolute influence of rampant teenage hormones enhanced by a cocktail of narcotics, the kids would nevertheless try to loot or destroy whatever dregs had been left behind by their masters. More police would be deployed to Enfield. And while the cops were busy grappling with children hardly strong enough to lift half the items they had supposedly looted, the businessmen would have moved to a different location to repeat the cycle; now operating with near impunity.

Other idle anxious and irritable youths from different areas, unable to afford the conventional night out, sat in front of TVs and watched their Tottenham counterparts doing the street dance with the cops. They were awed and envious, wishing this carnival would come to their town. The mood was set, the atmosphere charged and tense. All required was a spark, just one well placed message to drop within their social network and they too would be stepping out to the streets to start their own dance. Within days the pattern was being mimicked in other major cities and Great Britain was on the brink of anarchy.

The police would later suspect underground crime involvement. But without any breaks from within the gangs to help them figure out the finer details of the system, the cops resorted to their tried and tested routine; they simply rounded up the usual suspects, including Orelius, and took them down to the station for questioning.

They knocked on his door on the third evening of rioting and hauled him to a windowless room at the station where a pair of police interrogators, male and female, tried to put on a decent good-cop bad-cop routine for him. They asked Orelius if he'd been involved in the riots and he answered no. They wanted to know what he'd been up to in the last couple of days and he said he'd been at home, where they had found him, watching TV. Then the female one asked if he knew Mark Duggan and Orelius answered yes.

'Were you friends?'

Orelius shrugged. 'I'm friends with anyone who hasn't yet given me the reason to be their enemy.'

The male one smiled but he didn't look impressed. 'How exactly did you know Mark Duggan?'

'We were in the same year in school.'

'And you sat at home watching TV while all your people were out there expressing their feelings?'

'My people?'

'Don't try that with me, Orelius. You know exactly what I mean.' He cracked a dry laugh. 'Most of those rioters burning buildings out there have got no idea who Mark Duggan is. Yet you, a former classmate, are trying to tell me you didn't even throw a stone? Come on...'

'No, I did not throw a stone. And I'm not planning to either.'

'Noble, Mr Simm, that's very noble of you. So do you want to tell us what you've really been up to since the riots began?'

'Like I said, I have been mostly indoors, out of respect.'

Another dry laugh. 'Respect for whom, Orelius, the police or your friend?'

'Gandhi.'

'What?'

‘Gandhi. Mahatma Gandhi. You know, Asian dude... round glasses...?’

‘Does all this sound like a joke to you, Orelius? You think we brought you in here to entertain us with your wit?’ The male officer’s voice was rising. ‘Let me tell you something, mate, innocent people being burned alive in their shops on the high street is no–’

‘Mahatma Gandhi liberated an entire race without using a single weapon, not even a stone.’ Orelius had raised his voice just enough to be heard above the male cop’s. He watched the policeman’s eyebrows furrow as his lower lip dropped open slightly in bemusement. Realising he now had their attention, he evened out his tone accordingly. ‘I did not throw a stone, out of respect for Mahatma Gandhi.’

‘Ha,’ was all the man could manage.

*

Ten minutes passed while the pair just stood there at the foot of Northolt House, watching heaps of twenty-year-old vehicles nestled between the disintegrating struts of the ground floor car park. It was still early spring but the last couple of days had delivered midsummer weather. Stray leaves had swept through the car park on a swirl of loose brown dust stirred up in fluky gusts of wind. On one of the dust-covered windows of an abandoned wreck that had once been a Ford Focus, someone had scribbled in fancy graffiti-style letters the words:

She snorted something, then her shoulders started shaking as she sobbed quietly.

'You are committing rape, Anita. I wonder what your husband would think about that.' Orelius walked back to his chair and sat down. 'My little boy is missing. And I'm here because you happen to be especially fond of little boys. So I need you to stop crying and help me out here OK?'

She nodded and wiped her face with her hijab, but she was still crying.

'Where were you on Sunday?'

She took her time to bring her breathing back under control before opening her mouth again.

'Sunday was Shamim's birthday, my eldest daughter. I was here all day doing the party. My whole family was here, including Shamim's boyfriend and many of their friends, you can ask them. They didn't leave till after eight.' She snivelled, wiped her face and looked up at him.

Downing had moved from the kitchen to the bathroom and was now in the larger of the two bedrooms; they could hear the sound of drawers being pulled.

'My daughter is twenty-one,' the woman started again calmly, hugging the hijab close to her face. 'And do you know what? Sometimes I'm jealous of her. She's got a boyfriend now, she's had boyfriends before. They break up and get back together, or they move on... the usual. Shamim has

The lift screeched and clanked to a noisy stop a few inches behind the detective but he did not so much as flinch. Orelius automatically stepped to his left to peer inside even though he knew Kelly-Jo could not possibly be at her usual daytime dwelling today because they had dragged her to the station for questioning. Sure enough the car was empty, and for some reason this felt odd and disturbing, like Kelly-Jo's ghost was still in there asking them why they couldn't simply leave her alone. The doors slowly creaked shut again and the empty lift reluctantly croaked its way back up the Northolt Tower, leaving haunting echoes from the pit down below, where the elevator's power source was located.

Farm legend had it that a long time ago there had been worse technical problems with this lift, which somehow mysteriously self-remedied over time. Apparently, there had been a serious misalignment between the elevator car and the doors, which meant that sometimes the doors opened before the car was all the way down to floor level. This had allowed residents quick glimpses of the dark pit that housed the elevator's base station. They could smell the raw swamp that had once been Dudlham Farm Estate from down there. Naughty children used to be threatened with a trip down the stinking pit if they didn't behave. All residents, past and present, deny ever seeing anyone come to Northolt to fix the problem with their lift, but it went away anyhow. For years there would be heated debates about this mystery, but the one that ultimately gained universal acknowledgement was that it was a miracle.

As Orelius and Downing were about to find out from their next visit, miracles did in fact happen in Dudlham Farm.

CHAPTER 16

'Welcome, gentlemen, in the name of the Lord,' Pastor Sara Doyo said as she let them through her door. The first thing that struck them as they stepped in was the gulf in class between her and Anita Ahmed's living rooms. This remarkably magnificent lounge did not belong in Dudlham Farm. She had a massive L-shaped leather sofa complete with a footstool, and a frosted glass coffee table in the middle. There was a giant wall-mounted plasma screen with fitted glass shelves either side. The adjacent walls held a set of vibrant fabric decors, with a great canvas impression of Leonardo da Vinci's *The Last Supper* occupying the side opposite the TV. A big shiny black bible lay in the middle of the coffee table.

'Hi, Sara, I'm detective Gregg Downing,' Downing started, holding out his right hand, which Sarah took and shook vigorously, mumbling '*Praise the Lord*' repeatedly. 'And I presume you know Orelius.' He pointed towards Orelius with his free hand and Sara acknowledged with a nod, sparing him the mighty handshake. She directed them to the sofa with a swift spread of the arms as she herself took the leather tub chair opposite. 'I take it you've heard about the missing boy from Northolt,' the detective continued once their bottoms were comfortably planted on the leather sofa.

'I have, and we are all praying for him. The Lord will take care of him.'

After the detective's rant outside Anita's house, Orelius had tried to offer a half-hearted apology while they were still standing next to the Northolt lift. Downing had dismissed his efforts with a wave and suggested they go and try Markus Isaacs once more before they head for the appointment with his parole officer. Maybe the detective had been serious about coming back to close down this haven of crime, but Orelius did not fancy his chances. The trip to Isaacs's had once again proved fruitless but that didn't come as a big surprise because it had hardly been half-hour since their previous attempt. They had then decided that since they still had one hour before the meeting with the former parole officer, and the car was at Kenley, they could check on another of the listed names, Sara Doyo, at 83 Kenley House.

'Well... Sara,' Downing continued. 'Timmy's disappearance is the reason we are here. We need to ask you a few questions.' They had swapped roles now, with Downing carrying out the interrogation while Orelius looked around.

'Praise the Lord.' Sara seemed to be on autopilot praising the Lord, not showing any signs of being offended by the implication of their presence here. 'Ask me anything, I'd be glad to help.'

'We both know the reason we've chosen to come to you, so I won't waste time trying to make this sound nice.' The detective was looking her straight in the eye. 'Your husband is in prison because he ran a child abduction ring, right?'

Sara's reply was immediate. 'No one can be imprisoned if he has accepted the Lord Jesus Christ.' She clasped both palms together and drew them to her chest in a gesture of humility to the Lord. 'My husband might be behind bars and in chains, but he is free with the Lord.'

The UK courts had convicted her husband, George Doyo, for conspiracy to defraud, and only sentenced him to two years behind bars. But that was mainly because they were keen to get rid of him. After his sentence, they were handing pastor Doyo over to the Kenyan government to face more serious charges, including those for child abduction and racketeering. Pastor Doyo made babies happen for women who couldn't get pregnant biologically; the media had dubbed it the *miracle babies* scandal.

'We'll have to have a quick look around your house, Sara,' Orelius shouted from the bedroom, already pulling closets and drawers apart. 'I hope you understand. We are looking for a missing child...'

'My husband was convicted by people who are afraid to believe and have faith. He has never abducted a child.'

'But he somehow gave barren women babies,' Downing interjected.

'We help people accept that God's power is almighty. And with belief, miracles happen.'

'So how come you don't have children of your own, if your belief is that strong? Or could you be possibly selling your congregation ideas you don't believe in yourself?'

She kept her hands clasped tightly together and said nothing.

'How exactly do miracle babies happen, Sara?' Downing asked. 'Explain this to me, make me a believer.'

Sara closed her eyes and lowered her voice to almost a whisper, 'My thoughts are not your thoughts, and my ways are not your ways. Isaiah, fifty-five, verse eight.' Then she opened her eyes and assumed her normal voice. 'The Lord works in mysterious ways, sir. It is not for us to question.'

'Isn't it convenient when we can accept that some things are so great that we are unworthy to question them?'

'That would be wisdom, detective: when we simply shut up because we have no idea. Intellect is when you know, foolishness is when you don't know, and wisdom is when you know that you don't know.'

This brought a sheepish smile to the detective's face.

'Where were you on Sunday, Sara?' he asked.

They already knew where she was on Sunday. They had checked with two members of her congregation at Dudlham Farm Community Centre, the headquarters of Victory Gospel Church, an organisation registered as a charity to her husband's name. One of her alibis was in fact Timmy's mother: Nikisha and Timmy had attended the first service. The other was the cameraman who had filmed the two Sunday services in their entirety. Sara, now working alone with her husband behind bars, had conducted both services and not left the centre till after six p.m.

Her alibi for Sunday was as solid as a wall of lead, but their 'miracle-babies' scandal was a racket that did not require their direct involvement. It had been said to include an organised network of women who stole newborn babies from hospitals in Kenya and brought them into the United Kingdom. A desperate woman unable to get pregnant who donated enough to the church would be invited to a dark room at the Community Centre for a specially intensive session of prayers that included singing, humming, swaying and speaking in tongues. In the midst of this delirium a baby would fall from the sky. The mother would gracefully accept her blessing with more prayers and maybe another reading of Isaiah fifty-five, to reaffirm her faith in the Lord's mysterious ways. But deep down, they all knew the truth.

In answer to Downing's question, she said: 'I fellowship with the Lord on Sundays. That is where I was, with my Lord Jesus Christ.'

Orelius came out of the bedroom after fifteen minutes.

'Let's go,' he said to Downing, then turned to Sara, pointing a finger. 'This is not the end, Sara. So if there is anything you think I should know, you better find me with it before I find it myself.'

*

Anita Ahmed, along with her polygamist husband, belonged in prison. But she was nothing more than a lonely woman who had succumbed to temptation. The Doyos and the childless benefactors from their congregation were blasphemous frauds who all knew what they were doing and were heading straight to hell. But their scheme had only involved newborn babies. Those two had been very long shots, but the visits had nevertheless served a purpose. The list now felt slightly lighter Orelius's his pocket, with two fewer names to worry about. He drew two lines through them as soon as they got into Downing's Corsa.

Between their two unsuccessful visits to Isaacs today, he had received a phone call from Megaman which had swung the focus slightly back towards Isaacs. Two or three other people from Northolt had sworn to Mega that they saw The Bogeyman going up and down the stairs late in the night, not long before

Timmy disappeared. Sure, this sounded no different from the earlier Bogeyman myths, but combined with the fact that this man seemed to have taken flight, these myths were beginning to seriously haunt Orelius.

As a result, his first suspect had now changed back from Kelly-Jo to the missing old man. Maybe what he glimpsed inside the lift on Sunday and Kelly-Jo's subsequent mutterings at TJ was just the poor woman being herself. Isaacs's case was appearing more ominous with their increasing failure to find him. The twins' rushed scan of his house suddenly didn't seem so comforting anymore; he needed to conduct a proper search himself, and he couldn't do that while hanging around with a policeman who was still concerned about doing things legally. Sure, he knew he wouldn't find Timmy in there, but maybe there was a clue about Timmy, or the ears, or just an insight into the old man's thoughts. Who *was* Markus Isaacs? *What* was he? *Where* was he? There is never a clearer way of admitting guilt than by running. This was a man who apparently never left his house; it was very suspicious that as soon as Isaacs is told they are looking for him, he suddenly finds other pressing business to keep him away from home.

After a brief pause staring at the list, Orelius got the pen out of his pocket again and drew two big Xs across all the names above and below Markus Isaacs's. Kelly-Jo Pretty was not affected: her name had been scribbled almost illegibly at the footnote further down from the pack. The list felt a whole lot lighter, and the effect was almost exhilarating. It was now down to just two: Kelly-Jo Pretty and the elusive old man.

They had exactly thirty-five minutes to get to their meeting with his former parole officer.

*

Markus Isaacs:

My mother did everything to make my life bearable. She took some of the blows for me at home, and then, the following day, with her bruises still fresh, she would brave the curious stares and whispers and walk with me to school to discuss the bullying with the head teacher. The man she married turned out to be a monster. Had my mother known the real price she was going to pay for a British passport, I'm sure she would have found another way to give me a better life without leaving the land of our birth. He isolated us first, so he could be free to do as he wished. This was a man who enjoyed nothing more than the sight of my mother's battered face. But he soon learned that a disfigured face meant nothing to her; the only way one could ever really hurt my mother was by hurting me.

Everyone wants to know how I survived forty years in prison. Nobody asks about my mother: how she survived Dudlham; how she endured her days fighting my battles and taking my bullets; how she sacrificed her life and allowed herself to merely exist as an extension of her son. Sometimes I wonder if I should have reminded my mother that she had already given me the ultimate gift. She smiled at me through swollen lips and stayed up at night to watch me sleep. She gave me the most beautiful gift, just by being my mother.

Somebody spoke those words on that bright afternoon in the summer of '65. That person was not my mother:

'Today, son, you are going to fight back.'

CHAPTER 17

'We have to find him,' Orelius said as they cruised up Lordship lane. 'Get some help if we have to, but we have to find this man real quick.'

'You think it's him? A few hours ago you sounded pretty convinced it was Kelly-Jo. What's changed your mind so fast?'

'Innocent people don't run. It should be in his interest to find us and clear his name. Come to think of it, there isn't another human being in Dudlham Farm who could possibly possess five severed human ears. I was hard on Kelly-Jo; this is our man.'

They went past Bounds Green and turned into the North Circular Road.

'I did some checking on Isaacs after I left you yesterday,' the detective said after a long silence.

Orelius stared at the road ahead and waited for him to continue.

'I think once upon a time the system leant a bit too hard on this man. It could explain why he is running.'

Orelius turned to look at him. 'What's that supposed to mean?'

'I won't go into the details now, but from what I gathered the case against Markus Isaacs forty years ago could be the biggest miscarriage of justice I have ever heard of in the United Kingdom.'

Orelius arched his eyebrows. 'Well, that's new. I thought he was found sticking a knife into his mother's chest with the butchered bodies of his classmates next to him. And he confessed.'

'Which is exactly my point: he made a full confession. And did it buy him any sympathy? No, they still sent him down for forty years. I mean, look at the Bulger killers... they were about the same age. They tortured and killed a two-year-old boy who had done nothing to offend them. Heck, they didn't even know the child. And what did they get... six years? They were out in time to finish their A-levels. Markus Isaacs, on the other hand, snapped after years of abuse and killed his tormentors. The only mystery is why he killed his mother too, but that only justifies further the argument for insanity. Any half-decent defence lawyer would have exploited that. But from what I know it was never raised. No one cared about his side of the story, two white kids were dead and somebody had to pay. It was quite literally a thirteen year-old-boy against the world.' He emphasised the last sentence with well-placed dramatic pauses, then stopped to let him think about it. When Orelius didn't offer any input, he picked up once again with passion. 'And then to go on and lock him up with a bunch of violent criminals for forty-years... why didn't they just kill him? Oh no, they didn't kill him because that would have been merciful. They wanted him to suffer. Do you know what happens to people like Isaacs in prison?'

Orelius looked at him in dismay, shaking his head. 'I cannot believe you are sitting there trying to defend the actions of a man who is going around collecting people's ears.'

'I'm not defending anyone, but I'm not exactly proud to be part of the system that turned this man into what he is. I'm trying to prepare you for what we might be dealing with here. You don't release a man after subjecting them to forty years of torture and expect them to shake hands and gladly rejoin this big happy family we call society.' He paused and, perhaps realising his little devil's advocate act was going too far, evened out his voice. 'We have a subject harbouring an incomprehensible amount of rage for the system, and I've got a feeling we haven't suffered the worst of his wrath yet.'

Orelius thought about this for a few seconds as they waited for the lights at Henly's Corner junction.

'Maybe his victims forty years ago were abusive scum-bugs who deserved what they got,' he said quietly, not looking at the detective. 'Maybe it's someone else's fault that life dealt him such a terrible turn and made him the monster he has become. But it wasn't Timmy's fault. Tell me this story when we've found Timmy and this man is back behind bars where he belongs.

Then, I might be able to spare a thought for the reason this man became what he is. But right now is not the time, Gregg.'

*

Markus Isaacs:

We were in a foreign land and things were always going to start off tough. But they would soon get better, my mother always assured me. Things would get better and happiness would find us.

I remember the day my mother spoke to me about happiness.

'Education is key, Markus,' she said. 'Work hard in school and bring us success and happiness.'

Then she bent down and placed both hands over my shoulders, looked straight into my eyes and smiled at me through her swollen lips. I smiled back. I always smiled back.

And I asked: 'What about you, Mum? Why can't we run away, just you and me? We can go somewhere he can't find us. And I will still go to school because I'm not scared. But I don't like seeing you cry.'

She continued to look at me but her sweet smile slowly faded into the darkness. Her whole body stiffened and froze before my eyes. A network of old wrinkles invaded my mother's young beautiful face as her eyes welled up, and once again the tears began rolling down her cheeks towards the swollen lip.

One week later when I arrived home, my school shirt was ripped all the way across the back. There was blood coming from a cut on top of my left eye, which still had the nasty bump from the previous week's attack. I had bruises on my arms and knees, but not a single tear in my eyes. I never shed any tears. Before I entered the front door, I heard the familiar scornful howls from the bedroom. They were coming from the man my mother had married. So I waited outside till he stormed through the door, banged it shut and brushed past without him as much as noticing me. I could hear my mother's sobs from the bedroom. I stayed in the living room unable to face the damage caused by the man my mother had married. When she came out, she wiped her tears before hugging me tight, close to her heart. Then she washed me and nursed my wounds with a warm salty solution. She asked me the same three questions: 'Did you start it? Did you fight back? Did you cry?' I answered no, and she told me I did good; very good.

Even then, I should have known that grace is the cold water that quenches your inner fire; it's cheap, it's easy and it lasts. But someday you are going to need wine.

My mother's grace was never going to last forever:

'Today, son, you are going to fight back.'

CHAPTER 18

It took them forty minutes to get to Westminster. Clive House, the headquarters of the National Offender Management Service, was a nine-story granite skyscraper on Petty France, a five-minute walk from Buckingham Palace, about half a mile west of the Big Ben. There was a large, uniformed security guard in the lobby, who had been expecting Downing. He offered to walk them to their meeting venue, which turned out to be inside a deserted cafeteria on the first floor. It would be a working-lunch conference; this was a busy civil servant doing his best to squeeze them into his tight schedule at short notice. His name was Robbie Sergeant but according to Downing everyone called him Sarge. They found him sitting alone along the wall left of the door, at one of the Formica tables that lined the small restaurant. He was a lanky man with a few streaks of grey in his brown hair.

'Good to see you again, Inspector,' he said, pushing his chair back and getting up to shake their hands. 'And you must be the missing boy's father.'

He looked at Downing, and the detective gave Orelius a knowing nod. He had introduced him as Timmy's father.

'Yes, I am,' he said.

'I'm terribly sorry to hear about your situation,' he said. 'We are going to have to talk here, I hope you don't mind.'

Downing dismissed the apology with a quick flap of his right hand as he took one of the chairs opposite the parole officer. Orelius took the other one.

'Thanks for seeing us at such short notice, Sarge,' the detective started.

He nodded and gulped the remaining contents of the glass of dark red liquid in front of him. Then he wiped his mouth with a tissue before speaking again.

'So, how can I help you, gentlemen?'

Downing leaned forward and cleared his throat behind the clenched fists of his right hand.

'Like I said on the phone, Isaacs has emerged as a person of interest in Timmy's case. We need to talk to him. Only problem is we can't seem to find him. I assumed he was monitored closely on parole until very recently, and we thought maybe there could be something in his case files...' he shrugged, spreading his hands in front of him, '... about his contacts and behaviour after release that may help us locate him. Or better still, if there is anything in those files that would provided us with reasonable cause to search his house.'

Sarge swung his chair sideways and stared briefly at the table, as if consulting Isaacs's parole files, even though the table contained only empty plates, bottles and used cutlery.

'If you are asking whether he committed any crimes while on parole, then the answer is no, or we would have nicked him and sent him straight back to prison. As I explained, Gregg, I'm not allowed to take any files out. But I was responsible for him, so I'm reasonably conversant with what is in those files. And I can't think of anything off the top of my head that could possibly interest you. He was a pretty unremarkable character, never once came even close to breaching his parole regulations. He has no relatives or friends, lives on state benefits, walks in the mornings, prays a lot, and stays at home pretty much all the time. Made me wonder what the point was of releasing him from prison. All he's done is gone and imprisoned himself again in his house.' He chuckled, sombrely. 'Anyway, what I'm saying is I can't think of anything myself, but if there is something in particular you want to ask, I'd be very glad to help.'

'Was he on a tag for some time?'

'He was tagged for six months, meaning he was basically on house arrest for this period, except in his case we allowed him some restricted movement between the hours of seven a.m. to six p.m. in a three-mile radius of his address. After he was freed from this, we continued regular monthly checks on him for another twelve months by sending one of our officers down. This was basically to asses how he was rehabilitating back into society; to ensure he wasn't getting up to anything untoward. And like I said, nothing came up.'

'In those follow-up checks, did the officers have to visit him in Dudlham?' Orelius asked.

'That's correct, sir.'

'And this continued for year.'

'Twelve months, yes.'

'You sure? Because I come from Dudlham myself, though not close enough to Isaacs's block to know him. But I spoke to some of his neighbours and they have never seen anyone visit Markus Isaacs. Ever.'

'Well, they weren't exactly daily events that you would expect anyone to notice. These were occasional drop-ins. He was not considered a threat to society at that time.'

Orelius leaned slightly further forward over the table, both hands clasped together in front of him. He kept his eyes on the parole officer. 'There were at least ten official complaints from neighbours lodged to the council and the Justice Department when Isaacs moved into Dudlham Farm. They didn't want him there. Did any of these make it into the files?'

'Listen, all I can tell you is that from the documented information, parole follow-ups were conducted as required.'

'By whom? Who conducted the follow-ups?'

'Well... er... it wasn't always done by the same person, but I can assure–'

'Name one of them, off the top of your head. Just one.'

'I don't think it would be appropriate to divulge names.'

'OK, were they black or white?'

'What?'

'Black or white, Sarge?' he repeated slowly, looking straight into Sarge's eyes. 'Of what race were these parole officers that you cannot name?'

'Sir, I'm not sure–'

Downing cleared his throat again loudly. 'OK, people, let's take this easy,' he said, waving Orelius to calm. He turned to Sarge. 'We have a very delicate situation here, a child is missing and I believe you can understand Mr Simm's frustrations. We might need to see those files. How do we do that?'

The parole officer's eyes darted left and right. He had invited them for a quiet, friendly chat over lunch, and had not expected an ambush of this kind.

'Eeerm... I'm not sure–'

'Why aren't you sure?' Orelius banged the table furiously. 'Who were the parole officers? Where are the goddamn files? These are simple questions, Sarge!'

'Right, I think this whole thing is getting outside my territory.' Sarge was breathing uncomfortably. 'I don't believe I'm the right person–'

'Forfucksakes! Who is the right person then?' Orelius roared, waving his arms in frustration. 'You didn't really care once you dumped him in Dudlham Farm, did you? As far as you were concerned you had put him where he belonged, with a bunch of misfits no one would give a toss about if he slaughtered to extinction. I've got news for you, Sarge; Timothy Lewis is not a misfit. He is a ten-year-old boy, a good kid and a great tennis player, who works hard in school, and at home provides his mother's only source of joy. He wants to be the greatest tennis player in the world, but sometimes he also wants to be an astronaut. Dudlham Farm Estate is not entirely a den of outcasts. There are good kids like Timmy too.' His voice was getting throaty from the shouting. 'You failed a little boy.'

'Right, that's enough,' Downing snapped, grabbing Orelius's threatening arm and placing it back on the table. 'Apologies, Sarge. I really do apologise for all this.'

Robbie Sargeant nodded slowly as if to say *I understand*, but he remained silent.

'But I still need to see those files,' Downing said calmly.

*

'It's Wednesday today – about seventy-two hours since Timmy went missing,' Downing said as they walked back to his car. 'Our chances of finding him alive are dwindling, but they are still reasonable. And as long as those chances exist, anyone who agrees to help us should be treated as an ally. If these people made some mistakes that could have contributed to this, they would have to be dealt with in an inquest after we've established that our chances are gone. For now we keep them on our side and encourage them to do whatever they can to right their wrongs. The last thing we need is for the likes of Sarge to assume the damage has been done, because you know what would happen then, Orelius? Everyone is going to start running, taking evasive action, shifting blame, shredding and burying incriminating evidence...'

Orelius gave a few apologetic nods but kept striding briskly. He was keen to get back to The Farm, his territory, the only place he could make things happen.

'What I'm trying to say, Orelius, is that as a parent I understand your outburst back there. But if you can't control your parental instincts then you are of no use to me. You could be doing serious harm to the small chance we still have of finding Timmy alive.'

They got to the car and Orelius let himself into the passenger side without a word. He was not worried: despite the length of his speech the detective had remained very calm and it hadn't sounded like a lecture at all. Besides, he was still calling him Orelius. He had learnt that the time to start getting uncomfortable was when the detective was referring to him as Simm.

'What next, now?' he asked, as they strapped their seatbelts on.

The detective opened his mouth to answer, then stopped and held a finger up as his phone chirped with a piercing tone.

He spoke on it for about two minutes but Orelius didn't get much of the exchange because his mind was elsewhere.

'What's the next move then?' he asked again, once the detective had tucked the phone back in his pocket.

'I will take you back home and come back to sort the issue of the files. One way or another I'm getting a warrant tomorrow morning. The fact that we can't find Markus Isaacs should work in our favour.'

'And Kelly-Jo?'

'The psychiatrist came in very late. They are still talking to her. I'll let you know as soon as I know.'

But Kelly-Jo was very quickly receding into the background as a suspect.

Where on earth was Markus Isaacs?

CHAPTER 19

Orelius was back at Middlesex County Hospital before seven p.m. Nikisha had been transferred to a secure ward across the hall from the ICU and she was awake when he walked in. She lay on her left side, with only her heads and shoulders exposed above the blue hospital sheets that covered the rest of her body. There was an IV drip connected to her left arm near the elbow, with the wrist heavily strapped in a white bandage. Her skin looked dry and colourless.

She saw him, and her unusually white eyes rolled left and right, sizing him up. She shifted slightly on the bed. Her eyes locked onto his and held. But there didn't seem to be a person behind that ghostly stare.

'We haven't found him yet,' he said quietly. 'But I think we are close.'

He thought he saw her head move as if to nod an acknowledgment.

'You will be there for him when he comes home, won't you Nikisha?'

There was no answer, but he saw a lump travel across her throat as she swallowed audibly.

'I love Timmy. But I cannot pretend to understand what you are going through right now, how much you need your son.'

Orelius saw her bite hard on her lower lip. He leaned back against the wooden chair, his arms across his belly. He took in the fresh smell of disinfectant for the first time, and let his eyes wander around the ward.

The silence nearly lulled him to sleep before a squeaking trolley out in the corridor reminded him of where he was. He looked down at the bed. Her eyes were still wide open and empty, staring into space.

'Is it true that Nikisha means beautiful?' he asked her, casually, as though they had been chatting away all evening. She looked at him to acknowledge the question but made no effort to answer. 'Well...' he shrugged, '...I just thought I should ask. Timmy has said it a million times and I've never really thought about it till now.'

Orelius was not expecting a response and he did not get one. She didn't have her glasses on, and he studied her hazel eyes. They matched her chocolate skin nicely and he wondered whether she really needed those ridiculous glasses. Were they just another way of hiding her sexuality? The way she did with unflattering outfits that concealed the curves of her body? Maybe she blamed her beauty for the sins of the monsters who took away her womanhood in such a cruel fashion so early in life. Orelius leaned back in his chair and soon found himself dozing off with these thoughts. He jarred himself awake.

'Did you know that he asked me to marry you?' he said suddenly, picking up from where he had left off. That made her eyelids flutter over those hazel eyes, brought her back from that faraway unknown territory. His lips widened slightly into weak smile. 'He did. A few times, actually. You know, he is always going on about my mum this... my mum that... Sometimes when I'm feeling a bit low Timmy comes up with the most interesting statements like...' Orelius tried his best to do an impression of Timmy's young voice: '"*Oreeelius, did you know that even in the dark, a little smile can make your eyes twinkle like a star?*" Then Timmy nods his head vigorously, with his confident eyes daring me to disagree: "*Oh yes, it's totally true, my mother does it all the time. Maybe you should ask her to marry you so she can teach you her secret smile.*"'

Orelius looked into her eyes and saw a faint hint of a smile.

He lowered his voice almost to a whisper. 'What would I tell Timmy if I found him tomorrow and you are not here? What would I do if he asks me for Mummy's secret smile?'

He stopped and took a deep breath: she was now crying and it was getting to him. 'You told me he is your life. But don't forget that you are his life too, Nikki. Don't give up on him.'

CHAPTER 20

Downing called him at exactly fifteen minutes past nine the following morning, just as he was beginning to wonder whether it was too early to check on the detective himself.

'Good morning, Orelius, how are you feeling today?' he said cordially. 'Did you stay late at the hospital?'

Downing had surprised both him and Nikisha when he turned up at her ward unannounced, around seven-thirty p.m. He had brought flowers and candy, and stayed for about an hour. Orelius himself had not left till a few minutes before midnight, but he got decent uninterrupted sleep as soon as his head hit the pillow.

'I'm fine, thanks, Gregg,' he said. 'Did you get Isaacs's files?'

'I did, and we now have a search warrant. Now we have to hope we can find something in there to lead us to him. Depending on what we find in there, there is likely to be a general APB issued on Isaacs today. We could be posting his pictures in all media channels by midday if things go to plan.'

'So there is a whole new search team coming in?'

'Yes, but I will be there as well.'

'When will you be down?'

'They are prepping the search team as we speak. I'm making my way down in the next thirty minutes or so to meet them there. So if you can, meet me outside Stapleford House about ten. I will call you when I'm on my way.'

'OK.'

'And Orelius. I should let you know that they released Kelly-Jo this morning. The specialist's opinion was that she is a seriously imbalanced individual who could say anything to gain attention, especially about that lift at Northolt. She told so many different stories about her lift that in the end none of it meant anything.'

'Oh, OK.' Now he felt truly guilty for being so harsh on the woman. The incident at the pub on Tuesday suddenly seemed extremely cruel.

'But I insisted on checking the lift anyway to cover all potential loose ends. They are sending some crime-scene techs over there now. I want you to feel like we are making progress.'

'Thanks.'

'See you in a short while, Orelius.'

*

The detective's Corsa pulled up on Willan Road outside Stapleford a few minutes before ten. His blonde locks appeared slightly ruffled, as though prepared for the messy day ahead. The pair of jeans was the same but the T-shirt was different: beige with grey stripes. He was still very much in character as a

Farmer, side-by-side with Orelius, who today had chosen a plain white shirt with the Ralph Lauren logo on the breast. There was a sleeveless denim jacket on top of this which seemed out of place, especially in such bright weather, but Orelius needed it for its deep pockets. (There was at least one item in those pockets that he hoped his partner would never get to see.)

Downing let him into the passenger seat and briefed him on what would be happening. The search team would be arriving in patrol cars at any minute and proceed into Isaacs's flat. The aim of the search was to find any legal excuse to allow them to make Isaacs an official suspect, thus place a Wanted Persons Alert on him. Downing stressed that this didn't mean they were discounting everyone else. It was just a way of employing the necessary resources to find the mystery man and ask him some questions.

'So the other guys are still coming to do Kelly-Jo's lift?' Orelius asked.

'The techs are already there. They will be closing off that part of Northolt block for a while.'

Orelius saw the African woman who was Isaac's next-door neighbour, walking in front of their car, carrying two Tesco bags. When she looked left and noticed them, she stopped and doubled back. Then she turned round and started walking towards the Corsa. Downing began to wind his window down as she approached, as if to welcome her, but she stopped about five yards short.

'Let him be,' she shouted. 'He is a good man. Just let him be.'

'Excuse me...?' the detective started, sticking his head out of the window.

'That man has suffered the worst of this cruel, cruel world,' she spat, placing both her shopping bags down to gesticulate. She waved her clenched fists in the air, like a politician driving home a point. 'He lost all his life in prison for a crime he did not commit. The man lost his family and his life. He's lost everything. What more do you want from him? Let him be, people.'

'Have you seen him? Is he back?'

'He didn't do it.'

'OK, just take it easy, nobody said he did anything. We just want to talk to him. A little boy is missing, so please, ma'am... if there is anything you are not telling us...'

'I'm not talking about the boy. Markus most certainly had nothing to do with that. If I were you I would save myself the time and get on with finding the real culprit. I meant forty years ago... he did not do it, any of it. That man has never harmed anyone in his life.'

'And you know this because...?' Downing prompted as Orelius leaned forward. 'Ma'am, if you know anything about Mr

Isaacs' whereabouts that you are not telling us, I have to warn you that you could be committing a very serious crime.'

She walked straight up to the window, bent to Downing's face, and lowered her voice. 'When Markus was moved here from prison, everyone got up in arms, not wanting a murderer amongst them. They constructed horror stories about him, and neighbours avoided him like a leper. But I didn't. Because that is not the way I was brought up. My grandmother in Africa taught me to be wary of the weird ones and be scared of the normal ones, but to always give everyone a chance. I gave him a chance. In the end he opened up to me and I have spend my days since wishing I knew how to help a troubled soul like Markus, how to relieve him of some of that heavy burden. But I can't, no one can. All I can do is listen and believe him and pray that he finds peace.'

The detective didn't seem to know what to say.

'Let me tell you this, young man,' Miss Africa continued, raising an accusing finger, 'you might have heard the expression about the weight of the world being on one's shoulders. That is the only way to describe Markus Isaacs. All his life, that old man's frail shoulders have been carrying the weight of everything that is wrong with this society.'

'What did he tell you?' Downing had finally found his voice. 'What exactly did Mr Isaacs say?'

The woman stared at them in disbelief. She shook her head with an incredulous smile, as though dealing with a couple of stupid schoolchildren.

*

Markus Isaacs:

The next time, they followed me till right outside my door. I had managed to slip away and run as they tried to pin me to the ground. They all started chasing but most of them gave up along the way. Only Anthony Hart and Ian McHugh kept up the pursuit to its tragic end in Dudlham Farm.

I locked myself inside the house but I could still hear the boys screaming abuses from outside. For a moment I was so relieved to have survived that it didn't strike me how unusually peaceful the house was that day. I didn't hear any sounds from the bedroom, my mother's soft sobs or the thundering roars of the man she had married.

A slow-motion picture of the events of that afternoon is still lodged within the deepest grooves of my brain. These images go with me on my early morning walks and burrow deeper into the folds of my heart each day. They become my reality when I sleep, and my obsession when I'm awake. Sometimes I don't know whether I am asleep or awake because either way the scenes are always clear as day: the desolate living room, the sun's glare through the back window, the roaring torrents of obscenities from outside... everything. And I know these images will haunt me till the day I die...

My mother treads quietly out of the bedroom, almost on tip-toes, and shuts the door slowly and carefully behind her, as though trying not to wake a sleeping baby. The commotion from outside don't seem to bother her. The sight of my bruises registers, but this time, to my surprise, they don't set tears trickling down her cheeks. In fact, my mother is smiling. Her deep brown eyes are sparkling, radiant. I try to smile back but for some reason it chokes inside my guts. My stomach churns with a mixture of pain and trepidation when I realise that I recognise neither the smile nor the woman behind it. This is not the almighty smile that founded our special bond and rendered us invincible; the exhilarating warm smile that liberated me from my persecutors and promised eternal sunshine. This is something else, a living breathing thing that has morphed and taken the form of my mother; an invisible monster that creeps and crawls under your skin and makes the hair stand upright at the back of your neck.

She smiles again and a knot tightens inside my heart.

Then she extends her left hand towards me and I see the double-edged blade of a knife, nine inches long.

It is covered in blood.

'Here,' my mother says as she places the knife on my lap. Then, with the ghostly smile still on her face, she tilts her head

towards the chanting voices behind the front door. 'Today, son, you are going to fight back.'

I look at my mother's smiling face, and instead of smiling back, I start to cry.

*

'Madam, if you want to help Markus, we need to know exactly what he told you,' Downing tried again.

The woman's fiery eyes scanned them both, looking for any sign of sarcasm. Then her expression softened.

'You really have no idea, have you?' Her voice too was calmer. 'Yes, Markus did talk to me. And what he told me is something I'm sure the police had staring them in the face forty years ago. But they chose to look away because two white kids had been killed by a black person in a white man's land. That's all that mattered, not whether it was the right black person. An example had to be set for other black folk, to remind them of their place.

'You see, what really happened that day was that Markus's mother snapped after years of torture and killed her abusive husband, then her child's tormentors, and finally turned the knife on herself. It was that simple.'

She stopped to let them digest this. Then she leaned even further into the open window. 'Markus was trying to remove the knife from his mother's chest when they found him. He told everyone this. He told the police and the rogues they picked to defend him, and do you know what they did? They laughed. The very lawyer who was supposed to defend Markus actually threatened him... said if he wanted to try and tell a group of twelve middle-class white people this story and hope they believe him, best of luck, but he'd need to find another lawyer. Claimed he didn't want to be there to watch a little boy locked up for life in horrid prisons with horrid men who would do unspeakable things to him.

'So the lawyer tells him to do what is best and listen to his advice: Everybody knows you were being abused and bullied, this lawyer says. Hence you lost your head one afternoon, and did things you couldn't control for just that short moment. You are a young boy, people can understand that. They can sympathise with that. Now, whether or not it's true, that is the story you are going to tell, Markus. And the state will look after you.' The woman lowered her voice another notch. 'They set him up. They set up a fourteen-year-old boy.'

Everyone was quiet for a moment.

'Mr Isaacs told you all this?' The question came from Downing. 'How much time did you spend with the man, ma'am?'

'Just let him be,' she hissed angrily. Her palms hit the roof of the Corsa in frustration. Then she turned round, picked up her shopping and stalked into the block.

'Wow,' said Downing, settling back squarely into his seat. 'If that isn't love then I don't know what is. Thought this guy was supposed to be a loner.'

'You think they are having an affair?'

'Yes.' The detective was still watching the Stapleford block entrance even though the woman had long since disappeared. 'If we don't find anything in Isaacs's flat, we might have to search her place as well.'

Orelius shook his head vigorously, as though rousing himself from a daydream.

'You alright there, Orelius? Don't tell me that little performance has taken your breath away.'

'You know what?' he mumbled, staring blankly at the same entrance that had swallowed Miss Africa. 'I think it has, Gregg.'

'Really?'

'He didn't do it.'

'You are not serious, are you?' The detective leaned forward and turned sharply, to show Orelius his arched eyebrows. Then he settled back to a slouch in the driver's seat. 'OK, here are the facts: we tell him we want to talk to him... he knows what it's about... he decides to disappear. I know you are not a professional, Orelius, but those facts would look pretty ominous to anyone.'

'We've been wasting our time, Gregg, and it's entirely my fault. He didn't do it.'

'You really do amaze me, Simm.' Downing was shaking his head in disbelief. 'One minute you are a serious detective generating suspect-lists based on elaborate intelligence, and the next minute you are falling for the words of a love-struck housewife.'

'I wasn't alive forty years ago. I have never met Markus Isaacs. Unlike you, I don't have files to gather facts. Or, like Miss Africa there, the benefit of looking into Isaacs's eyes as he tells the story. But sometimes, Gregg, you don't need facts or evidence. Sometimes the truth just comes and hits you in the face. He didn't do it.'

Downing appeared to think about this. 'Gut feeling, huh...? Fair enough. Sometimes even the best investigators rely on it, so I'll give you that. But I'm also going to ask you one very important question: why the hell is he running?'

'While that woman was talking I was watching that man...' he pointed out a young man in a brown shirt who was just disappearing from sight round the bend on Willan Road, '... I saw him come out of his flat up there,' he indicated a door somewhere up Stapleford House with his chin. 'I watched him lock his door, then try it by turning the handle. And it reminded me of when we first went to Isaacs's door. I felt what that man probably felt: sometimes you feel a slight rattle of the lock within the groove, but you know the door is locked all the same. That was how Markus Isaacs's door was the first time. The second time, it felt tighter. And because this was just after his house had been broken into, I assumed that he had changed the locks, maybe replaced them with better quality–'

'Wait... wait.' The detective held up a hand, shaking his head confoundedly. 'Did you just say Isaacs's house was broken into?'

So the detective had completely missed Miss Africa's comment on Tuesday about the break-in. Orelius wasn't sure how to approach this. 'Erm... don't you remember on our second visit the woman mentioning a break-in... by some twin brothers?'

'A break in just after our first visit?'

'Yes... mmh... well, that's what she said.'

'Orelius, did you have anything to do with this break-in?'

He opened his mouth to answer but the detective quickly raised a hand to shut him up.

'You know what, don't answer that. Keep it to yourself.'

Orelius shrugged. 'I was saying that on that second visit the door felt different when I tried it. And because his neighbour said that he had only stopped over briefly and left again, I assumed the man had quickly changed the locks, re-locked his door and taken off. But what if he came back in after that and the woman didn't hear him, what if she just assumed he was out because of the silence from the other side of the wall? What if the door felt different because this time it was bolted from the inside?'

The detective just looked at him.

'What if Markus Isaacs has not been running at all and has been in there all the time?'

The detective turned and faced Stapleford, staring up hard at Markus Isaacs's door, as though trying to summon a hidden ability to see through walls.

Two patrol cars approached from Gloucester Road with lights flashing but without the accompanying sirens. They sped down the gravel path and parked side by side at the Stapleford entrance.

'I've got a bad feeling about what they are going to find in there, Gregg,' Orelius said as the detective's gaze shifted from Isaacs's door to the arriving police vehicles. 'Very bad feeling.'

*

Just like his life, Markus Isaacs's suicide was simple and unremarkable. They found his body hanging off a brown synthetic belt looped around his neck and tied securely to a wooden ceiling beam in his meagre, mould-infested kitchen.

He left no note. There was nothing else of note in his house. Unlike his arrival, the final departure of Markus Isaacs's body from Dudlham Farm was a non-event. Some residents gathered around to watch him being wheeled away on a stretcher. There were some curious whispers and murmurs, but no tears.

The only show of emotion came from Miss Africa next door, who went down on her knees and, with both hands up and eyes shut, mumbled the same version of some barely decipherable prayer repeatedly for the whole time they were there getting rid of Markus Isaacs's body.

CHAPTER 21

'We killed him,' Downing said, almost to himself.

Orelius turned to look at him, then turned his face back towards the police vehicles and curious onlookers. 'He was a very troubled man, Gregg. This was always coming.'

'He walked every morning and said his daily prayers. That doesn't sound to me like someone who was planning to kill himself. He had found a quiet, peaceful life after a forty-year nightmare. Isaacs would have lived it out had we not turned up on his doorstep.'

Orelius put both hands in the side pockets of his denim jacket and kept his eyes on the scene of Isaacs's final farewell to The Farm.

'Listen, I've got some news for you,' the detective said, and Orelius turned back to him, his hands still in his pockets. Downing folded his arms across his chest and said, 'I'm handing over this case to a new team.'

'Jeez, Gregg, we didn't kill him. Markus Isaacs was killed by the justice system forty years ago. I thought you, of all people, being from Scotland Yard and all, would understand that,' he hunched his shoulders inside the denim coat, 'or does the *white-collar inspector* tag disqualify you from being a real policeman?'

'If you must know, this is not my decision, and it has nothing to do with what happened up there.' He tilted his head in the direction of Isaacs's flat, ignoring Orelius's jibe. 'I informed you the other day that I may be pulled off this case at any time without notice, and that's what has happened. The Ear-Slasher case is being assigned to someone else. I've just been waiting for the right moment to tell you.'

'Well, this looks like a great moment.'

'Remember, the missing child investigation is still very much active. I gave detective Garret everything we have. He knows about the possible Ear-Slasher link and your suspect-list, but he won't be pursuing it for now. They will carry on their inquiry the normal way.'

'Shame, I was just beginning to like working with you,' Orelius said, still with his shoulders hunched, his eyes not leaving the scene. 'Do you know, I haven't even laid eyes on this Garret bloke who's supposedly running the official investigation?'

'Well, I've had a word with him about you and he will treat you as family from now on. He will keep in close contact and you will get regular updates along with Timmy's mother.'

'How about the Ear-Slasher... Who'll be running that now? Or have they given up on that one?'

'Not at all, they are just bringing the right people in to look at it. Like I said, it was an unusual set of circumstances that led to that file landing in my hands in the first place. But they were always going to get things back in order.'

Orelius nodded. 'For what it's worth, I believed your theory that these cases are linked. I still do, actually. We just took some wrong turns, but I will keep going.'

'You've got two more weeks of freedom before you appear in court; whatever you do with them is your own concern. I'd just advise that you be careful it does not involve further breaches of the law.'

'Whoever this new team is, tell them I can still give them the Ear-Slasher.'

'I'm sure they'll let you know if they need your help.'

'They will need my help.'

The detective let out a quiet grunt. 'I thought I needed you because this is not usually my forte, Orelius. The new team will be made up of real experts. People with more experience than you and me in such–' he lifted a finger, signalling for Orelius to hold onto the thought. He had been interrupted by the static-filled squawking of the police radio that was strapped to his belt.

'Inspector Downing... Inspector Downing. Could you please come in?' said the robotic voice.

He yanked the radio off his belt and brought it to his face. 'Yes. Inspector Downing here.'

'This is Northolt block CSI team.'

'OK, receiving you loud and clear, Northolt. Proceed.'

The words jarred Orelius to attention. His hands left his pockets, his shoulders straightened, and he found himself moving a step closer to the detective. He had almost forgotten about Kelly-Jo and the lift.

'Something is happening down here, Inspector,' the voice said. 'You might want to see this.'

*

They left the car and almost sprinted the hundred and fifty or so yards down the footpath. There were three squad cars lined up outside Northolt, with an unmarked white van between them that Orelius believed belonged to the same team. He saw about ten officers clustered around the entrance. Most were in uniform, some were plain-clothed, and, within the jumble, he made out at least two wearing full CSI regalia: plain jumpsuits with gloves and polythene coverings for their shoes. This was not the routine doubt-clearing sweep that Downing had suggested. These people were here on a serious mission.

A short, ginger-haired, bespectacled man who appeared to be the team leader approached them and took Downing to one side without acknowledging Orelius. As soon as the two turned their backs, Orelius stepped towards the blue tapes that had been used to cordon off the lift area. A pair of uniforms swiftly appeared from nowhere and held him back, both clutching him tightly by the arms.

'This is a crime scene, sir. You can't go in there.'

'Get your hands off me.' He tried to shrug them off. 'That is my boy in there.'

Another two officers came from within the crowd at the lift to help restrain him. Amidst the commotion, he tumbled and fell to the ground. He was still writhing under the force of four uniformed policemen when he heard Downing's voice.

'Let go of him, gentlemen. He is with me.'

They quickly backed off and Orelius got up, brushing dust off his shoulders and thighs. He had not given up the struggle, but a sense of calmness suddenly came and took control of him. He kept brushing off imaginary dust even after there was nothing left. Downing placed a gentle arm on his shoulder and led him round the corner, away from the group. He sat him on a ledge opposite the rows of beat-up cars at the lot.

'As you can tell, Orelius, they have found something,' he started. 'And they are very busy trying to ensure that it is dealt with in the right manner. So we are going to stay away. Richard there will be giving me instant updates as things develop,' he pointed towards the man he had just spoken to.

'What have they found? Is it Timmy?'

'I'll give you what I know,' Downing said, taking a seat next to him on the ledge. 'They brought in some special lighting equipment for the job but they couldn't find a mains connection within the elevator, so one of the techs went down the underground channel to find a connection. He accidentally dropped his light, and when he descended all the way to the bottom of the shaft to retrieve it, he found what looked like human remains.'

Orelius put his hands on his head, 'Oh my–'

'Wait. I have not finished,' Downing said calmly. 'What they have found, to be precise, is a heap of bones. Timmy disappeared less than a week ago, so you can do the math... it doesn't add–'

'Bones?' Orelius cut him short. 'They found bones?'

'Yes, and they are clearly a human skeleton. But these guys don't give out details until they have finished their tests.'

'It's not Timmy.'

'That is the general feeling. The bottom of that channel is still the foul-smelling swamp this estate was built on fifty years ago. If this lift has been serviced since, I would presume the engineers covered their faces with masks and got in and out as quickly as they could. So whatever was down there could have gone unnoticed for years.' He spread his arms and left the thought hanging. 'But like I said, they will not be making any assumptions.'

'I think this is from a very long time ago. Someone fell into the pit way back when the elevator still had that legendary fault, and got crushed under the descending car. It explains the mythical stench that people assumed was just the swamp.'

'Incredible,' whispered the detective.

'Twenty-six years ago a young single mother from this block vanished into thin air.' Orelius was now completely calm and straight-faced. He leant forward with his elbows on his thighs and moved his hands to cover his face. 'Last night her daughter sat with me at The Jolly and tried to explain that the lift took her mother. But because she didn't know how to, we shipped her poor soul to the police station and locked her up.' He raised his head but still didn't look at the detective. 'I think they've found Kelly-Jo's mother.'

*

The next morning Kelly-Jo arrived at the Northolt lift at seven a.m., about three hours earlier than usual. With a small folding chair and a large square carton box in front of her, like some kind of reception point for Northolt block, she set up a stall about ten yards left of the police tapes that still ringed lift's door. She sat on the chair, leaning forwards into her usual stance: open mouthed, right arm hanging at an angle. The early workers whispered their condolences to her without knowing whether or not she understood. Some dropped money and flowers next to her. The kids who had previously abused her or simply had fun at her expense stood and watched from afar, as Kelly-Jo Pretty mourned her only known relative in her own way.

She had spent twenty-six years a captive in that lift, waiting for her mother.

*

...As other toddlers enjoyed their toys and playground visits, little Kelly-Jo Pretty held on only to the smell of the last place she had seen her mother.

When normal children started school, made friends and acquired siblings, Kelly-Jo Pretty began her early pilgrimage to the Northolt lift to find her mother.

Others went back home to parental hands to lead them through the labyrinth of life and the mayhem of Dudlham Farm; Kelly-Jo Pretty walked back to the mental asylum to lay her mother's ghost for the night.

In their unruly teenage years they turned on her with sticks and stones, and Kelly-Jo Pretty stood firm in the lift and waited for her mother.

A few prospered and left Dudlham; Kelly-Jo Pretty kept waiting for her chance to truly mourn...

*

Twenty-six years she waited, only to learn that her mother was not coming back.

And after that day, no one ever again saw Kelly-Jo Pretty in Dudlham Farm.

CHAPTER 22

TJ was fairly busy for an early afternoon. It was a Friday in the school holidays, and for some the weekend had already begun. The sun was out again; five straight days of absolute sunshine now, and it was still only April. Some early drinkers were sipping cocktails under bright red umbrellas outside The Jolly. Children were out in full force in the surrounding playgrounds. Timmy Lewis was still missing, his mother was still straddling the thin line between life and death, but Dudlham Farm marched on.

'So, what are your plans now, Orelius,' Downing said, setting the mug of coffee back down on the table in front of him. 'You know, about the whole situation.'

'I don't know. I'm just another black man in Dudlham Farm. You are the authority, maybe you should tell me.'

It was the day after the discovery of the bodies of Markus Isaacs and Marianne Pretty. Each with widely different stories attached to them, yet both telling the same story; the ghosts of Dudlham Farm Estate.

The two men were sitting at the same table where Orelius had threatened Kelly-Jo three days before. There was slow music piping from the speakers above their table. Every now and then, rasping laughter thundered from the high round table, left side of the bar. Orelius recognised the source of the offending laugh as Callum Robinson, a gangly young ginger-haired white farmer who had his breakfast, lunch and supper in this pub. And none of it included any food. He had once heard a group of lads trying to persuade Callum to proceed with them into the clubbing circuits of Leicester Square to continue partying after TJ's closing time. Callum, who usually never left The Jolly, had by then put just enough alcohol into his system to give this proposition a serious thought. But after a moment of deliberation, Callum had decided he couldn't go to central London because he didn't want to be too tired for the next morning. Since the following morning was a Sunday and Callum wasn't particularly religious, the lads had inquired whether there was something special he needed to get up early for. *Not really*, Callum had said. *But I want to get back here nice and early tomorrow morning for a few more drinks*. So devoted was he to his drink that he couldn't bear the thought of being too hung-over to wake up and drink some more.

'You are making it sound like everything has been left down to me,' Orelius said after Callum's latest bout of laughter had passed. 'I haven't heard from detective Garret yet but I believe these people are now looking for Timmy's body. I want to know the whole story of what happened to Timmy, and I know this will come from the guy going around collecting white ears. If you told them about the connection, why aren't they buzzing about it? And who is the person in charge of the Ear-Slasher case now?'

'We probably won't know till Monday. I can assure you they are seriously considering the possible connection, but it would normally take some solid evidence to officially link cases.' The detective laced his hands together and set them in front of him on the table, gently tapping his two thumbs against each other. 'I know this might be hard for you but let's try and have some faith in authority this time, Orelius. This will work out better. I was just a temporary charge. These new guys are vastly experienced in cases like this.'

'If they don't need my help with that, and detective Garret is also keeping me at arm's length, maybe I should just go to sleep and wait for my day in court. And just trust that everyone is out there doing their best finding Timmy.'

'They *will* do their best. Believe me, we all want Timmy back unharmed. Besides, you might need the sleep. I know what's going on behind the scenes; despite my warnings, you and your friends have been keeping yourselves busy through the night after the uniforms have left.'

'What?' He tried half-heartedly to sound surprised.

'I know Isaacs's door was not the only one that was kicked in. There have also been reports of other residents being roughed up by local gangs looking for the missing boy.'

‘So you know,’ he said with and indifferent shrug. ‘I’m sure you’d do the same thing if your son was missing.’

‘If I believed it was the right thing to do, then, yes, I’d do it. But have your actions produced even one viable suspect? Have you considered that by putting fear in these people they may not be left with any sympathy? That you could actually be alienating some genuine well-wishers who might be able to help? I know your boy is missing but you can’t continue harassing innocent people–’

‘You know, the thing about a broken heart is that it’s the innocent people that end up with the pieces. That’s just how it is,’ Orelius cut in calmly. ‘Once upon a time, Gregg, that broken person was me, and the innocent bystander was a nineteen-year-old single mother. Luckily she had been dealing with a broken heart all her life and she knew someone who could mend one. She led me to him. She healed me by sharing her single source of happiness. Now that source of happiness is missing and the young woman is lying in a hospital bed waiting to die...’ His voice tailed off as his mind drifted back to that fateful meeting.

*

Before the beeping sound had snapped him back to life and led him to Timmy, there had been another sound that kept Orelius alive. Only this one was real. Her name was Amy Williams. Even though in his young life he frequently slipped and lost his head, she had always been there to keep his heart beating. He had travelled to Manchester that morning after one such lapse to get his heart beating again. This lapse, he vowed, would be the last, as he set off on his journey filled with hope, only to come back a few hours later a broken person: a twenty-three-year-old man staring head-on at the end of his life. The biggest irony of it all was that the morning had begun with so much energy and promise, dreams of a new beginning that he had considered a life-saving revelation. This was the day he decided to seek forgiveness for his past sins and start a new life as a better person. Only it turned out it was too late.

Eleven months after breaking up the relationship, Orelius had decided that morning to make the journey up to her family home in Manchester and attempt reconciliation. Amy's father had slammed the door in his face, threatening to call the police. Which, at the time, he thought was humiliating, but not the end of the world. The end of the world would come a few hours later, when he inquired about this uncharacteristic anger from Mr Williams, a man he had got along with well when he was seeing his daughter.

It turned out Mr Williams had buried his daughter only three weeks before.

There had also been a stillborn baby boy resulting from a complicated ten-hour childbirth in which too much blood was lost to save either mother or child. The baby in question was Orelius's.

Orelius had taken the news with a stoic nod of the head, and driven back to London wondering if he should see a psychiatrist about his apparent emotional deficiencies. In moments of frustration at his apparent indifference, Amy had more than once asked if Orelius was capable of ever letting anyone into his soul; of feeling the pain she felt when she gave love and got back only loyalty and respect. Too much attention from too many friends had driven an unbridgeable rift between them. But he knew none of the other strands of his chaotic lifestyle was real; he had always known. Amy Williams was real. She was the woman who stood by him when he was in prison; fought his battles for him and with him; and continued to love him regardless of the outcome.

This was the day he had gone to Manchester to offer Amy the whole of him. This was the day he was going to turn his back on his posse of friends and put an end to the petty crimes. He was sacrificing popularity and wealth for a simple life of loving and being loved back. But while he was planning all this, someone up there, that almighty being, was laughing. That someone taught Orelius a few painful lessons on this day. Despite his many failings, Amy had carried his child for nine months and not mentioned a word to him about it; he would never meet a stronger or smarter woman than Amy. He knew then, that at the age of twenty-three he had already met and lost the love of his life.

These were the thoughts of a young life wasted that had lulled Orelius into a trance behind the wheel of his BMW at the Northolt House parking lot.

Then along came that beeping sound...

*

'They saved my life, Gregg, and now it's my turn to save theirs,' Orelius continued. 'She might not be able to say it, but Nikisha Lewis is counting on me. Timmy, wherever he is, is counting on me too. I cannot let them down.'

'Sorry.'

'What for, Gregg?'

'For not being able to solve this case... for having to leave...' The detective couldn't find the words to finish. He stared blankly at his coffee for a few seconds, then looked up. 'Listen, I know you need to stay close to the investigations. I will try and explain to whoever gets the Ear-Slasher files what we've started here, see if they can come up with a way to let you carry on your quest in a manner that is legal and beneficial to everyone. Keith Garret, however, has a very serious missing child case, and he is understandably not too keen on letting you that close to his investigation. My experiment using you failed, and now I have to let them do their job. They will keep in close contact with you and Nikisha but it won't be the same kind of partnership me and you were attempting to run here. It's just how they want to do it. I'm sorry.'

'That's alright. It's not your fault.' Orelius looked up at the detective and added, 'Thanks for trying by the way.'

Downing nodded and took a sip of his coffee.

'I overheard your phone conversation with your chief the other day and it sounded like they were trying to get you back to your white-collar duties even sooner.'

This grabbed the detective's attention. He placed his coffee back down and stared up at Orelius disconcertedly.

'The phone call you received the other day, when we were here looking for Kelly-Jo,' he explained, even though he was sure Downing already knew what he was talking about. 'Sorry, I didn't mean to eavesdrop. I was just there, couldn't help it... what is your story anyway, Gregg? How'd you end up with this case if this isn't your area?'

'Long story. You don't want to know.'

'Sounded to me like you'd been having some time off and they wanted you back.'

'I wasn't having time off. If you really want to know, I was technically under suspension. There were some allegations that resulted in an internal investigation...' He stopped and changed tack. 'Listen, we are not here to talk about me.'

'Sounds very deep. Sorry, I guess.'

'It's OK. My job involves investigating stock market cheats and crafty corporate fraudsters who make a million by stealing a pound from a million different people. The kind of criminals no one really cares about. So it's not unusual for the investigator to be investigated every once in a while.'

'I take it you got cleared then. They didn't find anything on you.'

He nodded. 'That is why I'm going back to work on Monday.'

'So you only ended up with this Ear-Slasher case as a punishment?'

The detective said nothing.

'I'm not blaming you for anything. I'm just saying.'

'Orelius, you asked me to meet you and here I am. I doubt that my professional scandals were your only agenda.' He took another sip of his coffee and carefully placed the cup back on the saucer. 'I don't hand over the case till this evening. So if there's anything you want to talk about, this might be a good time.'

'I've still got the list and I will be going back to all the names we didn't clear.' Orelius dug his fingers into his breast pocket and produced the plain white A4 sheet. He started to unfold it, then stopped and tossed it on the table absently. 'I intend to talk to everyone on that list. Then everyone in

Dudlham Farm, and beyond, if I have to. I will not stop till I find him, Gregg.'

The detective picked up the sheet, finished unfolding it, and straightened it on the table in front of him.

'I hope you understand that even if you were to find your man, anything you do on your own will not help in a court of law.' He lifted the sheet and started tracing his left index finger down the list of names. 'In fact it would most probably harm any such case.'

'Well, what choice I've I got? You are quitting on me and you said the new guys won't work with me. I can't just sit around and wait.'

'Listen, I...' Downing looked up at him and hesitated; what he had been about to say he had already been through with him before, over and over. The bottom line was, it was not his call. He made another frustrated attempt to open his mouth but stopped almost immediately and went back to the list. 'Who is this MJ?' His finger had stopped on the third name on the list, amongst those that had been crossed-off.

'He is the next suspect I will be talking to. Maybe, since you are here and you are officially still on the case, you could come with me on this one. You know... to make everything legal.'

'I understand your urgency, Orelius. But sometimes it helps to take a short break to think things through maybe one more time. You sure this list is still the way you want to go?'

'That list is all I have,' he said, and the detective had nothing to say in reply. 'Tell me, Gregg, how would you feel if you were to learn tomorrow that Timmy is dead, but that he had been alive, waiting for someone to rescue him, right at this moment, as we sit here sipping coffee? And that we could have helped him? How would you feel?' He gave him some time to consider, before adding. 'There is no time to think, Gregg.'

Downing pondered this momentarily. 'We have gone through four names on your list and so far it has produced nothing but harrowing ghosts of a place I know nothing about. I was not even born when some of these things happened, yet somehow I find myself right in the middle of it. I don't know how I'm going to sleep again at night. So excuse me, but I hope you can understand my lack of motivation in pursuing that list.'

'This is what I could come up with. I will keep thinking of other ways but I won't stop in the meantime. I have to talk to MJ.'

'Who is MJ?'

'His name's Mic Bailey.'

'Mic Bailey?' he said thoughtfully. 'Why does that ring a bell? Have you mentioned him before?'

'We saw him the other day outside Stapleford. The kid–'

'With the BMX,' Downing finished, snapping his fingers with the deduction. Then he reverted to the questioning eyes. 'He couldn't have been older than twelve. How does he fit into this?'

'He used to go to Timmy's school and he's part of a family that is a right nasty piece of work. They hang around together with his cousin and uncle, and enjoy nothing more than causing trouble.'

'Is that it? You want me to go questioning a twelve-year-old about a possible multiple homicide because he is a known troublemaker in school?'

'Not too long ago they got caught on CCTV at Bruce Grove underground station trying to push some kid onto the tracks. When questioned by the police, their parents claimed that it was just a little fight that had spilled over from school and that they were merely pushing the boy around. They were *mortified* by the very suggestion that their eleven-year-old sons were attempting to murder someone. Thing is, none of them lives anywhere near the station or uses the train, so why did they have to have this fight there? From what the other kid said, they deliberately lured him out there. They used some colourful story about going to meet up with this other friend who had computer games to give away for free.'

The detective gave it a brief thought. 'Sounds pretty disturbing but I don't see a connection, not quite enough to warrant going round there making accusations of abduction and possibly murder.'

'Before this train station incident, the victim's father had made some noise about the Bailey kids giving his boy a hard time. Pushed the school to take action and threaten the Baileys with expulsion.'

'Orelius, I don't want to talk to a couple of ten-year-olds without any clear connection to Timmy's case.'

'A few of years back, when I first got involved in Timmy's life, I learned that these kids were bullying Timmy, so I went round to their house and had words with their mothers and the small-time dealer who lives there with one of the mothers. I put the fear of the Lord into them, and the bullying stopped. It must have really hurt their egos. I'm telling you, the Baileys don't like their reign being questioned. Maybe they were still holding a grudge.'

There was silence at the table as the men eyed each other. Then Orelius added, 'A bunch of people saw Mic Bailey floating around Northolt on Sunday.'

Downing kept his stare but slowly began nodding. 'OK, I suppose there's no harm in a having a word with them, just quick word.'

Just then, Oreluis spotted Gutierrez walking up to the bar with a brown tennis bag hanging over his shoulders, probably containing an array of merchandise he was trying to push.

Gutierrez bounced about, greeting and patting backs amidst cheerful laughter, as if he owned the place. He was taller, wiser and better-spoken than most of The Jolly's clientele. Only his slight frame and baby-face might have given away that he was not even old enough to be here. But no one seemed to care. The barman leaned over his counter and exchanged a few words before walking round to join him. Then the pair started towards the back door, three tables back from Orelius and Downing.

'Ah, just the man I was looking for,' Orelius called out to Gutierrez as they approached. 'You got a minute, mate?'

'Sure, Oz,' he said, walking up to their table, and took the empty seat. The barman quickly realised that his presence was undesired and walked back to his bar. Whatever deal he was about to close with Gutierrrez would have to wait.

'This is a quick one, son,' Orelius started, turning to face the boy. 'You know that Mic Bailey kid from the Willan Road houses, right?'

'MJ? Yeah, sure. Everybody does.'

'I want you to tell my friend here something about MJ,' he said, pointing towards the detective. 'The first thing you can think of.'

Gutierrez rattled straight on without thinking, 'Thirteen years old. Drinker, smoker, user and dealer. Carries a switchblade, and punctuates all his sentences with the word "fuck". Otherwise, just an all-round nice kid.' He said this articulately, without batting an eyelid, as though he himself was a responsible adult several decades older than MJ. It was easy to see why the Dudlham housewives had fallen in love with this boy.

Orelius looked at the detective with an unspoken question: *That good enough for you?* Then he turned back to Gutierrez and said, 'Thanks mate. That's all, you can go now.'

Gutierrez got up and hoisted the bag over his shoulder. 'Sorry about this thing with Timmy by the way,' he said, shuffling the bag into position round his back. 'You know, I watched him play tennis over at the club and I thought he was going to be a star...' He hesitated, not sure his sympathies were achieving the desired effect. 'You know what, Oz, we all keep hassling around here, dreaming of making it big and getting the hell out. The problem is, most of us have got no idea how to, because we don't see anyone ahead of us who's left and made it big. But Timmy... he was going places, man. Timmy Lewis was going to be our man, Oz. He was heading all the way to the top, to represent Dudlham Farm in the big time. To sing our song...'

And just like that, hypnotised in the cloud of a fifteen-year-old kid's passionate speech, Orelius Simm's rock-solid centre gave in and everything started to fall apart. Gutierrez's words became a distant background hum as he saw a baby's face floating before his eyes. It was a strange face, an infant, maybe smiling or maybe crying. It was hard to tell because everything was fuzzy. He blinked once and the face was gone, then he blinked again and it was back. And he suddenly knew. That face looked just like him; it belonged to the son he had never met. The baby he had replaced with Timmy Lewis had come back to haunt him. Because whatever Orelius Simm tried to be and whatever he did for Timmy would never absolve him of his past sins. He would never be forgiven for becoming yet another absent black father. The strange face lingered, swinging from one side then another of Gutierrez, whose lips were moving in slow motion. It occurred to Orelius that Gutierrez was really just a kid with dreams. He wanted to tell Gutierrez that he was wrong. That people did get out of Dudlham Farm and make it big. He wanted to tell him about people like Andre Boateng, who made it from The Farm, and probably wanted to sing the Dudlham song but couldn't; because sometimes true history has to be sacrificed in order for people to become who we want them to be.

When the face finally faded away, he realised he was sitting at the corner table in The Jolly on his own. There was no detective Downing, or Gutierrez, only a soft female voice from the speakers above him. The voice was soulfully lamenting why her lover wanted to hurt her when she already had enough trouble. Orelius looked around, wondering whether he had been dreaming, and whether he was dreaming now.

He felt an arm brush over his shoulders. He looked up and saw Downing. The detective was holding a small stack of cream-coloured tissues. So he had not been dreaming at all. They were really here at TJ, and he had in fact been talking to Gutierrez.

'Here, have some of these,' Downing whispered, sliding the tissues across the table towards him. 'I'm just popping to the restroom. Back in a minute.'

He was gone before Orelius could say anything.

Another chill enveloped him as he looked at the tissues in front of him and realised that they were in fact pure white. He saw three droplets of clear liquid directly below his head on the table, and another couple streaking along the breasts of his white shirt. Then he knew why Gutierrez had stepped away quietly, and why Downing had brought him tissues and left him alone.

He picked them up and dried his eyes. The voice above continued to beseech her lover not to hurt her.

CHAPTER 23

Although they were never charged for the alleged attempted homicide incident at Bruce Grove underground station, a young black psychology and social studies student at University College, London, would later use the Bailey kids as a case study in her thesis about the antisocial behaviour of young children in inner cities concentrating on pre-teens (the report refers to the boys two years ago at the age of eleven).

Antisocial Behaviour of Pre-adolescent Children in Inner Cities

By Melodee LaFaye

[extract from Section 2]

CASE STUDY 2: Three 11-year-old boys questioned and released without charge about the attempted murder of their classmate.

Subjects:

a) Miracle Jeremiah (MJ)

Age: 11 ************** Sex: Male ************** Academic record: Average to poor ************** Extra-curricular record: V. good ************** Anti-Social Behaviour Orders (ASBOs) record: 8 (for violence and drug-related misdemeanours)

b) Dwayne

Age: 11 ************** Sex: Male ************** Academic record: Poor ************** Extra-curricular record: Excellent ************** Anti-Social Behaviour Orders (ASBOs) record: 5 (for violence and drug-related misdemeanours)

c) Jordan

Age: 11 ************** Sex: Male ************** Academic record: Average to poor ************** Extra-curricular record: Good ************** Anti-Social Behaviour Orders (ASBOs) record: 4 (for violence and drug-related misdemeanours)

Report summary:

The three subjects all live in the same three-bedroom house with a total of eight residents, on a north London council estate. All have different mothers who live with them in the house. The only adult male presence within the residence is a twenty-one-year-old boyfriend of the oldest of the three women, Angela, who is thirty-nine. The other two mothers, Josie and Jessica, are both twenty-five. All three mothers are white. Their children are all of mixed heritage; black and white.

There are clear signs of lack of proper parenting in this household. On the Friday night before the alleged attempted homicide incident, the three boys had spent the night babysitting Angela's youngest child whilst the three women went out clubbing. They had also consumed a significant amount their mothers' leftover alcohol. On the morning of the incident MJ stole some marijuana from his mother's purse and smoked it with the other two.

Reports indicate that MJ, the dominant (alpha male) of the three, was an unplanned but nevertheless welcomed child. A fact reflected in his name, Miracle, and the unique circumstances of his birth.

Josie and Angela got pregnant at the same time when they were fourteen and twenty-eight respectively. The two pregnancies were common knowledge around the estate. The housemates' due dates were estimated to fall within two days of each other. And neighbours attest to their general excitement at the prospect of the big welfare cheques that would be gracing their household simultaneously. These same neighbours swear that the other fourteen-year-old girl in the household, Josie, was never pregnant. She might have gained a bit of weight, but that was it. However, a week before the two pregnant housemates' due date, they came home from a prenatal clinic to be greeted by the sight of uniformed paramedics in their house. The medics had just delivered a baby from Josie, the one that was never pregnant. She named him Miracle Jeremiah (MJ).

Angela and Jessica then went on to give birth on schedule a week later, within two days of each other, and named their babies Dwayne and Jordan respectively. Angela would give birth again, to a baby girl named Nicole, when the three boys – MJ, Dwayne and Jordan – had turned five.

A case of three newborn babies in the same household within a week should in itself indicate a potential welfare problem. This one, however, is further compounded by the relationships within the complex family tree of this household (as illustrated in Fig. 2.1 of the Appendix). All three women share the same surname, Bailey. Josie and Jessica are twin sisters and Angela is in fact their mother. Angela has given birth three times. The first time was *to* her twin daughters, when she was fourteen. The second time was *with* her daughters, when they were fourteen and she was twenty-eight. And the third time was when she was thirty-three and her daughter's children were both five (same age as her son). Meaning that at twenty-eight Angela Bailey became a mother again and double-grandmother at the same time. Then she went on to give her five-year-old grandsons a newborn aunty.

In short, MJ and Jordan are eleven-year-old cousins. Dwayne, also eleven, is their uncle. Six-year-old Nicole, who they occasionally baby-sit when the women go out clubbing, is their aunty.

In my opinion the Baileys' case illustrates a failing social welfare policy; a system incapable of acting, but somewhat fair in reacting.

*

‘Hey, Stop!’ Orelius shouted.

The white hooded top was bobbing up and down behind a small pointed head as Dwayne Bailey’s slight figure disappeared fast down Adams Road. MJ and Jordan were about five yards behind but Dwayne seemed to be gaining on them.

‘Hey, hold it!’ he tried again, but it was useless, as the three figures faded on the horizon.

They had just left the pub and were heading towards Adams Road when, by sheer luck, they spotted all three boys involved in a kick-about football game in Time Garden, right outside TJ. Dwayne, who was in goal and thus facing them, had spotted them first and started running round the back of the pub, then out of The Farm along Adams Road. The other two turned round, saw them, and immediately started sprinting after Dwayne.

Their reaction gave Orelius something to think about. Why were they running? The first time they did this, at their BMX show a couple of days ago, he had assumed that it was because of their antics with the angry driver. On second thoughts, he was beginning to see some problems with this presumption. For the Bailey kids, swearing and sticking up a finger at an adult was an everyday occurrence, something that was forgotten as soon as it happened. They shouldn’t have run away then, and they shouldn’t be running now. Unless they were guilty of something much worse.

‘I take it that is our friend Mic Bailey,’ Downing said, snapping him back to attention.

‘Yes, it’s them. MJ, his cousin and their uncle.’ He’d already told Downing their story. ‘Look we have to catch them. We’ll let Dwayne go for now but we’ve got to get those two.’ Orelius indicated the bend Dwayne had disappeared round, with MJ and Jordan quickly fading after him. ‘You keep going after them this way and I’ll cut through here,’ he said, pointing towards a barely noticeable alley between Lympne and Manston.

‘What, you think we can catch them?’

‘You don’t have to catch them, just keep following so they know you are behind. I know where they are going and I will be waiting for them when they get there.’ He was already jogging towards the alley. ‘I’ll call you when I’ve got them.’

CHAPTER 24

Orelius called Downing fifteen minutes later and asked him to proceed along Adams to get to Willan Road from the outside. He gave him Baileys' address and informed him he had MJ and Jordan and was taking them back to their house for a chat in front of their parents.

He got there ahead of the detective, and he saw the front door fly open before he was within ten yards of it. A young, long-faced dark-haired white woman in Adidas joggers stepped out, holding a cigarette. She was quick to let her feelings be known about seeing the two boys being frogmarched by the back of their shirts.

'Oh my fuckin' God, Oz,' she screamed. 'What have they done now?'

'Just get back in the house,' Orelius said. 'We are coming in to talk.'

There were two other women in the house; one looked older but they could have been sisters. All were smoking cigarettes. There was a daytime chat show on the old cathode ray TV in the living room.

'What the fuck's going on?' the older one shouted as she came barefoot down the stairs. The younger one shot up from the sofa and shouted the same question. Except for her blonde hair, she was the spitting image of the one with the Adidas joggers, who had now closed the door behind her and was also repeating the same question. It soon turned into an indecipherable shouting contest littered with profanities. The older one stepped right to his face, turned her cheek up, and she declared herself ready to be hurt instead of her boys.

'Calm down, ladies. I just need to ask these boys a few questions, and I will do so in your presence, then I will leave you alone.'

'What do you mean ask them some questions?' asked Adidas Jogger. 'What have they done? Why the fuck are you chasing them around the estate like criminals?'

'Chill out, darling. Someone is on his way up here from the Met Police. We'll ask them a few questions and be gone. But if you continue making things hard for us we can always shift them up to the station and do the questioning there.'

That seemed to give them something to think about. Their foulmouthed protests died down to muffled grumbles. It took another five minutes for Downing to get there. Unsurprisingly he didn't have Dwayne with him, but the two would do for now.

'So, boys,' Orelius started once they had all settled. He was looking straight at MJ. 'I assume you know why we are here. Is that why you were running away from us?'

'We ain't done nothing.' This came from grim-faced MJ.

'Don't make this hard, MJ, we already know what you did. You got caught on hidden CCTV camera just like last time.' It was a lie but a necessary one.

'What are they talking about, MJ?' asked Adidas Jogger.

'We ain't done fuck all, Mum,' he said. 'We just found him. And he was already dead, I swear.'

That hit them all like a rocket they never saw coming. Nobody spoke for almost a whole minute.

'You found who, MJ?' The question finally came from the barefoot older woman. She was looking back and forth between the two boys. 'Jordan, MJ what is going on?'

'We just found him, we didn't do anything.'

'OK, MJ, you need to tell us exactly what happened.' Downing spoke up for the first time. 'Where did you find him, and where is he now?'

'It was on the walkway at Rochford House. We just moved it into a corner to get it out of the way.'

'It...?' asked Orelius. 'You are talking about Timmy, aren't you?'

'Was that his name?'

'Of course that's his name, and do not pretend you don't know him because you *do*. You used to beat him up at school and I came here to talk to you about it remember?'

Now the boy looked genuinely confused. He started looking around for help; from his mother, then cousin, then aunty, then grandmother.

'I think they are talking about Albino Tim, from primary school.' His cousin came to his rescue.

'Oh, him? No, I haven't done nothin' to him.'

'So who are we talking about then? Who did you find?'

'We found the baby...' He wanted to say more but nothing came, so he looked over at his cousin again for help.

'It was like... an unborn baby...' Jordan picked up. 'A very tiny baby, about this big,' he separated his palms about seven inches apart to indicate the size. 'Everyone was saying that Shola dumped it there because Shola was pregnant and now she's not pregnant anymore.'

Orelius had been about to follow up on something else that had been said, but the shock of this new information stunned them all into silence. He forgot what he was about to ask but it didn't seem important now. He knew Dudlham Farm, and what these kids were saying was possible around here.

'Are you saying you found a baby?' Downing asked, just because something needed to be asked.

'So you don't know anything about Timmy?' Orelius followed up.

'No.' MJ shook his head. 'We went to the same primary school, but I don't even remember him.'

Further questioning only revealed that these kids knew nothing about Timmy's disappearance. Orelius and Downing had nonetheless clearly stumbled into something very disturbing. MJ later led them to a dark secluded intersection of the walkway in Rochford, and sure enough it was there. Shola's baby. The tiny shape of a not fully developed foetus, about seven inches in length, curled into a ball inside its transparent amniotic sack.

*

The emancipation of Shola Louise King

Two years ago, as part of an exercise in remorse and rehabilitation by the Department of Justice's probation service, some minor offenders serving non-custodial sentences were asked to write letters of apology to their victims. A one-time potential poetry prodigy named Shola King, then only sixteen and already boasting several drugs convictions, chose to write the letter to her mother:

Dear Mama,

I'm sorry that I never followed your advice to find freedom from the love of another human being. I'm sorry that I could only find freedom from a substance that costs money and wrecks lives.

Some people call you weak for allowing yourself to be broken by an act as commonplace as a man walking out. I want you to know that I know these people are wrong. I've always known. I know that you, mother, wield strength beyond compare. Like a wise man keeping his money in a bank, you packaged that strength and stored it in a divine unbreakable fortress, somewhere you believed it would never be breached. How were you to know that the bank would one day decide to walk out and start a new life with a white woman in Birmingham?

I know he stripped you of everything including your will to live or love. I know that I am alone because my father took away with him all the elements that made you, left you in the mercy of Dudlham's illegally supplied chemicals to fill the void and give you the illusion of being alive. I know that the powders from the man called Electric Dan that you sniff and inject helps. Because sometimes in those brief moments, when you are bouncing and jumping and dancing and laughing, I am convinced that you do indeed love me. But then they wear off and suddenly you are cursing and shivering and crying again, and I desperately wish for the powers of Electric Dan, to give you strength and make you happy.

I desperately want to be enough for you, Mama. I don't know how love works. I don't know if you once loved me on condition that my father was there to repay you back whatever love you gave. Maybe this is how love works; you get here, you give there. But I know that I will always love you, Mama; I will give and give and give, even if I don't get anything back.

I will understand that you have to pay for Electric Dan's solution with the little cash you receive from social welfare and that's why sometimes we have no food. I know when this runs out Electric Dan has to make do with a kind 'thank-you' gesture in the bedroom, as I sit alone in the living room watching TV at high volume. I understand that one day you will be too old for this gesture, and that you will need me to say 'thank you' to Electric Dan for you. I know that one day I too will discover the magic of Electric Dan's solution, so we can fly and be free together. Then maybe, just maybe, you will be able love me back.

I love you, Mama.

Yours forever,
Shola

*

This letter would pass through many hands, including parole officers, lawyers, judges, psychologists, academics and even politicians. Mailing it to its intended recipient, however, would have been tricky.

Shola Louise King's mother had been dead for six years.

‘Is it alive? I think it is breathing,’ Josie said backing away to hide behind her mother as if the thing was coming after her. All three women had made the journey to Rochford block to support their respective sons.

‘Course it’s not alive. Don’t be silly,’ retorted her sister, the Adidas Jogger, holding her ground two yards from the foetus.

‘Right, we are going to have to clear up now,’ Downing said, strapping the radio back onto his waist to wave away the small group that had begun to form. To remind everyone he was a law enforcement officer, he added, in cop-speak: ‘Move it along, people. There is nothing to see.’

Then he walked round to where Orelius was standing. ‘They are sending some guys over to deal with this,’ he said into Orelius’s ear. ‘But I think I’m done here, Orelius. Maybe you were right about me not being a real policeman, because, if I have to be honest, this place scares the hell out of me.’

*

Shola King was picked up later that evening on the Adams Road taxi rank opposite The Jolly Farmer. This is where a group of Farm girls, no older than eighteen and wearing short skirts, heels and heavy make-up, could be found after dark, waiting for unlicensed cabs to Soho. They brandished hollow smiles beneath weary looks as they set off to central London to make money. Their empty stares spoke untold stories: of needs to feed fatherless babies, or ailing siblings, or entire extended families in Africa, or incurable drug habits. Shola King belonged in the latter category.

The officers read Shola Louise King a range of charges, including prostitution, possession and distribution of Class-A drugs, illegal abortion, even child abuse and murder for good measure. Who knew – at twenty-six weeks the baby could have been alive and viable when it came out of her womb. They had to provide the judge with the full range of options to put this girl away for as long as possible. Shola's few friends didn't worry too much about her. She would do her time and come back to the streets, just like last time. Then she would be back in and out again... and again. Till one day someone would find her dead body, either in the showers of a maximum security prison, or nestled alongside rusty needles in a hedge somewhere in Dudlham Farm.

CHAPTER 26

The idea did not resurface till the early hours of Monday morning, when Orelius woke up from another of his recurring nightmares and walked to his bathroom.

He realised that the idea had always been there, ever since it was mentioned by one of the kids in the Baileys' living room on Friday. It had been pushed under the surface by the weight of subsequent events involving Shola's baby, then submerged even further by the implications of Downing's departure. But since that split second inside the Baileys' living room, when the information struck, something had always bothered him. He just had not been able to put a finger on it.

There was probably a reason why the pieces decided to fall in place while he was sitting on his toilet in the dark with his boxer shorts down around his ankles. Maybe it was the dead silence of the night or the relative lack of activity on that day that allowed his brain to finally piece it together. It started with the snippet of trivia from the Bailey kid, and a figment of his imagination. The two intertwined to create an idea. He explored the idea from one angle, then another, and every time, a piece of the puzzle fell in place. Soon everything was coming to him so fast, he had to force himself to stay sitting on the toilet and stop thinking for a minute. He relaxed, took a deep breath, then started all over again, right from the beginning. And it still made sense, all of it.

His first instinct was to call Downing even though he was no longer involved with the case. But on second thoughts he realised this was still a raw idea: it made sense to him, but maybe only because he so badly wanted it to. He had to have something more substantial, to bother the detective. So the first thing he did when he got out of the toilet was to fire up his computer and ask Google some questions. The computer spewed out answer after answer that fitted perfectly into the puzzle, as if it had been waiting all along for Orelius to ask.

He remained at his desk for more than two hours, filling in the blanks. Halfway through, he called Downing's mobile and it rang seven times before handing him over to voicemail. But maybe that was for the best, because this theory, while now much better than raw, was still not quite fully cooked. He needed to talk to someone, to back up what the computer was telling him. A quick scan of his memory for suitable candidates took him all the way back to his University days at Manchester, to a young woman named Joyce Mawenya. Joyce would know, and if she didn't, she'd certainly know someone who did. He had kept in tentative touch with Joyce and still received seasonal good wish messages from her, most of which he hardly ever had time to respond to. Now here he was, finding himself needing Joyce at three o'clock in the morning.

He dialled her number and got voicemail. Then, lacking other options, he tried Downing again, with the same result.

He was close to flinging the phone against the wall in frustration when the small clock at the bottom of his screen reminded him that maybe these people were not talking to him only because they were asleep.

CHAPTER 27

Downing's house was a gated detached mansion, tucked off quiet leafy St Margaret Street in Hampstead, a neighbourhood Orelius suspected was slightly beyond the means of an average police inspector. Either Downing was into some serious family wealth, or that internal investigation he had mentioned had something to it after all. This stretch featured plush homes with long green hedges and chain-link fences. Some of them had barbed wire in the mix for extra security. People here wore designer suits, drove fifty-thousand-pound cars, and couldn't tell you the price of a loaf of bread. This was the other side of London. Ten per cent of Londoners lived like this.

The gate to number 11 was not locked and Orelius pushed it open hesitantly, half expecting an alarm to go off. He walked down the concrete path, a ten-by-ten-yard square of impeccably trimmed grass and colourful flowers on his left. To his right was a paved marble driveway leading to a locked double garage. A black Mercedes SUV was parked outside the garage.

He pressed the doorbell and heard it chime. But in case that wasn't sufficient, he still went ahead to use the brass knocker and rapped it against the door twice. He noticed a CCTV camera mounted above the door to his right and looked straight into it, to give any prospective watchman a good view.

After about two minutes he saw a shadow moving towards him, and the door was opened by Downing himself.

'Hi, Orelius,' he greeted, tentatively stepping outside the door while still holding it open with his left hand. Then he raised his right hand towards his face and looked at the back of his wrists, miming a non-existent watch. 'A bit late for an announced visit, isn't it?' He smiled, but it was not pleasant.

'I tried calling, but–'

'I know, I know. I've been busy.' He stepped aside, pushed the door fully open and motioned him in.

There was a large hall with a curved staircase leading up immediately to the right. On his left was an open door leading to a kitchen with huge stainless steel appliances, gleaming marble and granite worktops and a large dining set in the middle. Downing led the way through the hallway to a door on the right into the living room. As they entered he noticed that the open door exactly opposite led to a spacious dining room, with another large and probably antique dining set – for the bigger occasions that couldn't be entertained in the kitchen-diner. The living room was all glass and leather furniture, a traditional fireplace, antique canvas paintings, a giant flat-screen with state of the art sound and home cinema systems.

There were two kids in the room, a girl of about twelve or thirteen and a boy slightly younger.

'Kids, say hi to Mr Simm,' Downing called out to them as he pointed him to the middle of the three-seat leather couch. He took the smaller version of the same sofa to Orelius's right. There was a glass coffee table between them, sitting on a furry cream and beige rug.

'Hi, Mr Simm,' they said, almost in unison, getting away from the TV and walking up to shake his hands.

'I'm Hannah,' said the girl, timidly offering her hand.

'Hi, Hannah, nice to meet you.' The girl was tall and slender. She walked on the tips of her toes, as if her heels were incapable of resting on the ground – probably a result of extensive ballet training. 'How old are you, Hannah?'

'Twelve.'

'And what about you, little man?' he asked, thrusting his hands towards the boy.

'Nine,' he said.

'Oh, *nine*... And your name?'

'Connor.' He looked exactly the same as in his picture, although the tooth seemed to have grown back.

'OK, you two are going to have to go and finish watching this upstairs now,' said their father. 'We have to talk in here.'

Another figure appeared at the door just as the children made their exit. She was lean and toned. Her blonde hair fell over her shoulders and curled at the tips. Orelius watched her long legs through the light blue bathrobe as she stalked

CHAPTER 25

Compared to the rest of The Farm, Rochford Block, at five stories high, was relatively low-rise. But it was long on the ground, forming a horseshoe over Nattons Garden east of the estate, opposite Martlesham. After the large ziggurat structure of Tangmere House at the centre, this was probably the next most conspicuous shape on the estate: structures running along the ground like snakes, turning sharply and running a bit more, before turning again the same way, as though out of track.

A small group huddled around the underdeveloped foetus on the floor on Rochford's first-floor walkway. They had watched Orelius use a stick to nudge it out of a small crease in the corner, where the two monstrous blocks of Rochford intersected. It had been wedged in there alongside cigarette packets, used syringes and dirty knickers.

'Guess you will want to do something about this,' Orelius finally said to Downing. Everyone else had decided that their shock would be expressed in gasps, wide eyes and open mouths, not words.

Downing unhooked the radio from his waist and clicked it on. Then he started pacing up and down the walkway speaking quietly as if to himself.

gracefully into the room like a peacock. And he decided that, despite the SUVs and giant plasma screens, this right here was the biggest proof that God loved D.I. Gregg Downing.

'Hi,' she said.

'Orelius, this is my wife, Joanna,' Downing intervened before he could reply. 'Joanna, this is Orelius.'

'Hi, Joanna, nice to meet you.'

'You too. I've heard a bit a about you.'

'Really?' He sensed some discomfort from Downing, and assumed that the 'bit' his wife knew about was not his best bit. 'Well I feel honoured you've heard about me at all. Beautiful home you have here.'

'Thank you. What would you like to drink? Coffee, tea or something stronger?' She had a loveable chirpy voice and, like her husband, was highly articulate. The detective's wife was no doubt a highflying professional too, which would explain how they could afford to live like this.

'Just some water will do, thank you, Mrs Downing.'

'OK,' she said. Then, just before disappearing round the corridor, she poked her head back through the door and added, 'You can call me Joanna, by the way.'

She was back almost immediately with two bottles of water and two glasses with ice. She set them neatly in the middle of the coffee table without another word.

'How are things going?' Downing finally said after a bit of uncomfortable chit-chat. 'How's Timmy's mother holding up?'

'Things are not going well, Gregg. Not at all. That is why I'm here.'

It was the Monday following Downing's withdrawal from the Ear-Slasher case, and it was still unclear whether that line of inquiry was still officially active. Nonetheless, the search for Timmy Lewis was still on, and there had been bursts of police activity around The Farm; but Orelius had had only twice spoken to the officer in charge, a small balding inspector named Keith Garret.

'Well, my situation is exactly the same as when we last spoke,' Downing said. 'I'm back to my usual role now at the White Collar Crimes unit. I haven't got any connections to the Dudlham cases anymore, and there is very little I can do to help in that regard.'

'I don't know anyone else who can.'

'I gave you the new contacts. Have you tried talking to Keith yet?'

'Keith hasn't got the first clue about Dudlham Farm.'

Keith Garret was the same rank as Downing, but that was where the similarity ended. Their looks, mannerisms and investigative methods were completely different. Orelius had first met him on Saturday afternoon, when the officer came in to see Nikisha at the hospital – and hated him immediately. The stumpy detective had answered all their questions with standard formal statements; it was all *our allocated manpower... our strategy... we are pursuing...* There was a ring of pomposity around Keith Garret that made him almost unapproachable.

Downing took his time, as if giving Orelius's statement a serious thought.

'There are people you can talk to about this,' the detective finally said. 'As you know, I'm just a white collar DI, I've never worked violent crimes. Heck, before last week I'd never even been to Dudlham Farm.'

'Neither have any other police officers. The uniforms we've seen down there recently are just going through the motions, they don't really believe they are going to find Timmy,' said Orelius. 'This case is probably going to be abandoned like all the others on the estate.' He paused and lifted the glass of water to his mouth. Then he put it back down without taking a sip. 'I need just one more favour from you, Gregg. I think I've figured out what's going on here but I need your help.'

'We've gone through all this before. We followed all your theories and half theories and they led us nowhere–'

'One more, Gregg. Just listen to me one more time.'

'But why me? I can't help you now. This is someone else's case, why me?'

‘Because you walked with me through Dudlham Farm and saw what it is really like. You saw Isaacs’s body hanging off his belt after a lifetime of heartbreak from being let down by authority. You saw what life in Dudlham Farm did to Shola King and Kelly-Jo Pretty.’

‘This is not fair,’ Downing hissed in frustration. ‘It’s is not fair for you to lay all this guilt on me. I haven’t done anything wrong. I have a family who rely on me, and to fulfil my duties as a parent I have to keep my job. To keep my job I have to toe the line drawn by my employers. What you are asking me, Orelius, is to help you with something that goes against my current terms of employment.’

‘Can you drop the formal talk, please? You are beginning to sound like Garret. Come on, man... this is you and me. You wore jeans and a cheap T-shirt and drove an old Corsa to tour the Farm with me. You ate lunch at The Jolly Farmer. I’m here to ask for your help as a man who may be the only cop in the country who really appreciates what we are dealing with here. You are a Scotland Yard inspector, Gregg. There must be something you can do for me.’

‘Yes, I work for Scotland Yard, and yes I am a detective inspector. But my area of expertise is not–’

‘Oh, OK, don’t worry about it,’ Orelius snapped. ‘You’ve explained it all before: you only solve white-collar crimes. You don’t get your hands dirty. My fault, I forgot.’ Orelius spat the words out. 'How can you sit there and talk about chasing after stock-market gamblers when a dying ten-year-old is begging for your help?' He paused, but not for long enough to allow a response. Then he spread his arms wide to indicate the magnificence of the surroundings and said, 'Well, I suppose if that is the job that helps you keep up this lifestyle... then maybe you've got your priorities right.'

Downing grunted, then opened his mouth to say something but thought better of it.

'You know, I'm not really sure what it is you do in this white-collar business,' Orelius picked up again, now with a trace of sarcasm. 'But it sure does pay well. I hope you feel proud when you walk down the streets and see all the difference your work makes to the average man.'

The detective began shaking his head slowly, and a dry, derisive chuckle escaped his lips. 'If I were you, Simm, I would be very careful before questioning the integrity of any profession. Sure, I spend my life hunting relatively harmless upper-class folks. I know I'm not exactly saving the world, but I make an honest living putting away dishonest people. You, on the other hand...' He pointed that same index finger towards his face, the one he'd threatened him with outside Anita Ahmed's. He kept it shaking in the air before letting it drop. 'Well, maybe you should remind me one more time what you do for a living, Simm?'

There was silence in the room as they eyed each other, then dropped their gazes almost simultaneously to their barely touched glasses on the table.

A small head popped through the door to rescue them from the simmering tension.

'Dad, can I read some Harry Potter?'

'Not after your dinner, Connor. You know that,' he said without raising his head to look at his son. 'You can go on the PlayStation for half-hour, then I'm coming to tuck you in.'

'OK,' the small voice said, without any further pleas or protests. As if he had expected this, and the whole trip down the stairs to receive the confirmation was the real adventure.

The two men waited in silence, listening to Connor's light footsteps disappear up the stairs.

'Aha... so reading is before dinner. PlayStation is after dinner,' Orelius said dispassionately, like the preceding exchange had never taken place. 'Very interesting. I suppose there is some logic behind this.'

Downing stared at him suspiciously, unable to fathom this sudden change of mood.

'They are just rules, Orelius. My wife makes them and I enforce them.' He leaned across to peer outside the door, making sure they didn't have an unwanted audience. Then he lowered his voice. 'Between you and me...' he edged forwards excitedly now that they were conspirators '...some of these rules don't make sense.'

Orelius looked up, slightly bemused, and caught the detective's eye.

His voice was slowly picking up enthusiasm. 'I tried questioning these so-called rules once, and Joanna was not impressed. She looked at me with this baffled expression, as if I was a child myself, and said...' he mimicked his wife's voice poorly, with exaggerated feminism: 'Never, ever question the rules, Gregg. We have to present a united front. These are kids and they have to have rules. Otherwise they will grow up running riot and eventually overthrow us in our own home.'

'Wow, I'm impressed. You are running a military regime here.'

'Apparently.' Downing snorted a laugh.

The laugh quickly infected Orelius, and they both descended into fits of suppressed cackling. The schoolboy giggles continued a little too long, outlasting the flavour of the joke. But they eventually came to an end, and the uneasy silence returned to capture the sweet lavender-scented air in the room.

'What exactly do you want, Orelius?' the detective finally asked.

'Listen, Gregg, I know what you think about my amateur detective work so far. I know I've only got emotions and not facts to go on. But I think I've finally figured this whole thing out and I need help.'

'How? What can I do that Keith and his team can't?'

'This goes back to the mysterious ears, where it all started. I think I've found the link between Timmy and the ears.'

'So, what's this link you've found?'

'I need to see those ears; that's how I want you to help me. Then I will sit down with you and tell you the whole story.'

'You want to see them?'

'Yes. I presume they will be in some police lab somewhere, and that you can arrange for me to physically have a look at them.'

Downing gave him a bewildered shake of the head, as if he was speaking a strange language. 'Why?'

'Just arrange for us to go and see the ears. I need to see and touch them, just for a minute. If I'm wrong, I will keep my stupid theory to myself and save us both any embarrassment. And I will not bother you again, Gregg.'

The detective took his time and made a good show of giving this proper consideration from all angles. But Orelius could already tell that he wanted to help.

'I'm not promising anything,' he said eventually. 'I will talk to some people first thing tomorrow and get back to you. This had better be good, Orelius. I really am pushing the boundaries this time.'

CHAPTER 28

They were outside the gates of the Forensic Science Service Laboratory in Lambeth before eleven the following morning. The building was enormous along the ground but only four stories high, with chimney-like extensions sticking up from the roof. Its exterior was dominated by clear glass windows that reminded Orelius of the campus blocks at his old university in Manchester. A concrete pillar inscribed with a big silver number – 109 – stood off its façade like a monument.

The detective appeared stressed and there had been little conversation during the journey. The forty-minute drive from North London had been made in the shiny black Mercedes SUV he had seen parked on Downing's drive the night before. He had asked him what happened to the Corsa and the detective had mumbled something about getting rid of it. Orelius had then joked that he preferred the Corsa, and got no response, not even a smile. Apparently Downing's superiors were not impressed by his continuing interference in Keith Garret's case, and the pressure was telling. Orelius prayed that his suspicions were right this time. This man had certainly tried his best for him.

One of the uniformed guards at the gate approached their car and asked two short questions. He wanted to know who they were here to see and have a look at their IDs. Then he walked back to his booth and they saw him pick up a phone receiver through the huge windows.

A grey-haired man in clean white scrubs arrived at the gates within five minutes and the guard finally opened up to let them inside the facility. The older man walked behind their car and waited for them to park, then approached and introduced himself as Dr Josh Kimble. He proceeded to lead them through a series of dimly lit corridors to an elevator that dropped them to the basement and more dark corridors.

'Big place, uh?' Orelius mumbled, to break the eerie silence as they went past rows of pull-out freezers that he assumed contained dead bodies.

'Indeed. But the recession and government spending cuts have hit us too. We won't be here much longer,' replied the doctor. 'They have decided to disband the Forensic Science Service and share out its duties between the Met's own labs and the private sector.

'Oh. When does this take effect?'

'The FSS stops serving in about two month's time. The full change should be complete before the end of the year. Some of us will effectively end up working for the Met Police and the others will have to try their luck in the private sector,' he said. Then in a quiet mournful voice, he added, 'I've been working here for thirty-five years.'

Even this immensely experienced man's future was uncertain. Orelius didn't know what to say.

'That's terrible,' Downing offered, shaking his head earnestly, as though this was news to him too.

They got to a locked door at the end of the hallway and the old man tapped lightly on it. It swung open almost immediately and two figures in white lab coats appeared. One, a bespectacled middle-aged woman, was clutching a clipboard against her chest with her left hand. The other was a young man with a permanent, somewhat nervous smile plastered over his face. Kimble introduced them as doctors Doreen Swift and Chris Forrest. Their credentials were provided so quickly and in terms so technical that the most Orelius could gleam was that at least one of them had something to do with the justice department, and that they had to be here for Orelius to be here.

'These two will come in with us as witnesses,' Dr Kimble explained while they were still standing outside the door. 'On top of that, everything will be recorded by our cameras and we will keep your time in there to a minimum. You asked for a minute, we will give you exactly two. I'll start my timer as soon as we enter the room.

'As far as we are concerned...' he indicated Orelius with a nod in his direction '... this gentleman here is an expert and you believe he can provide some useful input for your case. So we had to find a way of helping you without compromising anything.' He stated this purposefully, all business. The old man who had been bemoaning his uncertain future a couple of minutes ago was gone. 'It's mainly for your benefit, detective. This is the Met's case, after all. Now, if you step inside we will give you some protective lab gear to wear, then we are good to go.'

Five minutes later they were all outside another door barely ten yards away, on the opposite side of the hallway. Dr Kimble punched in a code to let them into what looked like an operating theatre.

On a shiny silver tray in the middle of an operating table lay five human ears. They were arranged neatly, in an almost perfect pentagon.

'There you are, Detective,' said the doctor, spreading his arms towards the table. Then he raised the back of his left hand, flicked a button on his wristwatch, and announced, 'Your time starts now.'

Both Orelius and Downing looked solemnly at the human body parts without saying anything. Then the detective turned towards Orelius and shot him a sharp glare that spoke his thoughts: *You better be onto something with this, mate.*

Orelius stepped forward, right to the edge of the table.

'May I... touch?' he asked looking back at Dr Kimble.

'Go ahead, you've got your gloves on.'

He picked the one at the top of the pentagon and saw Downing flinch as he gently pinched the flaccid earlobe between his thumb and forefinger and pulled it down to straighten the wrinkles. Then he lifted it up against the light for closer inspection. The detective folded his arms across his chest, trying to look unimpressed. Doreen Swift held on tightly to her clipboard and kept her focus. Chris Forrest appeared to be smiling.

Dr Kimble glanced at his watch again and said, 'One minute.'

'Don't worry, I think I've seen enough,' Orelius said, placing the specimen back on the tray.

'OK, let's all step outside. We can talk in my office if you wish.'

They used the same room down the hall to strip off the protective lab-wear, then Dr Kimble asked Orelius and the detective to head back upstairs with him. This return journey was made via the stairs which offered even more time for their silence to be ominous. But Orelius's mind was too preoccupied to notice. The fantastic figment of his imagination he had conceived in the middle of the night was on the edge of being the truth.

'Will you just give us a minute, sir,' Downing said when they stopped outside the doctor's office. He waved an apologetic hand towards the doctor and drew Orelius to one side. 'We may need to have a private word or two before we come back in and see you.'

'Sure, go ahead. I'll be right here.' He pointed them to a long, curved sofa that formed a semi-circle in front of the reception area at the end of the hallway. 'You can sit there and talk. It's normally quiet enough.'

The reception area was deserted and quiet, as promised. Orelius took a seat. The detective once again folded his hands across his chest and remained standing, his foreboding eyes hovering above Orelius like a hawk.

'You said all kinds of tests have been conducted on those ears,' Orelius started. 'They determined the approximate age of the people they came from and how long they'd been severed from their bodies.'

The detective kept his arms tucked and waited for a direct question.

'Is that right, Gregg?'

'That sounds correct, Orelius. I believe all those tests have been conducted.'

'The DNA matched nothing on the existing database?'

'No, there were no matches, but the database is not exhaustive. It only contains records of those arrested since the system came into place.'

'That idea... the one about a black serial killer targeting white kids, was that ever an official working theory by the police, or was it just a media gimmick?'

'Well, it would be a pretty easy assumption on the media's part, considering the circumstances,' the detective said curtly, and Orelius knew he was deliberately being vague, still trying to gauge where he was going with this.

'That was a big mistake, Gregg: that assumption.'

Downing arched his eyebrows and contorted his face in confusion. 'What are you talking about?'

'I'm saying that you have been trying to look for the people from whom those ears came. And you have all along assumed they were white kids.'

'What, you think they are not kids?'

'Oh yes, they looked like young human ears alright,' Orelius said, inching forward to the edge of his seat and glancing up at the detective. 'But, Gregg, all those ears belong to black people.'

The detective shifted his arms from across his chest and let them hang at his sides. He made a grunting sound but said nothing.

'Do you know what I was looking for when I picked one of them up and held it against the light?'

'I take it you were looking at the small indentation on the earlobe.'

'Yes, a piercing, on all of them. How come this was never mentioned in your reports?'

Downing shrugged again, 'We always hold something back. And we didn't see how this detail would have been important for the public appeal. If someone's had their ears chopped off, or knew of someone who had, they would surely come up and say something. The tiny piercing is a detail that makes no difference in that respect.'

'But they've all got the same piercing, and the holes don't look that tiny to me.'

'The ears were found tied together and looped with a string through those holes. We figured the perpetrator made the piercing after chopping the ears off so he could make some kind of twisted charm necklace with it. As a trophy.'

'Well that is one theory. But you all missed a very important point.'

'Enough with the cryptic clues, Orelius, spell it out. I ought to be back in my office.' He gave his wristwatch a glance to illustrate his urgency.

'There is this small African country known as Burundi, I don't know if you've ever heard of it...'

'Yes, I know where Burundi is. There was a massive genocide there in the early nineties.'

'That's correct, more than two million were killed, there and in neighbouring Rwanda. The world sat and watched–'

'Like I said, most people already know that bit.' Downing cut him short, trying to steer him back on track.

'There is a small commune in south-east Burundi known as Musongati. The Musongatis pierce the ears of their young boys as a right of passage at the age of five or six. They then gradually put various charm earrings on them, symbolising different cultural milestones as the boys grow up. At some stage the rings get slightly heavy on the ears and start stretching them, making the holes wider.'

He watched Downing's eyes widen.

'Yes, Gregg,' he said in response to the detective's unasked question. 'I think all those ears belong to young boys from the Musongati tribe in Burundi.'

Downing shook his head rapidly, as if he had just been slapped. 'You have been doing a bit too much thinking, Orelius.'

'You extracted their DNA and checked with the database,' he continued, ignoring Downing's remark. 'There was a widespread public appeal that lasted more than a week and nothing turned up. Doesn't that suggest that these people might not belong in this country?'

'Well... Well... But this cannot be right. Those ears look pretty white to me.'

'They do indeed, which brings me to my next point. Ever heard of albinos?'

'They did all kinds of tests on these ears... DNA and other tests to determine age of the victims... but I bet their race was presumed just by looking at them. Because that, as you said, was obvious: they looked white, and finding out exactly who they were would be the logical next step. Am I right here?'

'Ethnicity is one of the first factors they establish.'

'That sounds like a general statement, Gregg. Listen, my knowledge of police procedure is restricted to what I see on TV; when they find a dead body, they are on their radios describing it as a *Caucasian male* before even touching it, because these are things you can determine just by looking. So you tell me, is it possible that sometimes a test to determine something like this may be overlooked? I understand these things are handled by professionals with standards, but they are still human.'

'I know what you are suggesting here, and I can tell you that it is simply absurd... of course they would have checked.'

'They would have checked? Or they did check? Did you see anything in the file confirming the test?'

'Of course,' the detective fired back automatically. Then he hesitated for a beat before proceeding somewhat cautiously. 'They must have checked that, surely.'

'So you didn't see anything specific in the files.'

'I don't remember, but I'm sure there was something.'

'Well, I could wait for you to go and confirm the facts before I continue with what I've got to say. Otherwise I will just look like an idiot.'

'OK, Orelius, I will go with you for now. Let's say no one saw the need to check their race – so what?'

'Do you remember the story in the news a few months back about a British charity worker from London who was killed in Burundi and his body parts chopped into small pieces?'

Downing nodded, looking even more confused. 'Don't tell me you think that has something to do with this.'

'I think it does, Gregg. Because that man... his name was Bill Tierney by the way... his body parts were left outside the British consulate in a sack, like some kind of message. Bill Tierney had gone to take up charity work in Burundi after losing his wife, family and all his wealth in a bitter divorce. He took up coaching soccer with some local boys while he was out there, and was allegedly killed by his own players.' He allowed a few seconds for that to be digested before hitting Downing with the bombshell. 'It just so happens that his entire team, The Butterfly Wanderers, was made up of albinos.'

Downing ruffled the hairs on the back of his head vigorously, trying to think. 'Are you saying that someone murdered some albinos in Burundi in retaliation, and sent their body parts here to make some kind of statement?'

'That could be one theory. I've got another one that might sound better after we have confirmed the identity of these ears. I'm sure you will at least agree with me that if they do indeed belong to African albinos, then there is a connection with Bill Tierney. A white Londoner having his body hacked up by albinos, then albino body parts suddenly appearing in a London estate full of Africans two months later is too much of a coincidence.'

'Right,' Downing said absently, finally slumping onto the chair to Orelius's right, as if this was too much to take standing up. 'How does this connect to Timmy then?'

But before Orelius opened his mouth to reply, he saw that the detective had already worked it out.

'Yup, you guessed it,' he nodded. 'MJ's cousin Jordan said it first but we missed it that time. Then last night as I was trying to sleep those words came back and started bugging me: 'Albino Tim'. I've heard him called so many things, but not albino. In fact albino is not a term I hear often, but it suddenly strikes me that I have heard it on another occasion recently. Turns out it was in the news about a month ago, and guess what, it involved body parts. After this I can't sleep, so I go on Google and enter the words *Albino + Body Parts*. And the answers are right there. Just to check that I wasn't going crazy I also spoke to an old friend of mine from college who comes from that part of the world.

'I believe Timmy has been caught up in a tribal ritual, Gregg. Someone somewhere must have thought he really was albino.'

'I can't believe I'm beginning to buy into this.'

'You are the one who put that picture of Timmy side by side with your son's and showed me how easy it would be for an unsuspecting eye to misread Timmy's race. I don't think of him as anything but a mixed race boy, but that's only because I'm aware of his black heritage. Timmy suffered a severe case of Vitiligo disease a couple of years ago–'

'Viti...?'

'It's a disorder that reduces the production of melanin, which is responsible for skin pigmentation. It can affect anyone; black, white, young, old... and it is treatable. Anyway, Timmy had it, and even though he was able to regain some colour with just a course of anti-inflammatory drugs, his situation is particularly tricky because he is already a mixed race kid who inherited most of his skin-colour genes from his white father.

'Now, consider a stranger watching this white-skinned boy with almost no colour in the hair or eyes. He sees him being picked up from school by a mother as dark as charcoal. It would be very easy for this stranger to assume albinism.'

'You think this was someone from Timmy's school?'

'I don't know. I was only giving an example.'

'Oh,' the detective muttered wearily, too tired to protest.

‘All we need is to confirm that these are albino ears, Gregg. Then everything else falls in place. I know I’m right.’

Downing rested his forehead on both hands and closed his eyes, ‘Give me a few seconds, Orelius.’

‘Actually, we don’t even need to wait for that confirmation. We’ve got Dr Kimble here, haven’t we? Go in there now and ask him if a test was conducted for race. If it wasn’t, tell him to make a quick assessment and give you his opinion on my theory.’

Downing shot up from his chair and started walking towards the doctor’s office without another word. Orelius shifted to the other end of his sofa so he could watch them through Dr Kimble’s huge glass windows. He could clearly see them talking for about ten minutes. At one point the doctor got off his chair and stood still, with his right hand on the desk and his face down. He stayed in this position for about thirty seconds, as if thinking deeply, then went back to his chair and carried on their animated chat. Then the detective got up and left the office, closing the door quietly behind him.

He beckoned for Orelius to follow, and breezed through the double doors without breaking stride. Orelius followed him back towards the car park.

‘DNA racial profiling is still relatively new, expensive and somewhat controversial. So there’s a prevailing unofficial logic that if you don’t need to go that far, you don’t,’ he said once they got into the car. 'The ears looked white and they weren't looking for anyone in particular, so no one saw the need to go there.' He didn't start the car, just sat there, stroking his chin. 'I still don't understand how you came up with this, but he seems to think your theory is plausible. They will carry out a routine check and get back to me.'

Orelius said nothing.

'If you are right...' he started.

'If I'm right, we start everything afresh because now we know what we are looking for. You can put pressure on and help get a good team out to The Farm. We need to knock on doors with new questions.'

'No, we can't do that. We wouldn't want to storm The Farm with more uniforms giving away our new discoveries. The perpetrator will know we are on him before we are done with the first block. And if he's still got Timmy he might panic and...' He stopped, unable to say the words, and shrugged. 'What I'm saying is, this time, each and every one of our steps has to be calculated. We have to fully understand everything.'

'So what are we going to do?'

'If it turns out that you are right, Orelius, we will keep the new facts secret; tightly guarded under lock and key. Because this is our only weapon against the perpetrator: he doesn't know that we know. Then what we are going to do is get on the next available flight to Burundi. We have to get the full picture, gather all the facts and identify our suspect, if we can, before releasing this new discovery to anyone except those who really need to know.'

'We...? Did you say *we* are going to Burundi?'

'I never wanted to leave this case. You know that, Orelius. If we establish everything, I can go back to my bosses with a solid theory and ask to be put back on the case.'

Orelius nodded. 'OK, I just thought... well, when you said *we*, I thought you meant you could maybe arrange for me to be there as well.'

'I can try that too, but it wouldn't be easy. I'd have to convince them that you can help us with something in Africa that none of our experts can.'

'I need to be there.'

'Me too, Orelius. Me too,' he whispered solemnly, as if to himself. 'This case has affected me like no other in my career. I have found it hard to sleep since I saw Kelly-Jo's face after we told her we had found her mother buried in that pit after twenty-six years. And I can't get Markus Isaacs's dead body hanging off a sooty kitchen beam out of my head. I think I'm losing it. A week ago I was a happy father who couldn't wait to go home and be entertained by my family. Now I look at my wife and I can't stop thinking about Nikisha Lewis's loneliness in that hospital bed, waiting for the only person in this world who has ever loved her. I look at Connor, and I see Timmy

Lewis's terrified face begging for help.' He paused and swallowed the lump that was beginning to clog his throat. 'I want to look at my kids again, Orelius. I want to sleep again.'

BOOK THREE

The Butterfly Wanderers

CHAPTER 29

The incredible life of Jean-Baptiste Nimbona

I come from Gitaramuka, a small village in the Musongati commune in the Southeastern province of Rutana in Burundi. I was born here, I live here, and I will die here. But all I have left of Gitaramuka now are memories. My life now does not extend beyond this overgrown hedge around my homestead. I remember the days I used to watch the sun set upon the lofty green hills as I rushed home from school. The beauty of our small village could take my breath away. Some said that somewhere beyond those hills was another great country, Tanzania, but that was too much for our young minds to comprehend. It was hard to imagine a whole other civilisation out there. Gitaramuka was our universe.

I remember my friends from school. I remember Sylvestre, Jean Pierre, Louis and Cyprien. I remember the day Cyprien became my best friend. When he shared with me the cold boiled potato his mother had treated him to for being good with his household chores, and when he walked with me the daily five-mile round trip to and from school. I remember the day Cyprien invited me to their home, how his many parents and grandparents and uncles and cousins rejoiced at the sight of a guest, their son's best friend. How the small group of relatives gathered around the grass-thatched hut into which I was hosted. I remember the murmured conversations from the main room as I sat in the small windowless barn at the back of the hut with the door locked from outside. I remember being slightly concerned by the darkness in the barn. Because in that darkness, I could only hear the chirping of bats and rats and smell rotting flesh. I remember feeling rattled by the hushed conversations from the main room. Because in those quiet conversations, they were thanking their son for bringing them a special guest to solve their problems. I remember starting to cry when Cyprien's father began to say a prayer; because in that prayer, he was thanking the Lord for bringing them food.

I have got a hyena to thank for my life. As I waited for the door to open, gripped with terror, I realised that the pungent smell of rotting flesh in the barn was coming from the mounds of goats' heads lying next to me. The coming together of rotting flesh and hyena: it saved my life. When the ugly spotted beast came tearing into the barn, the bamboo door smashed and fell on my head, and I came face to face with it: a red-eyed hyena slowly smacking its black lips over a monstrous set of fangs. But I swear the animal looked more shocked than I was to find me in the barn. I looked beyond its rapidly drooping tail and saw, deep in the horizon, the sun setting upon the lofty hills of Gitaramuka. I realised at that moment that this animal was not the enemy. It was a friend, sent by God to free me. My left foot brushed its ears as I jumped up high, stretched my feet and let the wind carry me home.

The one time I looked back, I saw the hyena's head buried in the stacks of rotting goats' heads under the ruins of the barn.

This was two years ago, and I haven't been back to school since. I have in fact not ventured alone beyond the confines of my homestead. But I am happy. That I'm here today is testament to God's great miracles. Nithia Niyonkuru was not so lucky when her second uncle took her from her grandparents promising her a job in the capital, only to sell her to a witchdoctor in Bujumbura. Her severed head was found buried in a rich man's living room; to protect his wealth. Anatole Nkomerwa of Bukemba was not so lucky when his science teacher took him to his home, chopped his body into little pieces and sold the parts to different people around Rutana; to bring them good luck. I speak for Nithia, Anatole and many other children like me all over Burundi and Tanzania who did not make it.

My name is Jean-Baptiste Nimbona. I am twelve years old, and this is my life; because I am an albino.

*

'This is incredible,' Greg Downing whispered, wiping a bead of sweat off his forehead with a handkerchief.

Everyone else remained silent. Most of them seemed to be sweating even though it was still before ten o'clock in the morning.

'Why do they do this?' he asked, and he knew the question sounded hollow. All the conversations were being conducted through Mfura, their Burundian translator, who was also a policeman.

Mfura answered this one himself. 'It's a sacrifice: for peace, rain, good luck, wealth, or even to give babies to mothers who can't have children. It's a common belief that albino body parts have magical powers, that they can solve any problem.'

'Incredible,' Downing repeated.

Aside from Jean-Baptiste and his large family, a group of no less than nine outsiders had gathered around the ancient table in the small single room of a grass-thatched hut, to listen to the boy's horrific tale. Matt Mansford, the deputy UK ambassador to Burundi, had brought with him two military attachés from the British embassy office in the capital, Bujumbura, along with a female MI6 agent named Michelle Ryan. Michelle was the only female in the group, a blue-eyed brunette, nearly six foot tall and exhibiting all the signs of a woman who could handle herself. With the local embassy having no MI6 presence, agent Ryan had been summoned from neighbouring Kenya. She would report anything worth noting from this tour back to her superior in Kenya, who would then add it to their East Africa files and send it to London. Who knew, maybe one day such information would become useful for the security of the good British people. They called it Intelligence.

There were also two local male police officers. One of them, Luca, had doubled as the driver of their minibus for the three-hour journey to this remote village in the south-east. The other was Mfura, the translator.

The final group consisted of Gregg Downing's contingent from London. This included only two others: Keith Garret, the lead detective in the Timmy Lewis case, and a young black man ambiguously described as an African-British crime consultant. Downing had made up this title and gone to great lengths to sell it to his superiors so that Orelius Simm, a well known thug from Dudlham, could make this journey at British taxpayers' expense.

'So you never played football for Coach Tierney, then. Did you know about his team?' This came from Mansford, and Downing thought it a silly question. They all knew this kid never even left his house after the incident. Jean-Baptiste himself had said it: he was a prisoner in his home.

The boy shook his head.

Although Jean-Baptiste's skin colour was not too dissimilar to Downing's own, there was something about his build that distinguished him as a person of African origin. His hair was thin, and cream-white. The skin was blemished with red inflammations, probably from mosquito bites and other rough conditions of rural Africa not suited to a white skin. He had a wide nose and there was a bump above his right eye, as though he had taken a punch up there recently.

They had learnt that The Butterfly Wanderers was a term used in this region to refer to all albinos and not just Bill Tierney's team. Jean Baptiste Nimbona was the last of the Butterfly Wanderers in this village. A year ago, Coach Tierney had managed to find fifteen albino boys of the right age to build a junior football team. By the time he died, two months ago, there were only ten left. They had been hunted down one by one, despite Tierney's efforts to stop this horrific ritual. And in the end the pain became too much for him to bear. Of the ten members of the team Coach Tierney left behind, only four were alive now. And that was only because they were safely locked up in a maximum security prison in Bujumbura. They were all serving life sentences for the murder of their coach.

'Can't you move away somewhere safer, maybe to the capital?'

Again Mfura answered this without relaying it to his intended target. 'This isn't England, Detective. You can't just uproot your family and plant them somewhere else. People belong where they belong; this is their ancestors' land, and so will it be their children's and great-grandchildren's.'

He looked over at Orelius, who had remained a subdued figure in the background since they landed in Burundi. His silence suited Downing fine: unlike The Farm, this was not his territory. This group was filled with senior government officers who were better served if Orelius's real identity remained secret and his role in this mission vague. There was an odd spot or two of perspiration on the Dudlham Farm crime lord's brown skin, but the early morning heat didn't seem to bother him. He remained still and emotionless, letting everyone else ask the questions.

'We are going to talk to this man and probably arrest him. What I want to know now is where does that leave you in terms of your and your family's safety?' Downing asked the old woman who was Jean-Baptiste's mother. The potential fallout from their actions in this village was an issue that could not be ignored. Jean-Baptiste had never been safe. They all knew this because they had interviewed the four prisoners in Bujumbura a few hours after they landed. They now knew everything they needed to know about the Tierney case; their stopover at the Nimbona homestead was just a courtesy. Their main mission in the village was to talk to a witchdoctor whom they hoped would explain how albino body parts ended up in London.

The woman didn't seem to get his question, so he tried to clarify, 'Do you think you'll be any safer after this man is gone? Is there anything we can do to help?'

Mfura listened to her attentively, then relayed the answer back to all the visitors, 'Taking away the *umupfumu* is not going to make us any safer. If the rains fail this season and the drought hits, everyone gets desperate. These witchdoctors need body parts for their rituals but they don't usually snatch the children themselves. The people who require these rituals bring in the albinos. And when times are bad and everyone is desperate for a miracle, that person could be my next door neighbour or even my brother.'

Umupfumu was the local language, Kirundi, term for witchdoctor, *wamupfumu* being its plural form. So significant was their role in this community that they were also commonly referred to just as *Muganga* (Doctor).

Downing put his hands on his head and kept his face down. He stayed in the same position for a whole minute. Less than two weeks ago he was a happy father of two with a lovely wife and a secure home. He worked for a living and paid his taxes. He was a noble God-fearing man trying to bring his children up to be good citizens of the world. Why had he been picked for this journey into the mire of everything that was wrong with this world?

He must have drifted into a trance because a sharp voice from somewhere roused him with a start.

‘Maybe should get moving now.’ It was Michelle Ryan, sitting across from him. ‘I can’t wait to have a chat with this *umupfumu*.’

*

They drove down a series of dirt paths, with overhanging branches constantly scratching the body of their minibus. About three miles from the Nimbonas, they came to a riverbank and the drive came to an end. They left the driver and one of the security attachés from the capital in the bus to guard it; the rest crossed the river via a flimsy footbridge and started walking through a seemingly endless plantation of sugar cane.

The African contingent – Mansford, his remaining military man and Michelle Ryan – soon struck up a conversation about politics on this continent. Most of their chitchat inevitably centred on corruption, with each sharing funny anecdotes based on personal experiences with corrupt governments. Downing tried to do the same with Keith, thinking that two Scotland Yard detectives would surely have enough interesting stories to relive while tackling an African jungle. But he soon realised this wasn’t going to work: Keith Garret measured all his words carefully, as though he was being assessed, and he wouldn’t stop referring to him as ‘Sir’ or ‘Inspector’. He tried instead to inquire about Orelius, and the Dudlham mafia don grunted that he was fine and killed the conversation right there. Mfura, the local police officer, was nice, but his grasp of

English, while decent enough for translation duties, was just a bit slender for fun banter.

In the end, to accompany his arduous trek through the jungle of a little known African country, Downing was left only with the haunting thoughts of the heartbreaking discoveries they had made since landing here yesterday.

*

'Is anyone out there aware of this practice?' he had asked Matt Mansford in Bujumbura, on their way to interviewing the imprisoned Butterfly Wanderers. 'Surely the world must know.'

'We know it happens; there was a fairly well publicised case in Tanzania when someone smuggled a Kenyan albino in and tried to sell him,' replied Mansford. 'It's especially bad on Zanzibar. That's because they have a greater population of albinos. A few lesser-known charities have tried making some noise but I don't think it makes any impact. You have to consider that the local governments are constitute mainly of people who share the same beliefs.'

'And what is the world doing about it? I mean, I, for instance, watch the news every day. They do regular features on Africa, talk about corruption, tribalism, AIDS... but I've never heard a word about this.'

'I would be lying if I told you that the UN or any other such organisation is looking at this situation. We are aware of it but no one knows the full extent of the crimes related to it. You have to remember we sit in the best office available in Bujumbura and work only on information and intelligence that we deem pertinent to the security of the UK and any British citizen who happen to be here in Burundi. Our job here is to protect the British interest. And same goes for the Americans, the Germans, the French... everyone is just looking after themselves.'

'This is a travesty. We are busy invading Iraq, Afghanistan and Libya, trying to install democracy, and we don't care about this?'

Mansford sighed. 'You are asking the wrong man, Inspector. I'm here to serve the British interest.'

'And I have no doubt you've done that to your best ability, but look where it has led us. I heard President Obama say some time back that if your neighbour's house catches fire, you help put it out, not necessarily because you care about your neighbour, but because you know that sooner or later that fire is bound to spread to your own house,' said Downing. 'I couldn't think of a better analogy. Now these people's sins have found their way to our doorstep. The body-parts business is thriving right in the centre of London. And of course Bill Tierney was a British citizen. So maybe you would like to reconsider your definition of *the British interest*.'

'We are going to give you all the assistance we can, Inspector.' The diplomat didn't seem to have taken Downing's onslaught personally. 'First we are going to interview those football kids again and get to the bottom of what happened to Bill Tierney. If he killed himself as a sacrifice to save a persecuted race, we will accord his memory the honour he deserves and set the kids free. We will take full responsibility for anything we overlooked with regard to Tierney. The body-parts thing, however... that is a case that began in London, and it is your job, Inspector Downing. All we can do is support you while you are down here, and keep you safe.'

They had been granted access to the prisoners within three hours. The four footballers were all on lockdown at the Mpimba maximum security prison in Bujumbura. Downing had conducted the interviews in the presence of an international lawyer provided by the British mission, and a representative from the local prosecution service.

All the kids had told the same story: the coach had left a note in a sealed envelope with Sylvie, the team captain, asking him to open it on the day before their next game. The boy did as directed, only to find out that it was a suicide note with instructions on what to do with the coach's body. Sylvie had then gathered three other members of the team and they had gone over to Tierney's lodge in Musongati, where they found his body hanging off the roof. And they had all been in tears as they dismembered his body parts to mimic the horrific local rituals, as per his final request. All four had travelled to Rutana with

Tierney's body parts in a sack, and dropped it outside the British consulate. Somebody would question why this happened to a British citizen. Then maybe someone with enough power would realise that there is a secluded jungle somewhere within their world, where this is common practice.

As young as these kids were, they had known that their actions could condemn them to life in prison; but considering what else was awaiting them out there, this was not the worst option. The suicide note was supposed to be their defence: in it the coach explained that the police would analyse his handwriting and believe their story. He had also warned of the risks. In case it all went wrong and the authorities didn't buy it, it would be life in prison. But there could never be a worthier course to die for; they would be bringing the attention of the world to the plight of their forgotten race.

Only things didn't work out as expected. And they would have stayed that way had Timmy Lewis not gone missing.

Bill Tierney, they all now understood, was a man who left London at the height of his depression, with nothing else to live for. Then he came to this place and developed a special bond with the albinos. The fight to free them offered him a new lease of life. He started a selfless battle, and almost lost it. But, like pastor Sara Doyo had stated, the Lord works in mysterious ways. It had taken the disappearance of Timmy Lewis in

London to finish the job started by his compatriot Bill Tierney in an obscure African jungle thousands of miles away.

Following their interview with the boys, a meeting had been held by the British Ambassador and certain government officials. Lawyers had been called in, and they were still in the process of reviewing the evidence against the members of The Butterfly Wanderers football team. There was no doubt the charges would be dismissed. It was ridiculous that the kids had been convicted in the first place.

CHAPTER 30

The *umupfumu* turned out to be a short old man with a thick, greying, unkempt beard. His voice was deep and had a hoarseness that suggested he had spent his long years chanting and shouting, like all self-respecting local *wamupfumu*, otherwise known as *waganga,* were expected to do as part of their trade. Once again, Mfura took charge of the questioning.

They had discussed a strategy during a short meeting at the British embassy, at which it was decided that, to ease the flow of information, the local cop would present them to the witchdoctor as foreign academics who were here to research medieval African sacrifices and their spread in western Europe. The man had been forewarned of their imminent arrival, and even offered an advance payment for his services. They would secretly record everything, and arrest the *umupfumu* as soon as they were satisfied they had enough. It was a deliberate ploy to lie to a suspect, which was in fact illegal in England, and probably in this country too. But thanks to their lawlessness, they were going to get away with it.

'Many of us fled this country during the war in ninety-two,' the *umupfumu* said via Mfura, their translator. 'People would first move into neighbouring countries like Tanzania, Congo and Uganda. Then from there they could apply for asylum in

French-speaking European countries like France and Belgium. My guess would be that those who made it to the UK would have got there via France. It is well known that the refugees in France are always trying to get into the UK, believing life is much better there.'

'Would we be right to assume that these *waganga* would carry on this practice wherever they ended up as refugees?'

'Yes, as long as there is a group to cater for, we've always got a job to do.'

'And they would need albino body parts to do this job.'

'That's correct.'

'Then what happens once your get the albinos? What exactly do you do with them?'

'If someone brings us body parts, we check that they were blessed first or the sacrifice won't work. But we prefer to get them alive so we can do the blessing ourselves.'

'Blessing?'

'Yes. This is what we do to make the albinos pure before sacrificing them to the gods, to bless the soil and bring rain, among other things.'

'And how do you do this?'

'We have to keep them for about a week, feeding them only termites and water, and praying for them twice a day. That is the only way to make them pure for the sacrifice.'

'Did you say about one week?' This came from Orelius, speaking up for the first time.

Downing knew why Orelius had reacted. He was himself already doing the math in his head. Timmy had been taken last Sunday. It was now Thursday week: eleven days since Timmy disappeared. If they kept their victims alive for *about* a week, then maybe, just maybe, there was hope.

'Yes, a week of nothing but termites and water, to make sure they are pure for the sacrifice.'

'Is this an exact time?' Downing asked with similar enthusiasm. 'A week, as in seven days...? Or could it be maybe eight... nine... ten days?'

'It could be more, but a week is normally enough.'

Downing exhaled audibly. He saw Orelius lean forward. Keith was busy scribbling some notes.

'Where would the body parts come from?' Keith asked without looking up from his notebook. 'I mean, they are in a foreign country, these *waganga* refugees – they don't know where to hunt for albinos. And even if they did, security is tight in these more developed countries, and the consequences would be severe. Would it be feasible that they could use their contacts from back here to traffic albino kids into Europe?'

'Yes, that is indeed what happens. That is what they do.'

'And you know this for a fact?'

'Yes.'

'Have you ever personally helped traffic an albino child or body parts into Europe?'

'No, the *waganga* in Bujumbura do this, but not me. They have friends overseas. I have been told about this well-known *muganga* in the Mugere slums who has smuggled a few children out of the country. They forge documents or just bribe someone to issue genuine ones saying these kids are reuniting with parents who ended up in Europe during the war. The albinos and their families are of course happy because they think these are good people, friends doing a good deed by sending their children to Europe for a better life.'

The foreigners stared at each other, all thinking the same thought: the *muganga* in Mugere slums. That was the person they needed to talk to. Their quest was heading right back to the capital, where they had just come from.

Downing asked a few more questions and got the best instructions he could from the witchdoctor on how to trace his well-connected counterpart in the capital: the crucial bridge through which the body parts made their way into Europe.

As they began gathering their things, Mfura stepped forward and removed a pair of handcuffs from his back pocket.

*

They were back in Bujumbura before sunset, and all agreed that the trip to Mugere could not wait. After quick refreshments it was decided that only the London contingent –

Downing, Keith and Orelius – would accompany the two local cops to the shantytown in a smaller car, an old Peugeot Estate more suited to the hostile slum territory.

A dim speck of setting sun was still visible in the horizon as the old Peugeot rocked over the violently bumpy dirt roads of Mugere, threatening to collapse at any minute. They had tried opening all the windows for some fresh air but it only led them to nearly choking on the swirling dust. They stopped outside a tin-roofed building, about fifty metres long, with rotting wooden surfaces, that housed a row of shops. This was the glamorous stretch of Mugere, a golden island in a sea of crumbling mud-walled shacks that were smaller than most toolsheds back in England. Mfura got out and spoke to one of the shop owners for about two minutes, presumably about the safety of their car. Then he asked them to follow him through a sewage-covered alley. Half-clothed malnourished children stopped their activities and stared. The party ignored their curious looks and ducked through the low-hanging roofs and zigzags of rugs on makeshift clotheslines between shacks. Their destination was a relatively erect wooden structure at the end of a small cul-de-sac, about half a mile from where they had parked the Peugeot.

Mfura knocked on the flimsy-looking bamboo door as hard as he could without breaking it, and waited. They heard a sound from inside, someone talking rapidly in low tones. He knocked again twice. The monotonous sound from within persisted and there was no movement towards the door. The two cops looked at each other and exchanged a knowing nod. Then Mfura backed up a step and kicked the door in.

An old man, his face covered in thick grey hair, was in the middle of a space the size of an average kitchen. He was down on his knees with both hands in the air. His eyes were closed, and he was mumbling a series of indecipherable words. The only semblance of a reaction to the commotion of their breaking and entering was a slight change of tone. The man stayed on his knees just as they had found him, with only his voice gradually getting louder. The words sounded like a language from outside this world.

The five men stood in the small space and waited for about three minutes, but the prayer, or whatever it was, still did not show any sign of ending.

Mfura hunkered down close to the small ears that were barely visible through the grey bush, and shouted. 'Hey!'

Nothing happened; the grey bush did not sway, the hands stayed aloft and the eyes remained shut. Only the mumbles got louder.

Mfura removed a black baton about fifteen-inches long from his waist straps, and started poking him lightly on the shoulders with it. Downing stepped forward and held Mfura's wrist.

'Wait,' he whispered, easing him away from the old man and gesturing for everyone to step back.

They huddled close to the broken door and waited another two or three minutes. Then the man stopped abruptly, lowered his arms and slowly opened his eyes. Still kneeling down, he raised his eyes up towards them with a smile, and whispered something – two words – in a strange language.

'What's he saying?' Keith asked.

Mfura stepped forward and exchanged a few words with the old man in their vernacular. Then he turned back to them.

'He said the man you are looking for lives in Paris. His name is Abdoul Rahim Umuvango.'

And as if by magic, he had Abdoul Rahim's photograph too.

*

One hour later, Matt Mansford made a call to the British embassy in Paris. Everyone waited in his office for the call back, which came just before eight p.m. local time. It had taken the French police less than an hour to establish that a Burundian refugee known as Abdoul Rahim Umuvango lived in Les Bosquets, a high-rise estate north of Paris, not too dissimilar to Dudlham Farm. Downing was sure they all got the irony, but no one mentioned it.

They had interrogated the *umupfumu* back at the Mugere slums a bit more about this name, and he remained adamant that it was a revelation he had received from the spirits. But Downing was convinced he was actually Abdoul Rahim's source of albino body parts. News about their inquiries had somehow filtered down to the slums and he was trying to save his own skin by snitching his counterpart. When they had everything they could get from the *umupfumu* and were back in their Peugeot, Downing had asked the two uniformed cops to make sure they came back to arrest the man.

'I can arrange a direct flight to Paris ASAP,' Mansford said once he had finished the telephone conversation with the Paris embassy. 'The embassy has been notified and they'll be waiting for you.'

'That would be wonderful.'

'Get back to your hotel and catch some sleep while you can. The flight could become available any time. Perhaps earlier that you think.'

Mansford picked up the phone again and asked for the driver to take the three back to their hotel. Downing started hoisting the small brown bag with his notes and case files over his shoulders. Keith was already up but he noticed that Orelius was not moving.

'Can you get me on a flight back to London?' he heard Orelius ask the Deputy Ambassador. 'I'm not going to France.'

That came as a shock to everyone. Downing's initial thought was that the Dudlham Farm mafia lord had finally lost his will to see this through. It would explain the sudden change in his demeanour that seemed to have occurred as soon as they landed in this country. Was it fear? Had the pressure got to him now that they were getting so close to finding out what really happened to Timmy?

'You don't want to come to Paris?' Downing asked him.

'No.'

'Why?'

'Because I can't stop thinking about Nikisha in that hospital bed on her own with no visitors.'

Downing had known this man less than two weeks, and every day Orelius did something that amazed him. 'You are going back because of Timmy's mother?'

'She needs a friend, Gregg.'

That was true, but it was not an answer to his question. Downing considered asking him again but thought better of it. He already knew why Orelius Simm had suddenly decided to go back home. He was going back to The Farm because the *umupfumu* had said they kept their victims alive for about a week, and Timmy had been missing for eleven days. Downing was taking Keith Garret with him to France and they would do their best to get a swift result. But he knew there was a chance that, by the time they got back, Orelius and his hooligans would have already torn Dudlham Farm Estate to shreds looking for his boy.

This was his theory on what was going on in the gangster's head. And if it was true, he was glad Orelius was keeping it to himself. Because had he hinted that these were indeed his intentions, as a law enforcement officer, Downing would have been obliged to stop him.

And for once he didn't feel like stopping him.

CHAPTER 31

Road Runner: The narrow escape of Mpendulo Mburu

My name is Mpendulo and I live in a notorious Seine-Saint-Denis estate north of Paris called Les Bosquets. The French president once referred to places like Les Bosquets as ghettos, and their residents, 'lawless scum who should be washed away with a power hose'. All the evils and dregs of Paris live in Les Bosquets: violence, drugs, prostitution... you name it, it is here.

But for me, Les Bosquets was my saviour.

I have not always lived here. Once upon a time my home was a small African country known as Rwanda. That was back in 1992.

I remember no time in my life better than February 1992. I was eleven years old, sitting in the back row in Mrs Kivu's maths class learning about fractions. Gatonye and Gume had been made to kneel in front of the class for chattering behind Mrs Kivu's back as she wrote on the blackboard. The class was now as quiet as a tranquil sea, with only the grating sound of Mrs Kivu's chalk disturbing the silence. That was when I heard some kind of commotion outside. It came from the opposite block, which housed the office. I looked out of my window and saw a group of teachers approaching down the flower-laden path between the two blocks. They were heading towards the office and seemingly growing in size as they got closer. The procession reminded me of an approaching bus, picking up more teachers along the way to join the march towards the office. When they got to my class, Mrs Kivu put down her chalk and jumped on the bus.

A whisper or two rippled through the tranquil sea Mrs Kivu had left behind, then a few murmurs, then some jostling for a better view. And soon everyone was hooting and shouting. I could see from my window that the scene was being replicated in all the classes across the way and along the block. Loud verbal communications started flying inter-class and inter-block, and somehow the messages got through. Rumour and speculation went back and forth, growing more fancy tails and wings in the process, and before long it landed in class 5A.

The president was dead. His plane had been shot down somewhere in Burundi, or Congo, or Tanzania, or was it here in Rwanda? Probably right here in Kigali, but maybe it was his limousine, not a plane. Maybe he was with Burundi's president, and maybe he was dead too. The bottom line was that our president was dead. Our president had been killed.

'Our president has been killed, by the Tutsi cockroaches.'

It started as a murmur then grew into a chant. From my window I saw a small altercation develop outside the office, when Mr Munene started pushing Mr Butare around;

shouting, pointing and shoving him hard on the chest. Mr Butare stumbled and regained his balance, then stumbled again, and this time plunged headlong into the ground.

A sudden freezing chill engulfed my entire body. Mr Butare, the man lying helplessly on the ground, was a Tutsi.

I was a Tutsi.

Mr Munene was soon joined by three or four other male teachers, and the altercation turned into all-out pandemonium. Mrs Gumede, also a Tutsi, tried to get in between them, and within seconds both she and Mr Butare were on the ground getting kicked by almost everyone, including the female members of staff. I saw Nyungwe from class 7B jump through his classroom window and start running towards the gate, with other pupils spilling out of doors and windows in pursuit. Someone else was in the middle of a student lynching near the toilets. Two other Tutsis were running for their lives from the senior block. I looked back into my classroom and saw a group of older, Year 7 boys walk in and shut the door behind them. They were looking straight at me. All my classmates turned round to face me amidst chants of 'Tutsi Cockroach... Tutsi Cockroach!'

I had played a fun game of football with most of them during the short break, less than an hour before. My team had won the game, mainly because of me. I was fast, and my pace had terrorised the other defence, a fact they lamented at the end of the game. A deal had been made that next time there would be a coin toss to decide which team I play for, because everyone wanted me. Everyone wanted the fast player. I remembered this as the bigger boys charged towards me: that I was fast. So I jumped out of my window and started running. I saw the other groups catch up with their quarries and begin the lynchings. Two huge flames had gone up in the football field, and I realised that someone I knew, maybe even a friend, was in those flames. But I did not slow down. I kept running and running and running...

My name is Mpendulo Mburu, and I have never stopped running.

*

Mpendulo raised the picture close to his eyes, and kept it there for too long. The room was suddenly dead silent; the French officers had stopped their animated debates to listen to their African friend. They all knew critical decisions would be made, based on what the man could tell them about this photograph. The picture was of a certain Abdoul Rahim Umuvango; a Burundian refugee in France, a *muganga*, a man alleged to have received African albinos both alive and dead, a man in close contact with other men like him in Africa, France and beyond; a man who would probably know of others like him in the United Kingdom, and possibly about Timmy Lewis. Mpendulo's intelligence was going to be the key in cracking

Timmy's case, but its implications would reach far beyond that. It had now been established that they were dealing with a huge criminal ring operating in both Britain and France, and probably in other Western countries too.

The tense silence in the room captured the gravity of the situation. Only the small African's heavy breathing disturbed the air, but he seemed unaware as he continued to stare at the picture. He was a small man with a slight frame and hair shaved skin-bald. Fine beads of sweat glistened over his shiny head, and his blue shirt was sticking to his body, with patches of sweat showing under his armpits and around his chest.

'You didn't run all the way down here, Mpendulo, did you?' Downing asked, just to break the silence. The man had declined the offer of a police ride and had made his own way down to 36 Quai Des Orfevres, a journey of about ten miles.

'No, I took a train to central Paris then ran the rest of the way,' he said, placing the picture on the table face down. His English was fairly good, better than the French policemen's.

'Isn't there an underground station just outside this building?'

'There is. But I like running.'

Downing nodded. 'So, Mpendulo, do you know the man in the picture?'

The African inched forward over the table and smiled. They were all huddled in one corner of a long conference table that extended to the other end of the room. Mpendulo threaded his hands together and rested his chin on them, his eyes darting between Downing and Garret. 'Did you say you are the British police, or spies? You know... like MI5, MI6–'

'We are the police, Scotland Yard detectives.'

'Wow, Scotland Yard,' he beamed. 'I like Scottish people. Scottish people are nice.'

'I'm sure they are, sir. But we are from London, England. Scotland Yard is just an informal name for London's Metropolitan Police headquarters.'

'Aha. I see, I see,' he nodded cheerfully, as if everything clicked into place. He continued to smile absently as his smooth black head bobbed up and down like a pulse. He seemed to have forgotten why he was here. The French officers sat silently, arms folded across their chests, and made no attempt to get involved. Aside from their boss, Henri Laurent, the other French cops had shown at best a sketchy grasp of English. Downing wondered whether they were still following.

'Do you know the man in the picture, sir?' he tried again.

'Yes, I do.' The African's eyes dropped to the picture. 'He lives in number 219, block G.'

Instant result. Downing felt his heart skip a few beats but he tried not to show it. It was not quite the moment to jump off his chair and punch the air in jubilation. They were on the home stretch but not quite there yet.

The *umupfumu* in Bujumbura had given them a photo, a name, and a location, which they had used to find the exact address of their suspect in Paris. But the French police needed something more substantial to storm the residence of a citizen accusing him of murder. So they had called in Mpendulo Mburu, a man whose role in the French police Downing still didn't fully understand. Inspector Laurent had referred to him as a man who helped them with odd jobs in the inner city, which downing assumed meant he was their undercover informant from Les Bosquets.

Mpendulo was still breathing heavily.

'What can you tell us about him?' Downing asked, accepting the picture back from him and placing it in the centre of the table between them. There was a familiar stirring in his gut that usually signalled a case coming to a satisfactory conclusion. He was confident that they would come to the end of their pursuit with answers – but the possibility of saving Timmy was still as remote as it ever was. This informant had just confirmed the existence of their man, an African witchdoctor they had first learnt about in Burundi. He lived less than ten miles from where they were sitting. And he probably had all the answers to what was going on in Dudlham Farm.

Orelius was back in London. Downing's only partner now was Keith Garret, and he was still finding it hard to believe that they were in France. They had been picked up from De Gaulle airport by a black Land Rover with diplomatic plates and brought straight here to 36 Quai Des Orfevres, the French equivalent of Scotland Yard.

Often referred to simply as 36, the headquarters of world-famous *Direction Règionale de Police Judiciaire de Paris* was a gigantic fortress whose exterior looked aged in a charming way. The interior, at least the bit Downing had seen so far, was a dull, faded white, devoid of any decoration, with linoleum floors. Downing had napped through the journey here and missed the mid-morning Paris scenery. In fact, since leaving Mansford's office in Bujumbura last night, naps in taxis to and from airports was all the sleep he'd had. But there were enough French accents in this room to remind him exactly where he was.

'He comes from Burundi.' Mpendulo said in answer to his question about their suspect. His bald head was pointed directly at the picture with almost visible intensity, as though there was much, much more he could say. 'He is a Burundian refugee. That's in Africa, by the way, next to my country.'

'We know where Burundi is, my friend. We've just come from there,' Downing said with a tired smile and Mpendulo smiled back, probably thinking this was a joke. 'What does he do for a living?'

'I don't know. He's a quiet old man who keeps to himself. But there are a lot of rumours about this man...' He hesitated, looking for encouragement.

'Rumours...?' Downing prompted.

'Yeah, they say he is involved in witchcraft. You know... African black magic.'

Everyone looked at each other. Hit number three.

They had their *umupfumu*.

All the pieces seemed to be slotting into place, but would it be too late for Timmy Lewis?

Downing faced the French officers with arched eyebrows and asked, 'Do we really need any more?'

Inspector Laurent was the only one of the French policemen not in uniform. He had a full head of neatly cropped, jet black hair, which didn't seem to match his coarse facial features. He stroked the inside of his wrinkled double-chin, nodding slowly to himself, before turning to his colleagues. Then they started murmuring animatedly in French, clearly planning their next move.

Downing had initially thought the French would find it hard to believe a story about the import and export of human body parts taking place in their country. But they surprised him when Laurent produced a stack of files they had on an array of ethnic ritual crimes not too dissimilar. They were aware of some problems among the immigrant population. And, as was standard practice for places like Les Bosquets, they had informants in place, an invaluable law-and-order tool in French inner cities. And right now Downing felt nothing but admiration for such policing methods, because Mpendulo Mburu had delivered.

'That's all, Mpendulo,' Inspector Laurent finally said. 'Thank you very much for coming at such short notice.'

The man's eyes darted around the room as if he was not yet ready to leave. He continued chatting to the officers rapidly in French for a couple of minutes as Downing and Keith Garret started gathering the documents from the table and putting them back in their respective files.

They offered Mpendulo a ride back to Les Bosquets but he declined and jogged back down the street. Then Inspector Laurent brought two more uniformed officers into the room and, alternating between English and French, started briefing everyone on the impending operation in Les Bosquets.

There was going to be a raid, and Inspector Downing would be part of it. This was the right way to solve crimes, the police way. And yet there was a different kind of raid that Downing was sure would be happening at around the same time in London's version of Les Bosquets. It made him anxious, but he didn't know whether it was dread of a portending catastrophe that by rights he ought to avert, or whether he was secretly willing it on, for Timmy and Nikisha Lewis's sake.

CHAPTER 32

Orelius was back at Middlesex County Hospital on Friday afternoon. He had barely time to rush back to his flat for a shower and change of clothes before heading out. Nikisha was sitting up in bed, and gave him a weak smile as he walked in. But Orelius could see fear behind that smile. It had been the same every time he walked into her ward: she would first stiffen, setting herself for bad news, then relax a little with the knowledge that at least someone was out there looking for her son.

She gave him an intense stare and held it for about a minute without saying anything, searching for answers in his eyes. Then she leant forward on her thighs and rested her head on her palms, as though it was too heavy for her narrow shoulders to hold. She closed her eyes but Orelius knew she could still see him.

'We went to Africa,' he said.

She opened her eyes, then shut them.

'Some clues came up and we had to follow them.'

'Is Timmy in Africa?'

'No, I think he is in Dudlham Farm.'

She opened her eyes and stared blankly at the floor.

'We got some significant information in Africa and the detectives are still following it up. I came back because I think Timmy is still at The Farm and I don't want to waste any more time. The police are taking too long.'

'What are you going to do?'

'There's only one thing to do, Nikisha. Tear it down, the entire estate.'

'Are you going to hurt people?' she asked.

Orelius glanced at her and their eyes met. Then he dropped his gaze to the floor and, as if to himself, said, 'Waiting patiently by the riverbank with a bait to hook a trout is a game; sweeping through the river with a net is fishing; but if it comes down to an issue between you and the fish, be prepared to drain the entire river to pick up the lot.' His voice had dropped to almost a whisper. 'I got that from my grandmother, she was always full of them,' he explained with a joyless smile. 'I was fishing before, but now it has gone beyond fishing.'

*

He left Nikisha's ward at five, promising to be back in the morning. The doctors still weren't sure when it would be safe to discharge her, and no one else seemed to be worried. So all responsibilities, even for the essentials she needed for her hospital stay, fell to him. He would be back with some shopping, and maybe some good news about her son.

He got his mobile out to call Cory Dillinger as soon as he left the hospital. He needed to check on how his plans were progressing back at The Farm. He had left Dillinger and Mega in charge of prepping the team for tonight's operation. He had identified ten hardened Dudlham Farm thugs and had personally called them for this favour. All had agreed, some with more excitement at the prospect of some action than he was comfortable with. This had made it necessary for him to stress that they were not going to twist arms and break bones for fun. They were looking for an abducted child who might still be alive. He had then left his two trusted friends to iron out the details.

Cory answered on the first ring, with his standard opening. 'Cory D. Talk to me.'

'Hi Cory, this is me. How are things down there?'

'All good, bruv. Mega and I are on top of things. Everyone knows what they are doing. They've all put together their little teams of helpers... we'll be ready, soldier.'

Mega was going to be the muscle behind this operation, and Cory, the brain. Although big-talking Cory Dillinger was sly and street-smart, he was relatively harmless. He had the cunning ability to stir trouble and yet somehow manage to stay away from the consequences. He needed Cory to make sure Megaman didn't turn tonight's mission into a bloodbath.

'Cory, will you check out those little teams of helpers as well? I don't want anyone getting too drunk or stoned and taking this for a carnival of violence. Make sure they know what we are doing.'

'Did that already, everyone's been vetted. I got this, bro, you just chill... Oh, by the way, Trig wanted to swap with the Kimani brothers so he could have Tangmere and the twins take Hawkinge. But we said no chance.'

'Tell Trig that he doesn't have to be involved in this. But if he wants to help he's going to have to do it my way. He's not going anywhere near Tangmere.'

Trigger Ty was a twenty-seven-year-old big-time dope supplier. Real name: Tyson Flynn. Trig, only recently freed from prison, had a long-running beef with all the residents of Tangmere and wanted to use tonight's operation to settle some old scores. He still believed that one or more of them snitched him and led the narcotics squad to his flat in Tangmere House, which had been converted into a cannabis farm. This was despite the fact that everyone else knew that the problem had come from his electricity supplier. The power company had raised numerous concerns about his abnormally high consumption, and had even requested to inspect his installations for possible faults, to save him money. Ty had declined. He was quite happy to pay his bills just as they were, thank you very much. But Trigger had been drawing seventy times more power from the grid than the average two-bedroom flat, and the electricity company alerted the authorities.

'Oh no. Ain't nobody quitting now, Oz,' Cory stated confidently. 'I told Trig how it is; he and his team will take Hawkinge, the Kimani twins have Tangmere. End of story. We'll be ready tonight, bro.'

Throughout the search, his friends had remained as useful as they could behind the scenes but their work had been restricted by the police presence around The Farm. Orelius understood tonight could get ugly, but that couldn't be helped. These were desperate times. He had tried things Downing's way. It was time to go back to the old school.

'Good, everyone knows the drill, right? The times and who we are targeting?'

'Loud and clear, bro. Start at the same time and work fast. Don't allow time for word to go round. And target Africans, but if you don't know someone, assume they're African.' He recited them like a set of scout laws. 'I had them singing that over and over again.'

'Good, Cory. Pass my thanks to Mega as well, I owe you both big time. I'm coming back in a few minutes and we'll go over everything again before we begin.'

'No worries, Oz. We always got your back, you know 'dis. We family. And tonight, if he's out there, we are bringing Timmy home.'

Orelius was about to tuck the phone back into his pocket when a text message alerted him that he had five missed calls from Downing. Downing had promised to keep him informed of their progress in France, and had there been only one or two calls, he would have assumed it was a routine update. But five?

He felt his heartbeat quicken as he called the detective's number. He was still at the hospital's car park, and his original idea had been to make this international call in around two hours' time, from the landline back in his Dudlham flat. He had planned to let the detective know what he was about to do, seconds before it went down, right at the eleventh hour, with no chance of him doing anything to stop him.

But the five missed calls suggested an emergency.

'What's happening?' he asked as soon as Downing said hello.

'Let me call you back,' the detective said.

'We found the man, Orelius,' Downing started when Orelius picked up. 'It's just like we suspected: some albino body parts made their way into the UK from France in the back of a lorry.'

He paused before dropping the bombshell.

'There is a man in London, an *umupfumu*. There is probably more than one of them but this French guy claims he only knows and deals with one. And this one sounds very much like our man.'

'Did you get this guy's name and location?'

'He claims he doesn't know his address: these things are couriered through corrupt lorry drivers who are part of an organised crime network. You give them your packages and pay the fees and they give you a reference number to give to the recipient. The recipient provides this number on the other side and receives his package, no questions asked. They don't care what's in the packages.

'Some of these *wamupfumu* are just frauds who don't even believe in the rituals. They peddle these bizarre beliefs simply for commercial gain. So there is a very good chance this guy knew that Timmy was not an albino but took him anyway because he looked close enough – his customers wouldn't know the difference–'

'Gregg,' Orelius said, 'we can do the psychology later. Right now I need facts. You said you've got our man.'

'I believe we have. This guy basically told us that his London partner calls to arrange delivery and to get this reference number for the couriers, and that the calls always come from different numbers. So we seized his phone and checked the received-calls log. A couple of them came from within a mile of Dudlham Farm; one from a payphone and the other an internet cafe on Lordship Lane.'

The origin of the calls was not a surprise to Orelius. 'How about a name? Did you get his name?'

'Yes, a certain Mr Jona Buyoya?'

The name meant nothing to Orelius.

'An old refugee from Burundi, who got into the UK via France,' Downing continued. 'He's in his seventies and is apparently hard to miss because of his seriously disfigured face from the war. The last time this French guy saw him, our man had a cleft palate with most of the upper lip missing, leaving two unusually huge front teeth sticking out.'

'Like a warthog...' The words left Orelius's mouth but he wasn't conscious of speaking them. 'The Hog.'

How could he have missed this? A chill swept his body and his head went blank, then started spinning violently. Of course, now everything made sense, things always made more sense in hindsight. Timmy had last been seen on the deck outside his front door. When the Turkish woman from Lympne said she saw an old bearded black man inside that van, she had not been wrong. Only the old bearded black man was not Markus Isaacs. Their search should have stayed right here in Dudlham Farm, where it all started. Right there, less than five yards from the balcony where the boy was last seen, on that Sunday afternoon.

'Hellooo... Orelius, you still there?' Downing's voice sounded like a distant echo.

'I know that man, Gregg.' His words were soft and quiet. 'He lives at 92 Northolt House, *right next door to Timmy.*'

There would later be inquests, accusations and counter-accusations regarding how something so fundamental could have been overlooked. Meetings would be held, conclusions drawn, and findings published and distributed to the right people, to help avoid similar mistakes in future. The wonders of that abstract notion called hindsight; a parachute that only opens when you are already down.

In reality, though, those long journeys were a crucial step towards finding the truth. They had to travel halfway round the world, not only to learn that Timmy had been taken by his next door neighbour, but also to discover the existence of that secluded place of secret people and a mysterious culture, a world unknown to all but its own.

EPILOGUE

London's Grosvenor House Hotel was swarming with well-known personalities from various walks of life. There were politicians, pop stars, movie stars and sports stars, all in glamorous tuxes and frocks. It was the time to mingle before the start of the Pride of Britain Awards, and the stars did this with flair, moving gracefully, waving, posing and smiling for the cameras, displaying their designer clothes and hair and teeth. The common folk, who had been billed as the real stars of the night, tried to match them, but there was no contest. They were mere mortals – notwithstanding the borrowed designer suits – and they would never match the celebrities' panache. Their nervous smiles alone were a sure giveaway. Nevertheless, this was their night. The Pride of Britain Awards were for the ordinary people of Great Britain who had overcome extraordinary situations in the past year. Tonight they were the stars. The celebrities were here to pay tribute to them.

One of these average Joes, a small, light-skinned boy, seemed particularly popular, and the clamour for his attention was almost chaotic as he got whisked around from superstar to megastar for photo opportunities. He was wearing a black suit over a neat white shirt, and a bowtie. Detective Inspector Gregg Downing stood about ten yards behind him with the other commoners, and watched as the Prime Minister bent down to shake his hand and then crouched almost to his knees so their eyes were almost level amidst a flurry of clicks and flashes from the cameras of the jostling paparazzi. He saw the boy smile timidly at the Prime Minister's quiet joke. The boy then wrapped his right arm around his mother's hips and allowed himself to be led away from the pack. The pair turned round and walked towards Downing. The mother marched gracefully, like a catwalk model, in a pair of shiny three-inch heels and a stunning navy blue gown that traced her small waist, hugged her hips and fell all the way to her feet. She was not wearing her glasses, and when she smiled as she approached him, a charming set of dimples lit her chocolate-coloured face.

He smiled back, then lowered his eyes towards the boy and said, 'Hi, Tim.'

'Hi, Detective Downing. Guess what, I've just met Simon Cowell.'

'I know. You are quite a star aren't you? I've just seen you posing for a photo with the Prime Minister too.'

The boy squinted in confusion. 'Who... when?'

Downing laughed. 'Never mind, Timmy, I'm just saying you are the real superstar.' He then turned to the boy's mother. 'Hi, Nikisha.'

'Hello, Detective.'

'How is your new home?'

'It's great, thank you, sir. We are settling in fine.' She sounded composed and articulate, a new woman. The Housing Association had moved them to a two-bedroom terraced house in Finchley after their Dudlham Farm ordeal.

'He's not here is he?'

She shook her head. 'No, he isn't.'

'I personally delivered his invite.'

Nikisha said nothing.

'Do you know why he didn't come?' Downing asked. He knew that, as per the deal, the man in question had appeared in court to face a weapons charge, and had managed to get off with a fine and a twelve-month suspended sentence.

'I understand he went away,' replied Nikisha. 'To the Caribbean, I think.'

'Oh, he flew out to see his dad?'

'I didn't know he had a family.'

The detective smiled. 'You don't know much about him, do you?'

'I know he loves my son,' she said quietly, looking down at Timmy, who seemed distracted by a group of reporters who were talking to a celebrity couple. 'For me, that is enough.'

Ten minutes later, all attendees were called to order and asked to take their seats.

Detective Inspector Gregg Downing's award was presented almost an hour later by a rock star who described him as *the*

Batman of our time. A white-collar officer who happened upon a place neglected by the law and decided to do it all on his own: he put down his pen, hung up his suit, and travelled to the remotest corners of the earth to save an abducted child.

Thunderous applause accompanied him to the podium.

'Thank you... thank you all so much,' he started, trying to cool off the audience. He had made presentations and delivered speeches before but this was the most nervous he had ever been in front of a crowd.

'I'd like to thank the organisers for giving us a forum where we can say a simple thank you to ordinary, unsung heroes. Thanks to all of you in this room who have inspired me today with your extraordinary stories of courage. I am just a policeman who was only trying to do his job two months ago. And with the aid of a few good men of Dudlham Farm and some good fortune, we got a breakthrough and managed to rescue young Timothy Lewis.'

Another round of applause, which he allowed to go on for about ten seconds, then waved for calm.

'I am unworthy of this honour, ladies and gentlemen. I am unworthy to be amongst you great people. So why, you might wonder, am I standing here holding an award that I do not deserve? I asked myself that question when I was first told about my nomination. I questioned whether it was right for me to even set my foot inside this room. In the end I decided that I needed to be here. I had to be here for the sake of the real heroes I met during our two-week search for Timmy. I stand here on behalf of those heroes, who will never have the chance to stand here themselves and receive their due: small people in small places, who make big sacrifices for others and expect nothing back. I believe they too should be heard, and honoured.

'I'm here to tell you about a young man called Orelius Simm, who does not fit in amongst us fine upstanding citizens. But to the people who need him most, he remains a gallant captain, fighting their small everyday battles so they can see tomorrow.'

In the third seat of the second row, a quiet snivel escaped Nikisha Lewis's nose as a tear rolled down her left cheek.

'I want you all to know that there once lived a man called Bill Tierney, who gave his life to liberate an obscure race that most of us have never even heard of. Bill Tierney was a hero, ladies and gentlemen. I am nothing.'

Nikisha's tears were slowly spreading to a few others around her and beyond.

'I also stand here to apologise for the others I met along the way who desperately needed a hero but did not find one. I want to say sorry to Markus Isaacs, Kelly Jo-Pretty and Shola Louise King and her unborn child. Let's spare a thought too for Jean-Baptiste Nimbona and the persecuted albinos of Burundi. Their names might not mean much, but we know these faceless people. We see them everywhere. They clean our houses, mow our lawns and care for our elderly. Sometimes we wave and smile at them. But when the sun goes down, we lock our gates, put our feet up in front of our plasma screens, and forget that places like Dudlham Farm even exist.'

If you liked this book, you may also enjoy the author's other works, including his previous novel:

THE DALLAS MERCENARY

Visit www.michaeloren.co.uk for more information

AUTHOR'S NOTE

The social issues raised in this book are real. The pattern of urban decay depicted here is representative of most inner cities. The persecution of Albinos in certain parts of Africa happens. I point the issues out and try telling stories around them that will, hopefully, touch or move my readers in some way. But make no mistake; this is not a social or political commentary. This will remain a work of fiction.

ACKNOWLEDGEMENTS

My most heartfelt thanks are always reserved for those who buy and read my published books. Some go a step further by offering feedback and encouragement through reviews and at times even direct contact. You are my heroes. Because of you, I might one day be able to call myself an author. Many others contribute to getting the books there and, as usual, rather than going through a list of names here, I will take my time to thank the individuals personally outside of this page. However, because I don't want any issues with law enforcement authorities, an exception will be made this time for Adrian F. Allen of London's Metropolitan Police. He told me what I needed to know. If I then went on to distort this information in the name of fiction, I will take full responsibility.

Lightning Source UK Ltd.
Milton Keynes UK
UKOW051820050912

198550UK00001B/8/P